Copyright 2015 by Michelle St. James aka Michelle Zink

Cover design by Isabel Robalo

ISBN 978-0-9966056-1-8

1

Angelica assumed she was just being paranoid. She'd run errands before her shift at the Muddy Cup, stopping at the grocery store, picking up the heeled boots she'd sent in for repair, and paying a past due parking ticket. None of it was unusual for a Wednesday afternoon, but she'd had the heebie-jeebies all day, dogged by the feeling that someone was watching her. She was relieved to finally step inside the coffee shop that night. Surrounded by the overstuffed sofas, old chairs, and worn counter, her paranoia faded into the background.

She'd been working at the local coffee shop since before graduation, and while she knew deep down that she needed to figure out a long term plan, she couldn't seem to take a step in any direction. She was paralyzed, frozen and embarrassed by the post-grad apathy she despised in her generation.

She spent the next few hours slinging coffee drinks and retrieving the key that everyone seemed determined to leave inside the bathroom. By closing time, she'd completely forgotten her earlier unease and was contentedly mopping the floors when her cell phone rang. She pulled it from the pocket of her jeans, smiling when she saw the name on the display.

"Hey, loser," she said, propping the phone between her ear and shoulder while she continued mopping.

"Very funny." Her brother, David, laughed on the other end of the phone. "Especially since you're still working that shitty job."

"Touché," she said. "What's up?"

"Not much. Just finished mid-terms."

She reached back to tighten the hair tie holding her long, blonde hair in a half-assed ponytail. "Fun." She hesitated. "Is everything okay?"

She and David were close, but they usually texted. Calling was reserved for relationship and life crisis.

"Yeah, sure." He said it a little too quickly, then sighed. "Have you heard from Dad?"

"Not for a couple of weeks. Why?"

"I don't know," he said. She could almost see him drumming his fingers, an old habit from childhood, on the beat up desk in his dorm room. "I left him some messages. He hasn't called me back."

She chewed on her thumbnail, measuring her words. David's relationship with their father had been strained since David came out last year. In an age when it seemed everyone and their mother had accepted homosexuality as no big deal, their old-school, Italian father could barely look David in the eye. She hated it, but there was nothing she could do about it other than make her feelings known. Which she'd done. On several occasions.

Their relationship had been distant since he sent them to boarding school after their mom died, but David's admission had only increased the tension. Their father was avoiding both of them now, and Angelica spent half the time thinking he could go fuck himself and the other half desperately trying to come up with a way to bridge the gap.

People will tell you who they are if you listen.

It was one of her father's favorite sayings, and she was still trying to figure out if he hadn't yet told her, or if she was just too stubborn to believe what he was saying.

"Well, if it makes you feel any better," she said, "I haven't heard from him in at least that long."

"It doesn't," David said. "I'm sorry."

She used the mop handle to push the wheeled bucket toward the kitchen. "It's not your fault Dad's a homophobe."

He laughed, but it sounded hollow to her ears. "Good point. So what else is new?"

She balanced the phone on her shoulder while she wrung out the mop and dumped the water. "Literally nothing. My life is about as exciting as watching paint dry."

He seemed to hesitate before speaking again. "You can change that, you know."

She sighed. "Yeah. I just don't know what to do next."

"You have a degree," he said.

"In Philosophy." It felt like the punchline to a bad joke, and she laughed as she turned on the faucet.

"True, but I'm sure you could find a job somewhere. You could teach. Maybe overseas?"

She thrust her hands under the hot water. "Maybe. I'll figure it out."

"If you say so. Just promise me you'll get out of there, Ange." David always used the nickname, even though everyone else called her Angie. Everyone but her father, who used her given name, Angelica. "You're too good for them."

"Now you're just kissing my ass," she said.

He laughed. "You wish."

For a split second she could see the smile on his face, and she missed him so much it hurt.

"Visit soon?" she asked.

"I'll see you next month at Thanksgiving."

"Sounds good. I love you."

"Love you, too," he said.

She hung up and slipped the phone in her pocket, then grabbed her jacket, turned out the lights, and headed for the door.

It was only eleven, but the streets were nearly empty. She remembered what David had said about mid-terms. All the state colleges were on the same schedule, which meant business would be slow for at least the next week.

It was late October, but winter was a ghost in the air, and she drew her jacket more tightly around her body as she turned to lock the door. She had just put the key in the lock when she felt the gun against her temple.

"Move and you're dead."

She felt a pinch in her neck just before some kind of bag came down over her head. Then everything went dark as unconsciousness claimed her.

2

Nico Vitale was kneeling in one of the pews at St. Monica's, praying for his mother and father. They'd been gone two years, but the pain of losing them still lingered. He had only been twenty-eight when they'd been killed, and he'd expected to have them for many more years, to give them the daughter-in-law and grandchildren they had wanted.

Their future had been stolen. From all of them.

He forced down the fury that had become all too familiar. Anger was good. Productive. It's what drove him to seek justice, to right the wrong perpetrated against his family, against the honor code that had survived decades under the rule of some of history's most violent men.

But this wasn't the place for anger. This was the place for peace. Repentance. He took a deep breath and tried to calm himself.

His mother had always gone to St. Patrick's, but Nico made a point of moving around the city, sitting in any church with an open door. He liked the anonymity of it. Liked knowing that no one would know him or remember his parents.

His faith was only a shadow of the belief that had sustained them. Nico didn't believe in the edicts of the Church. It had been organized by man to benefit man. He worshipped his own god, and his god didn't turn the other cheek. He might forgive, but that forgiveness didn't preclude a punishment justly earned. Still, he liked to sit in silence and remember, to send love to his parents, wherever they were, and to stand on the side of any god who believed in vengeance.

He was reciting the Lord's Prayer when he felt a tap on his shoulder. He instinctively shook off the hand. When he turned to see who had interrupted him, he was even less pleased.

"What is it, Dante?" He forced his voice even as he took in the leather jacket and jeans worn by the man in front of him. A dress code was part of Nico's organizational reboot, but keeping cool was a point of pride, part of his mission to remake his father's business for the twenty-first century. And having a reputation for being calm only made him more formidable when the situation called for his wrath.

Dante shifted in his seat, his face flushed, eyes feverish with excitement. "We got her," he said. "We got the girl."

Nico looked around before tipping his head at the church's massive double doors. "Not here."

Dante stood, hurrying down the aisle. Nico followed slowly, letting the peace of the church wash over him as he made his way out the door.

He took his time following Dante down the steps of the church. When they reached the sidewalk, they stepped back to stand near an adjacent building.

"Any trouble?" Nico asked.

Dante shook his head. "She didn't see it coming."

Nico didn't like the note of excitement in Dante's voice. Nico's father had ingrained old-fashioned chivalry in his bones, and Nico never sanctioned hurting women. These kinds of things were a necessary part of doing business, not something he enjoyed.

"You didn't hurt her." It wasn't a question.

Dante sighed, and Nico caught a hint of annoyance in the other man's face before he could hide it. "We did it just like you said. Knocked her out, put her in the van, took her to the basement. She's fine."

Nico nodded. "Good. Make sure she's comfortable."

"Comfortable?" Dante's laugh was bitter. "Why do we care if that bitch is comfortable?"

Nico clamped a hand on Dante's shoulder and squeezed until he flinched. "We don't call women bitches in this organization. Ever. Understand?"

Dante nodded, his eyes lit with the fire of indignation.

"Good." Nico released his grip. "Now go make the pick-up."

"Will do." Dante rolled his shoulders, like doing so would free him of Nico's grip when they both knew only death or dishonor would do that. "Want a ride back to the office?"

"No." He didn't owe Dante an explanation.

Dante nodded and headed for the car double parked at the curb. Nico watched him get in and drive away. He waited for the car to disappear into traffic before he started walking.

Dante was a problem. Nico understood it, but he was still trying to settle on a strategy for dealing with it. He knew Dante resented him. That Dante believed his father, Gabriel Santoro, should have been Underboss to Nico's father before his death. If that had been the case, Dante's father would be Boss now, and Dante himself would be the crown prince of the New York territory.

Instead, a year before his death Nico's father had inexplicably turned to Nico, pleading with him to step in as Underboss. Only twenty-seven at the time, Nico wasn't ready to take on the mantle of responsibility held by his father. He didn't even believe in the mob. Not the way it was then; stealing and killing and raping in the name of money. In the name of power.

But his father had been unsettled. Even Nico, as young and wrapped up in himself as he'd been at the time, could see that. And his father -- his family -- meant everything to him. So he'd gotten his act together and joined the business, learning it from the inside out. He was just beginning to feel like he had a handle on the basic operations when his parents were murdered, execution style, outside the restaurant where they'd met over three decades ago. They had been celebrating their thirty-second anniversary.

Nico had spent the two years since remaking his father's legacy. Raneiro Donati, head of the Syndicate that acted as governing body to criminal organizations all over the world, had stepped in as a mentor and father figure, guiding Nico through the early stages of grief and the rage that threatened to undo him. Gradually, Nico had found a focus for his fury, and he'd poured every ounce of his energy into targeting that focus and reimagining his father's legacy.

Some of Nico's soldiers embraced the change. Others, like Dante, clung to the old ways. Nico understood, but the reorganization wasn't optional. They would comply or they would be gone.

Nico didn't like taking the girl. A decade ago, something like that would be off the table, a blatant breaking of rules that had been in place since before the Syndicate formally existed. But nothing could be rebuilt without first dismantling the rotting foundation of what had come before.

And unfortunately, the girl was part of that foundation.

He checked for traffic on 2nd Avenue and crossed just before a taxi barreled through the intersection. He felt liberated by his time at the church. Lighter on his feet. Maybe he would call one of the women who acted as a physical companion when he felt the urge.

After all, he wasn't a saint.

3

The first thing she noticed when she woke up was the sledgehammer chipping away at her brain. She had a sudden flash of memory; the man's voice in her ear, the gun at her temple. It was dark, and she thought the bag might still be over her head, but when she made a concerted effort to open her eyes, everything slowly came into focus.

She was laying on a mattress, surrounded by four nondescript walls. She groaned as she sat up, putting a hand to her head like that might stop the war waging inside her skull. Nausea rolled through her stomach, and she took a few deep breaths, willing herself to pull it together. Someone had kidnapped her, drugged her, brought her to this room. She needed to figure out what was going on.

When the worst of the nausea passed, she slowly stood, bracing herself against the wall with one hand. Then she looked around, taking inventory, trying to figure out where she was and how she could get out of here.

The room was tiny, but surprisingly neat and clean, although there were no windows. A writing desk stood next to a twin size bed, but the room was otherwise devoid of furniture. There were two doors, and she felt a flare of hope when she realized one of them was open about an inch. She crossed the room, hoping it was a way out, and was disappointed to realize it was a small bathroom, complete with a sink and shower.

Her gaze was drawn to the closed door, and panic clawed at her chest as the reality of the situation hit her. She had no idea who would want to kidnap her, but it was the question of what would come next that terrified her.

Were they going to kill her? Worse?

She thought about all the documentaries and news stories she'd seen on human trafficking. Was it possible something like that had happened on the streets of a sleepy, American college town? She didn't know, but the door might be her only way out. The odds that it was unlocked were slim, but she had to try.

She made her way across the room. Her head still hurt, and she felt a little dizzy, but she got to the door and put her hand carefully on the knob. What would she do if it was unlocked? If someone was on the other side with a gun?

She didn't have a clue, but instinct told her paralysis would be deadly. She couldn't afford to freeze. She needed to think. To act.

She turned the knob slowly in case someone was listening outside the door.

It was locked.

She was scanning the room for another way out when she saw something on the floor near the foot of the bed. It only took a second to realize what it was, and she hurried as fast as her leaden limbs would allow and dropped to her knees.

She picked up the lip gloss and held it in her palm. Already it seemed like an artifact from another life. When she ducked her head to look under the bed, she saw the rest of her belongings scattered across the tile, her purse gaping open near the wall. Someone must have tossed it on the floor when they'd brought her to the room.

She reached under the bed and gathered up everything, including the bag, then sat with her back against the bed frame to take inventory.

The first thing she noticed was that her wallet was still there - money, credit cards, and all. *Not a garden variety mugging then,* she thought. She didn't know if the knowledge was comforting or terrifying.

It only took a minute to realize everything else was accounted for as well -- everything but her cell phone.

Damn.

She looked around the room and thought about her options, fighting the urge to curl up on the bed and sleep away the fog in her head. One locked door. No windows. No cell phone. She could wait for what was coming or hurry it along. The thought scared her, but sitting there like a sitting duck, waiting for the other shoe to drop, scared her more.

She got up, went to the door, and started banging on it.

"Hello!" she shouted. "Hello? Is anybody there? Let me out!"

She pounded the door with her fists, yelling louder. The more she screamed, the better she felt. At least she was doing something. It felt so good she forgot to be scared.

A couple minutes went by before she heard the sound of a key in the lock from the other side of the door. She stepped back, her heart thumping wildly.

The door swung open, and a dark haired man with a thin face strode into the room. His purposeful stride took her by surprise, and a second later she felt something hard and unyielding strike her face.

Her hand went reflexively to her cheek. The bastard had backhanded her.

He was so close she could feel his body against hers. When she looked up, it was into eyes so dark they appeared black. She expected to see anger there, but they were completely vacant. The man's physical violence -- or the anger that had prompted it -- was obviously nothing unusual.

"Shut your mouth, bitch," he snarled. "Or I'll shut it for you."

His eyes traveled the length of her body, and she suddenly felt naked despite the jeans and peasant blouse she still wore from her shift at the Muddy Cup.

He shoved a paper bag into her chest, his hands lingering there even after she'd taken hold of whatever it was he was trying to give her. The back of his hand pressed against her breast before he lowered his arms with a salacious grin.

She licked her lips, her mouth suddenly dry. "What... Why are you keeping me here? What do you want?" she managed to croak.

"I'm not keeping you anywhere. I'm just following orders." His voice was as cold as the rest of him, and he spit out the last word like it tasted foul in his mouth. "As for what I want..." His gaze dropped to her chest, and she had the irrational feeling he could see everything, even though her blouse was nowhere near low cut. "Don't worry, I'll tell you what I'm going to do to you ahead of time. That way you can really enjoy it."

Her step away from him was instinctive, and she felt the bed hit the back of her knees. Nowhere else to go. She was debating the merit of screaming like crazy and hoping for a miracle when someone spoke up beyond the man's shoulder.

"Dante. What are you doing?"

She dared a look over the man named Dante's shoulder and spotted another man, this one slightly smaller, although he had the same dark hair.

When she looked back up at Dante, his eyes were still on hers. It seemed like an eternity before he took a step away from her.

"Nothing. Giving the girl food like the boss said."

The other man folded his arms over his chest. "It doesn't take five minutes to hand someone food."

Dante turned around to face the other man. "Fuck, Luca. What are you? My babysitter now?"

"I'm responsible for her, too," Luca said. "Let's go."

Dante looked back at her. She had to fight not to shudder. His eyes were almost reptilian, and a chill slithered up her spine.

"Fine," he said, turning away and heading for the door. "She's just a spoiled bitch anyway."

Luca held the door open for Dante while Angelica clutched the paper bag to her chest. When Dante was clear of the room, Luca met her eyes.

"You okay?" he asked softly.

She nodded, which was ridiculous since she was nowhere near okay.

"Eat," he said. "You need to keep up your strength."

She didn't have time to say anything else before the door closed. A second later the lock clicked into place.

She dropped onto the bed, exhaling a breath she hadn't known she was holding.

4

They brought her lots of food after that; cold take-out hamburgers, hot dogs, sandwiches, and once, spaghetti. She stopped eating somewhere around the second day. It was the only way she could protest, the only way she could gain some kind of control over the situation.

She hadn't tried banging on the door or yelling again. She was too afraid it would bring Dante back into the room. She could still see the dead look in his eyes, feel the hard crack of his hand across her face. Instead, she stayed quiet, trying to strategize another way out. It must have worked, because he hadn't been back since the first day. She started to feel a little safer. Luca was polite, and she thought she saw something kind in his blue eyes when he entered the room to give her food.

She had used the bathroom to wash her face and brush her teeth with the toothbrush left there, but she hadn't dared to shower. The idea of stripping when she had no idea what was going on beyond the walls of her room, no idea who was holding her or why, made her feel vulnerable and scared.

Refusing to eat was a last resort, and she spent the time between Luca's drop offs sitting on the bed or pacing the room, thinking about her father and brother, wondering if they knew she was missing. She didn't have many friends, just Lauren, a fellow holdover from college. Would she be worried when Angie didn't return her texts? Would Angie's boss, Josh, check up on her when she didn't show up for her next shift?

Thinking about the few people who might miss her only made her feel worse. She'd been living like a shadow since college. She just hadn't wanted to admit it to herself. The truth is, she'd had trouble connecting with people since the death of her mother, and while she'd hoped college would be different, it was obvious now that nothing had changed.

When wondering what was going on outside started to make her crazy, she replayed everything that happened the day she was kidnapped, searching her mind for a clue to the question of why somebody would want to hold her hostage. It didn't take her long to land on the only logical answer.

Someone was holding her for ransom.

Her father wasn't a billionaire or anything, but he was rich. Really rich. Responsible for the development of half the new Boston skyline, he had enough money for limos and private jets, expensive boarding schools, and vacations at private, far-flung resorts usually reserved for celebrities trying to avoid the paparazzi. It was why she'd decided to go to a state school in New York despite her father's protests. She wanted to be normal for awhile, minus the paranoid eye of her father's bodyguards and all the people whose only purpose, it seemed, was to make sure she and David had anything and everything they needed.

It was only their father's presence, his attention, that was out of reach.

But she'd stopped feeling bad about that a long time ago. She wasn't going to play the poor little rich girl card. She knew they were lucky. Knew there were people who went hungry in every city in America, not to mention the whole world. If the price she and David paid for their security was their father's absence, well, it seemed like a smaller price than most people had to pay for their survival.

The idea of a ransom gave her comfort. Her father would pay whatever they asked. Despite the recent awkwardness because of the situation with David, they were loved. Her father would do anything to get her back.

The sound of a key in the lock broke her away from her thoughts, and she scrambled to her feet, bracing herself for the door to open. A couple of seconds later, Luca stepped into the room. His eyes dropped to the unopened paper bag on the floor.

"Still not eating?" he asked.

She crossed her arms over her chest. "I'm not hungry."

His brow furrowed a little while he considered her words. "The boss wants you to eat."

"The boss?" Maybe if she could get some information on who was behind her kidnapping, she'd be able to find a way out of it.

"You're going to want to eat." He glanced back at the half open door, then looked at her, speaking more softly. "You don't want to make him mad. Trust me."

"Dante?" she asked.

He shook his head. "The boss makes Dante look like a two-year-old throwing a temper tantrum. Just eat. You'll be out of here before you know it."

"Tell me why I'm here," she demanded.

"I can't," he said.

She recrossed her arms. "Then I can't eat."

He sighed, and she didn't think she was imagining the concern in his eyes. "I'm trying to help you."

"Yeah? Well, I'm trying to help myself."

A wall came down over his face. "This isn't the way to do it, but it's your funeral."

He retreated from the room and locked the door.

She dropped to the bed, his final words ringing in her ears.

It's your funeral.

5

Nico bounced on the balls of his feet in the middle of the boxing ring on the first floor. He was dripping sweat, although from the looks of things Marco was no better off. Nico read the other man's body language, trying to determine Marco's next move, as they circled each other with their arms up.

When Nico got bored, he stepped forward, opening the round with a vicious left hook to Marco's face. His neck snapped back, and he immediately put his hands up in front of his face, ready to block Nico's next move. He was on the defensive now, which was exactly where Nico wanted him.

He faked a right hook, then raised his left leg, kicking Marco in the stomach just hard enough to send him flying into the ropes. He recovered quickly and came out swinging, but he was tired. Nico could see it in his gradually slowing movements, his hands just a little too low to really block his face.

Nico was still feeling good, and he circled Marco a couple more times, still bouncing, trying to wear out the other man before going in for the kill.

The sparring sessions -- a combination of Muay Thai and conventional boxing -- were part of Nico's initiative to minimize the use of weapons. The family had relied on them long past their usefulness. Guns were noisy and unwieldy, and knives were difficult to control. Nico's soldiers were mandated to train in street fighting, tactical combat, and at least one martial art. The massive gym at Headquarters -- built by tearing down the walls between three rooms -- had become a social hub for the organization, and it was almost always full of men working with one of the experts that coached there on a rotating basis. For Nico, sparring with them wasn't a matter of pride; it was one of leadership. They had to know he could hold his own, especially since he was so young. It was the only way they would respect him.

And he only led by fear when respect didn't work.

Marco was on the verge of exhaustion now, his feet dragging, arms threatening to drop altogether. Nico backed him into a corner and pummeled him with three quick jabs, then gave him enough room to stumble off the ropes before finishing him with a light kick to the chest.

Marco fell back, hitting the floor with a dull thud.

Nico took off one of his gloves and removed his mouthguard while one of the trainers helped Marco up.

"Good fight," Nico said, tapping the other man's glove with his own. "You kept me on my toes."

Marco took out his mouthguard.

"Thanks, boss."

They stepped out of the ring. Nico grabbed his towel, stopping to say a few words to the men gathered in the gym, making a point to ask about their families. He'd learned this brand of personal attention from his father, who always said family came first. And he didn't just mean blood.

For Nico's father, anyone working under the Vitale umbrella was family, and he'd spent much of his time attending weddings, funerals, and christenings, always leaving a thick envelope of cash as a gift.

When Nico had first started to learn the business, he'd asked his father why he bothered. He was the Boss. His people followed his orders because they wanted to be in the business -- and if that wasn't reason enough, because they might not see another sunrise if they didn't. Nico's father had used violence less than the Boston branch of the Syndicate, but it had still been on the table.

They'd been walking in Brooklyn at the time, meeting a bookmaker his father had suspected was skimming money. They had stopped in the street, and his father had pulled Nico to the side and placed a firm hand on his shoulder.

"In the wild, the weaker members of a pride or pack see to the day to day details, details that insure the survival of the group. Why do they do this while their leader sits by and watches?"

"Because the leader provides protection," Nico had said, chafing at the simplistic description.

His father had nodded. "And in our world, how often do we have a chance to demonstrate a willingness to protect what is ours?"

Nico had thought about it. "It depends."

"It's a rare circumstance in which one of our soldiers is repeatedly under threat, when we have a chance to prove our worth as head of the family."

"But going to weddings..."

"Not protection," his father agreed. "But we prowl the perimeter of our pride, stay on display. Both for the animals who might attack us when we're not looking, and for those who require reassurance that we're still vigilant on their behalf."

Nico swiped bitterly at his face as he left the gym. All of his father's strategy had been for nothing; his death had come at the hands of someone on the outside. The loyalty of the family hasn't saved him. It hadn't saved Nico's mother either. Their murder made Nico want to rage.

"Nico."

Luca caught up to him in the hall.

"What is it?" Nico stuffed the memories down as he headed for the stairs.

"Can I have a word?" Luca asked, tucking a large manilla envelope under one arm. "In private?"

"Can it wait?" Nico asked.

Luca shook his head. "I don't recommend it."

Nico fought against the weariness that seemed to lurk in his bones the past few months. He was tired. Tired of maintaining a constant wall of strength, of surveying the shadows for the next threat. It wasn't supposed to be this way. There were supposed to be certain protections inherent in his position. An honor code that insured his safety as long as he followed the rules. The execution of his parents had proved that theory false, but Luca was a good man, probably Nico's best. If he said he needed a word, it must be important.

"Walk with me to my office," Nico said, starting up the stairs.

They made their way to the third floor and Nico's private suite of rooms. There was an uptown office for MediaComm, the legal arm of the Vitale family holdings, but Nico had the brownstone renovated after his father's death as a way to bring the family's other enterprises under one roof. Consolidating the illegal part of the business under the guise of a private residence meant it was harder to get a search warrant, although not by much thanks to Homeland Security. They kept it clean, just in case. The little paper they used was immediately scanned and shredded, and their digital files were encrypted by some of the best coders in the world, constantly tested for vulnerability by two notoriously brilliant hackers, one of whom Nico had recruited from the FBI.

He'd taken heat from some of the other families for his "new age" way of doing business, had even been forced to defend the move with Raneiro, but in the end Nico had been right; the Vitale family was more efficient than ever, and his men -- and a few women now -- seemed to feel more like a cohesive unit.

The renovation had included a private office for Jenna, who managed his personal affairs, a digital lab for the increasingly important business of cyber theft, and the large gym. The basement was soundproof and held rooms for those occasions when they needed to detain someone -- like Carlo Rossi's daughter, who was down there now. But the third floor was all his, complete with an office, a bedroom, and a private bathroom. In some ways it felt more like home than his penthouse near Central Park. Here he could hear the sound of people hurrying up the stairs and down the halls, could feel the energy of the finely-tuned machine he was building.

His apartment was like a tomb. Silent and sterile.

He stepped into his office and stripped off his sweaty tank top, then grabbed a clean T-shirt from the second drawer in his desk. He would shower and clean up after his conversation with Luca.

"What's up?" he finally asked.

Luca handed him the manila envelope. "We have a problem with Dante Santoro."

Nico opened the envelope, skimming the report before he dropped it in the shredder. Then he turned his attention to the photos. He forced his face to remain impassive. The girl's face was a mass of blue and purple bruises, her lip split, her nose at an angle that could only mean it had been broken. The rest of her body was more of the same.

Nico put the pictures back into the envelope.

"What does he say?" Nico asked.

Luca shrugged, but Nico could see the anger burning in the other man's eyes. "Sex got rough, but it was consensual."

"Is she asking for anything?"

"No, but she doesn't have much. We might be able to offer help with medical bills and something for pain and suffering."

"Is that what you recommend?" Nico asked.

Luca's mouth twisted in disgust. "I recommend we take Dante out behind the woodshed and show him how it feels to fight a man."

"That's not off the table," Nico said. He paused. "Has anything like this happened before?"

"A few bar fights, domestic claim from a girlfriend who later recanted, scrap with an off duty detective... but nothing like this, no."

"Offer the girl cash, and plenty of it. Tell her Dante is being dealt with. He won't hurt her again. Then you and Marco deal with Dante. Make it look good. I want the others to know I won't stand for this."

Luca nodded but made no move to leave.

"Is there something else?" Nico asked.

"Carlo's daughter still isn't eating," he said.

Nico sat back in his chair. Kidnapping Carlo Rossi's daughter had been a last resort. It was necessary, but that didn't mean he liked it. And he sure as hell didn't want anyone saying he'd starved her if she made it out alive.

"How many days?" Nico asked.

"Five," Luca said. "Any word on the old man?"

Nico shook his head. "We put the word out, but nothing so far."

"You don't think the bastard would leave her to us, do you?" Luca asked.

"I don't want to believe it, but it's hard to say," Nico said. "Word on the street is the son's gay. Carlo hasn't talked to him since he came out."

"Not surprised. Half the goombahs in the northeast would still feel the same way," Luca said. "Like it's the fucking dark ages."

Nico frowned but let the cursing go. He didn't allow his soldiers to curse while on the job. It was part of the reorganization -- the building of a modern, efficient army with the intellect and respect of a more elegant time. Call it the Broken Window theory of mob management. But he and Luca were alone. And they weren't exactly boy scouts.

"Angelica is his only daughter," Nico finally said. "He'd have to be the devil incarnate to leave her with us."

"From what I've heard, that's not as far-fetched as it sounds," Luca said. "What should we do about her?"

Nico stood. "I'll be down after I shower and change."

6

She was almost elated. Now at least, something would happen. The knowledge that she probably wouldn't like it was responsible for the knot in her stomach, and she spent the next couple of hours staring at the door, feeling slightly nauseous.

She forced herself to remain seated when she heard a key in the lock on the other side of the door. She wasn't going to give the asshole -- whoever he or she was -- the satisfaction of knowing she was scared. But all of her big plans went out the window the moment the man swept into the room.

He was tall and powerfully built, his broad shoulders straining at the rich fabric of his designer suit. Everything about him was leonine, from the thick, dark hair combed back from his face, to the pronounced cheekbones over the strong set of his jaw. He moved quickly and gracefully toward her, not a shred of indecision in his gait.

But it was his eyes that made her stand, that forced her back against the wall.

They might have been brown, but the flecks of amber glowing from their depths made them look almost green. She had a flash of the black panthers she had loved at the zoo when she was little. Their unflinching gaze had been predatory, the raw power in their prowl both frightening and awe-inspiring. They had drawn her like a magnet.

Now, she had that same sensation. Like she was helpless in the face of him, forced to wait until he devoured her. She felt like she couldn't breathe. Like this man, whoever he was, had sucked all the oxygen out of the room with his mere presence.

He didn't stop until he was right in front of her, and her breath came fast and heavy as he stared her down, eyes locked on hers.

Finally, he spoke. "Is there a problem?"

His voice was deep and sure, with the diction she recognized from her wealthy classmates at boarding school. The question threw her for a loop (who was she kidding? *he* threw her for a loop), and it took few seconds to summon the anger that had been her companion during her hunger strike.

"You bet your ass there is." She pushed her chin into the air. "Your men drugged me, kidnapped me, and kept me prisoner. I'd say that's a big fucking problem."

"My men didn't do any of that," he said.

She didn't know what she had expected, but it wasn't that. "Then who did?"

"I did." He leaned down, his face mere inches from hers, and she caught a whiff of something musky and elemental laced with soap. She had a sudden flash of herself naked, wrapped in his suit jacket, infused with his scent. She was trying to shake the image from her mind when he continued. "And that's because nothing happens here without my approval. Nothing. Do you understand?"

He held her captive with his eyes, and she hoped he couldn't see the rapid rise and fall of her chest. Or that at least he would think it was fear. Because now that they were face to face, fear was a lot more palatable than the lust fighting for position in her body. And there was no denying the desire coursing through her veins. She felt it from the surface of her skin, only inches from the crisp wool of his suit, to the longing that beat like a drum at the center of her body.

She wanted to slap herself for nodding.

"Good," he continued. "Because while you're here, you will abide by the same rules as everyone else. Which means you will obey my every order without question. That includes eating. And if you don't, I might have to bring your brother in to keep you company."

His mention of David was like a slap to her face. "David…"

"… will be fine," he finished. "And so will you, as long as you do as you're told."

"What's the point of eating if you're going to kill me anyway?" she finally asked.

He didn't flinch. "As long as you're quiet and cooperative, you'll be set free as soon as I get what I want."

So she'd been right. Ransom. "Why should I trust anything you say?"

He stood a little straighter, pulling back enough that she felt like she could breathe again. "Whether you trust me or not is of no concern to me, Angelica." She was still recovering from his use of her name when he turned around and headed for the door. "But you do have my word."

She was reeling from her contact with him, questions swarming her mind. He was almost out the door by the time she fought through the noise in her brain to find the one thing she was desperate to know.

"Who are you?"

He stopped walking but didn't turn around. "I'm Nico Vitale," he said. "And I can either be your greatest ally or your worst enemy. It's up to you."

7

Nico pulled on gray sweats and left his building before the sun came up. He jogged toward the river, keeping the pace light until he hit the Parkway.

He'd slept fitfully, his altercation with Carlo Rossi's daughter running loops in his mind. He didn't know what he'd expected. He'd seen pictures of her in the planning stages of the kidnapping, but the photographs hadn't done her justice. She was beautiful, with golden hair that fell in waves to her waist and green eyes he'd almost gotten lost in. But it was more than that, more even than the soft swell of her curves, a contrast to all the women in the city who honed themselves to lean, hard planes that offered little in the way of comfort.

It had been in her eyes; something familiar and lonely. It had connected to a hidden part of his psyche, and in the moment he'd stood in front of her, all he'd wanted was to banish it from her forever.

He pushed himself to pick up the pace, a kind of punishment for his lack of discipline. His hormones were obviously out of control. The girl was a very important pawn in a very important game of chess; his only hope of getting the security tape that would incriminate Carlo Rossi in the death of his parents. He could sleep with any girl in the city.

But not her.

His senses felt oddly sharp in spite of his lack of sleep, and he continued past the point where he normally turned back toward his apartment, hoping to banish the distraction. It worked to some degree, and he turned his thoughts to the more practical aspects of holding Carlo Rossi's daughter hostage.

That she wasn't eating was a problem. He was already in violation of the Syndicate's code — the kidnapping and murder of family members was prohibited unless a very specific set of benchmarks had been met. They hadn't been, although it wouldn't have been necessary at all if Carlo hadn't first violated the code. Still, Nico was walking a fine line, and the survival of his organization depended on his ability to stay on the right side of it.

Kidnapping Angelica was risky. Letting her starve would be suicide.

He headed turned up West 90th Street and headed for the apartment, his limbs warm and loose. The run had gotten his blood pumping, and he was annoyed to find his thoughts drift back to the girl. This is what happened when you were used to getting what you want. The first time you saw something you couldn't have, it became an obsession. Not because you really wanted it, but because you knew you couldn't have it.

Still, it wouldn't hurt to be kind to her. It wasn't her fault her father was a bastard.

She had to eat.

8

She inventoried her purse for the hundredth time, peering at herself in the pocket mirror she rarely used but had been carrying around since Lauren gave it to her two Christmases ago. Her hair was disgusting, and her face had taken on the pale, translucent look of the very ill.

Or the perpetually imprisoned.

Her thoughts drifted back to Nico Vitale for the hundredth time in the two days since he'd invaded her room with his edict to eat. Her proximity to him had awakened some kind of primal need inside her, something that made her either crazy or ridiculous or both.

"You really need to get laid when this is all over, Angelica," she muttered under her breath, closing the mirror.

Her lack of sex life was the only possible explanation for her attraction to the man responsible for her kidnapping. She wasn't some dysfunctional ingenue with daddy issues. Okay, maybe she had some daddy issues, but Nico Vitale was anything but fatherly, and she'd worked through her feelings about her father, both alone and with the help of the therapist she'd seen on campus sophomore year.

No, what she'd felt when Nico's body had been close enough to touch was primal, physical. Probably had to do with pheromones or something. Lust was like that. Or that's what she'd heard anyway. She hadn't had much experience with it outside of a couple drunken frat parties when she'd first come to college. Then she'd just been happy to be free of the constraints of her Catholic boarding school, and for awhile, she lived it up with the best of them.

By her second year of college it had gotten old. Watered down beer didn't flip her switch the way it used to, and she'd started to feel sad and pathetic fending off the advances of her fellow students until she could reasonably make a break for the dorms. She hadn't had a boyfriend since junior year, and while there was a time when she'd been frequently asked out, eventually everyone stopped asking. It was a small town. Word had probably gotten around that she was frigid.

Or maybe they just thought she was a bitch.

She didn't really care. Things were easier when she only had to take care of herself, and sometimes that felt like more than a full time job. Her weakened sexual appetite didn't worry her. She always assumed it would reawaken when the right guy came along. Except now she suspected that her libido was on drugs, because the right guy was definitely not Nico Vitale. She knew this both because he was the man responsible for her current predicament and because she'd finally realized why the name sounded so familiar.

Nico Vitale was head of the Vitale crime family, one of the most notorious underground criminal organizations on the eastern seaboard.

She didn't know much about the mob, but she'd heard the Vitale family mentioned on the news. According to reports, Nico Vitale headed up a ring of organized crime that made money on everything from bookmaking to human trafficking, all of it shielded by a massive -- and legitimate -- international company called MediaComm. But the Feds never had enough to charge anyone, and people in the city had gotten blasé about the occasional arrest -- and about the fact that they never seemed to lead to a conviction.

You have my word, my ass, she thought.

She wondered how much honor a mobster could have, and if she could really take him at his word that he wouldn't hurt David. Nico had certainly felt dangerous when he'd been standing in front of her, although if she was honest with herself, that hadn't all been on him. Her physical response to him was enough to get her in trouble all by itself.

But at least now she knew for sure this was a ransom kidnapping. Obviously the Vitale family augmented their other illegal activities by kidnapping the brats of wealthy parents.

Herself included. How cliche.

She heard the key turn in the lock but didn't bother getting up off the floor. She'd stopped standing on ceremony with Luca some days ago. They had their routine down. His assertion that she should eat. Her refusal. The shake of his head when he told her Nico wouldn't be happy. The tightening of his jaw when she told him she couldn't care less if Nico was ever happy again.

It was a good routine. Solid. She could do it in her sleep.

The door swung open and Luca stepped into the room, this time empty-handed.

"No more offerings to the goddess?" she asked.

He sighed. "It's too late for that."

She stuffed down a thrum of alarm. "What's that supposed to mean?"

He removed the gun from his belt. "It means you're coming with me."

She got to her feet, her earlier bravado gone. "What's going on?"

"I can't tell you anything. You know that."

"Are you..." She swallowed hard and steadied her voice. "Are you going to kill me?"

His expression softened. "No one's going to kill you."

She tried not to hear the unspoken words; *Not right now, at least.*

She crossed her arms. "I want to know where you're taking me."

He stepped farther into the room, and she realized that he was taller than she'd originally thought. At least as tall as Nico, although Luca had the kind of compact muscle that was more distance runner than heavyweight boxer.

"I'm trying to be nice here," he said, "but I can use the drugs — and the pillowcase over your head — if you'd prefer it."

Regret shaded his voice, and she understood that he didn't want to use those things, but he would do it if she forced his hand.

"And if I come on my own, you won't put the pillowcase over my head?" She was as afraid of the darkness as she was of drug-addled oblivion.

"I'll still have to cover your eyes eventually," he admitted. "But not until we leave the building. And I'll forget the drugs if you come on your own and promise not to do anything stupid."

She wasn't crazy about the pillowcase under any scenario, but at least this way she might get a clue about where she was being held. "Okay."

"You'll be good?" He asked the question like he almost didn't believe it. "You promise?"

She sighed. "I promise."

She didn't think twice about the lie. She wouldn't hesitate to make a break for it if an opportunity to escape presented itself. It's not like these guys had any honor.

"Good." He looked down at the gun in his hand. "This is only a precaution. We're going to make our way through the building, and I'm going to put the bag over your head before I put you in the car out back."

"The car?" Hope blossomed inside her. "Does this mean my father has paid the ransom?"

"The ransom..." Luca looked confused in the moment before a wall of impassiveness dropped down over his features. "Not yet. But trust me. Nothing bad will happen to you tonight."

She raised her eyebrows. "Trust you?"

"I've kept you safe so far, haven't I?" he asked. And then, more softly, "Kept Dante out of here?"

The name sent a bolt of dread through her body. "Okay," she said. "Let's go."

9

She tried to look around the hallway without being too obvious, but there was nothing to see; just the same beige walls, different closed doors.

Luca opened a door at the end of the hall, and they ascended a narrow staircase. She could feel the gun pressed into her side, but just barely. She wasn't afraid. For some strange reason, she trusted Luca. He wouldn't hurt her as long as she held up her end of their bargain. And she would hold up her end of their bargain until she had a reasonable chance of escape with enough time to warn David to make himself scarce.

They exited the staircase into another hall, this one paneled in gleaming mahogany, and her feet sunk into thick taupe carpet. For the first time in days, she could hear the noise of other people moving around.

Luca stopped walking and looked down at her. "I'm going out on a limb here. Be good."

She nodded, a little overcome by the knowledge that there were other people in the vicinity. Not because she thought any of them would help her escape -- whoever was in this building obviously worked for Nico, and you didn't cross a man like Nico

Vitale -- but because the sheer proximity of other human beings meant she wasn't alone for the first time in days.

Light shone from one end of the hall, and she guessed that was the front of the building. Luca headed the other way.

She tried not to wonder why he was doing this for her. Wasn't he worried that she would see something -- or someone -- she shouldn't? And if not, was it because they planned to kill her after all?

She did her best to glance into the rooms with half-open doors while Luca moved her along, but what she saw didn't exactly clear things up.

The first room they passed was large and brightly lit, filled with tables topped with what looked like hi-tech computer equipment. The work stations were manned by men and women in suits and skirts. It could have been any office building anywhere in the world, and the sound of fingers tapping on keyboards lingered even after they passed the room.

They were approaching another door when she heard the sound of a woman's voice, professional and very British.

"That's correct. The donation should be listed as anonymous on your tax forms."

They passed the room, and Angelica got a glimpse of a straight-backed woman, hair pulled into a taut bun at the back of her neck. She was sitting at a carved desk, head bent to cradle the phone as she spoke.

"Mr. Vitale simply wants your word that all of the money will go to provide for the children," she said as they continued down the hall.

A donation? To children? What kind of mobster donated money to a kid's charity? Or was it some kind of bribe? Hush money for an under-the-table favor. And why was an infamous New York mob guy working out of what could have been a swanky office? She was still puzzling over the questions when they came to a set of double doors. They were both closed, but she could hear thumping coming from within the room, and occasionally, a grunt or yell.

Her gaze cut to Luca, hoping for some kind of explanation, but he kept his gaze focused on the door at the end of the hall. When they reached it, he stopped.

"I have to cover your eyes now." He reached for something, and for a few seconds she was free, one of his hands on the gun, the other reaching for his pocket and the dark pillowcase he would put over her head.

She felt a surge of adrenaline. She could bolt for the door. It was right in front of her. But if Luca was taking her that way, someone was probably out there waiting for them. And while the house -- or whatever it was -- seemed civilized enough up here, she had no doubt she would be stopped before she made it down the long hall to whatever exit had to be at the front of the building.

She tried not to feel defeated when Luca took hold of her arm again. She couldn't afford to be stupid. She would make a break for it when she was sure she could get out alive.

"Sorry about this," Luca said, lifting the pillowcase over her head and pulling it down until the edges brushed her shoulders. "It won't be for long."

Everything went dark, and she fought a wave of panic. "Are you... are you sure it's going to be okay?"

She felt the gentle pressure of his hand on her shoulder. "No harm will come to you tonight. I promise."

She nodded, too relieved by the promise to focus on his use of the word "tonight" and all the uncertainty it implied for her future.

She heard the door open in front of her, then felt the touch of fresh air on the bare skin of her arms. For the first time since they'd taken her, she was going outside. She wanted to weep with the joy of it, and also with the unfairness of having her head covered so she couldn't look up at the sky.

"Any trouble?"

She froze in her steps when she heard the voice. Dante.

"It's okay," Luca said softly. And then, louder, "No trouble."

"You're not going to leave now, are you?" she asked Luca, her feet still rooted to the ground.

"I'm not going anywhere. Dante's just driving," Luca said. "Come on."

She reluctantly moved forward under the gentle pressure of Luca's hand on her arm. She was helped up into some kind of big car. Luca slid in next to her, and the door closed behind them. They were encased in the muffled secrecy of the vehicle in the seconds before Dante slid into the front seat.

"I can't believe the fucking boss is doing this," he muttered.

"You don't have to believe it," Luca said. "That's why he's the boss."

"Don't fucking remind me," Dante said.

The car started, and then they were in motion. She lost track of time as they navigated the streets, but she knew for sure now that they were in a city, probably Manhattan. Everything was muffled from inside the plush interior of the car, but she could make out the sound of honking, the clang of a fire truck, and once, someone with a distinctly New York accent yelling something obscene.

The car zigged and zagged as Dante yelled under his breath. The gun was still at her side, but looser now. Good. Let Luca think she was a complacent little lamb. All the better for the moment when she would make her escape.

She started to get car sick. She prayed to whatever god might exist that they would arrive at their destination soon, then felt the familiar sting of Catholic guilt. If she was going to pray, she should be praying to Jesus, or at least to the Virgin Mother. But she hadn't attended mass since she'd left boarding school. She wasn't even sure she believed all the propaganda she'd been fed since she was a child, but it's not like she could tell her father that. He'd been going to mass nearly every day for most of his life, and she really didn't want to be responsible for the heart attack that killed him. Plus, he was still getting his head around the situation with David.

David. Did he know she was missing? Had he tried to text her? What would he do, who would he call when he realized something was wrong?

The car stopped with a sudden jerk. She waited, wondering if they'd hit another red light. But no. One of the front doors opened, and a few seconds later she heard the noise of the city and felt a cold wind on her face.

The pillowcase was pulled off her head, and she squinted against the faint light of dusk.

"What the fuck are you doing?"

She flinched when she heard Dante's voice next to her and saw that he was standing at her right shoulder. A dark purple bruise covered his left eye, a crack in his lip dried with blood. His eyes roamed her body, and she turned her attention to the building in front of them, anxious to break eye contact with him.

They were standing in an alley outside what looked like the rear entrance to a high-rise building. A service entrance, she guessed. She looked around, hoping for a delivery or maintenance person, anyone who might report the fact that two men were holding a woman at gunpoint outside the building.

But there was no one, and she wondered suddenly if they'd been paid to make themselves scarce. Pulling those kinds of strings would be easy for someone like Nico Vitale.

"I'm taking her up," Luca said. "And stop swearing. The boss doesn't like it."

"The boss doesn't like anything," Dante said, his voice cold. "Turned into a little pansy ass, and took the rest of you along for the ride."

Was he really calling Nico Vitale a pansy? Angelica didn't know Nico at all, but she didn't want to think about what might happen to anyone who talked that way about him. She could still feel the chill of his eyes, the animal energy that emanated from him like a warning.

"Watch your mouth," Luca growled. She turned to look at him and was surprised to see that his brown eyes had gone cold. It was the one and only time he'd seemed as dangerous as everyone else.

"Someday you're going to see that I'm right," Dante said. "Then you'll have to pick a side."

"I've already chosen a side," Luca said.

"What am I supposed to do while she's up there?" Dante asked.

Luca nudged her toward the doors. "I don't care. Just be ready when I call."

They stepped inside the building and started down a long concrete hallway.

"What are we doing?" she asked.

"Following orders," Luca said, his voice suddenly impersonal.

She kept quiet after that, assuming Luca was agitated by his conversation with Dante. Clearly they had differences, and while it was obvious Dante was less than loyal to Nico, that didn't do a thing to help her. Nico scared her, but only because of the raw power she sensed in his presence. Dante was something else; a loose cannon with an undercurrent of for-the-hell-of-it violence. She didn't know much about the real life mob, but she was pretty sure there was some kind of honor code. That was something, and if it was true, she'd rather wait it out with Luca than roll the dice with someone like Dante.

They came to a bank of elevators, and Luca pushed the Up arrow. A minute later a set of doors opened, and they stepped into a plush, mirrored elevator that stood in stark contrast to the concrete hallway they'd left behind. No one was inside. Nico's men had covered all the bases.

Luca inserted a key next to the button marked with a"P", and they stood in silence as the elevator began to ascend. She was acutely aware of the fact that she hadn't had a shower, hadn't been able to wash her hair in days. She almost felt sorry for Luca until she reminded herself that he was at least partially responsible for her current predicament.

She watched the numbers climb past the sixtieth floor before the elevator slid serenely to a stop at the penthouse level. The doors opened, but Luca remained in place.

She looked at him. "What now?"

He relinquished his hold on her arm and folded his hands in front of his body, still looking straight ahead. "Now you go inside."

"What is this place?" she asked, daring to hope that her father might be waiting, that maybe this was some kind of drop-off point.

"It's fine. Just go inside," he said. "I'll be back to pick you up later."

Her stomach dropped a little. No end to her imprisonment then. Not tonight. At some point she would be back in the little room under Vitale headquarters.

"Thanks for nothing," she muttered, stepping out of the elevator.

The doors closed behind her with a soft hum, and she turned her attention to the expansive room in front of her. It was all white furniture and gleaming wood floors stretching to a wall of glass, the city sparkling in the setting sun, lights just coming on in the skyscrapers scattered like jewels across town.

Definitely New York City.

"I see you made it."

A fire was already starting in the center of her body as she turned toward the voice.

Nico Vitale stood against the wall, arms crossed over his impressive chest. The suit was gone, replaced by a pair of jeans that hugged his thighs like a caress and a long-sleeve t-shirt that covered everything yet somehow made him seem more erotic than ever.

It took her a minute to find her voice. "What am I doing here?"

His eyes burned into hers. "You're here because I want you here. And that's all you need to know."

10

Nico leaned against the wall and watched her. She stood straight, the only sign of fear the fists clenched at her sides. She'd been through a harrowing ordeal, but she still seemed up for a fight. He had no doubt that she wouldn't go quietly, however this ended for her.

"Follow me." He pushed off the wall and started walking down the hallway.

"And if I don't?"

He didn't turn around. "You will. One way or another."

"You don't even have a gun," she said behind him.

He turned around, meeting her green-eyed gaze. "Do you think I need a gun to get you to do what I want?"

She licked her lips, and his eyes were drawn without his permission to their velvety softness. "I... I don't know," she admitted.

"Then I suggest you don't test the theory," he said, resuming his walk down the hall. "Besides, I assume you might like a shower."

He felt her presence behind him a moment later.

He led her to the guest bedroom where he'd laid out clothes on the bed. "There are fresh towels in the bathroom. Take your time. I'll be waiting in the living room."

He left in a hurry. He didn't want to stand close to her, didn't want to imagine her taking off her clothes in the steamy bathroom, letting the hot water wash over her alabaster skin.

Closing the door behind him, he took a deep breath, then headed for the living room where he poured two fingers of vodka into one of the crystal glasses that had belonged to his parents. He drank it all before crossing the room to the wall of glass overlooking the city.

The sun was almost gone. Central Park stood below him, spots of light illuminating large expanses of darkness. Beyond were the lights on the high rise buildings of 5th Avenue, and beyond it, those of Madison and Lexington Avenues. It was a multi-million dollar view, but he didn't enjoy it the way he usually did. He was too aware of Angelica in the other room. Too aware that they were alone in his apartment. That he was treading on dangerous territory allowing her a glimpse of his private residence.

Of course, once she realized her place in the grand scheme of things, her lips would be sealed about everything that happened to her while she was under Nico's control. It was the only reason he'd been able to risk having her at Headquarters, that Luca and Dante had been able to show her their faces. She didn't know it yet, but she had every reason to keep quiet about her abduction.

He ran a tired hand through his hair and watched as his reflection performed the same image. He felt like he'd aged ten years since his parents' murder. Taking over the family had been a big enough undertaking; remaking it had taken monumental effort. The mafia was old-school, built around rules and traditions that had existed for more than a century. Many of his father's men hadn't taken kindly to Nico's vision for the organization. Carmine, the Consigliere and advisor Nico had inherited from his father, had questioned the wisdom in limiting the use of weapons, developing a cyber division, letting go of the men who were unwilling to embrace change.

Nico had done it all anyway, giving generous retirement bonuses to the ones he fired -- those who went quietly anyway -- and even more generous packages to the ones he kept.

It had been an uncertain time, but the proof was in the result; a team built on respect and dedication instead of fear, and a hundred and twenty percent increase in revenue due to their interests in high-level hacking and information exchange. Thanks to their new business endeavors, Nico had been able to phase out some of the more distasteful income streams, many of which had sustained the family for generations. The New York City territory was now the Syndicate's most profitable, outpacing even the operations in countries where law and order was essentially non-existent, and Nico made a point of giving a significant portion of his profits to the philanthropic organization run by MediaComm. Even Raneiro had been forced to admit that Nico had been right.

The scent of garlic and basil drifted through the room, and he turned away from the windows and made his way to the kitchen.

He picked up a wooden spoon from the counter and stirred the clam sauce -- his mother's recipe -- in the pan on the stove. His men had given Angelica nothing but take out food since they'd taken her almost a week ago. No wonder she wasn't eating. He'd thought about having Maria, his housekeeper, make a meal before she left for the day but had decided at the last minute to do it himself.

He didn't want to think too long about his motives. The girl had gotten under his skin the day he'd confronted her in the basement, and he wasn't quite sure why. He told himself it was because he'd been sleeping with prostitutes too long. A product of his busy, and very private, lifestyle. He'd gone right from post-college bachelorhood to the all-consuming need for revenge and the high-octane task of running the Vitale family interests. He didn't have the time or inclination for anything real. Sex, by necessity, was like everything else in his life; all business. He had a couple of escorts that he met in high-end hotel rooms, but he'd never had a woman in his apartment.

He put down the spoon and turned off the heat on the sauce, then dumped the pasta he'd started before Angelica arrived into a colander in the sink. When he looked up, she was leaning against a wall in the living room, staring at him.

His breath caught in his throat at the sight of her. She was wearing the drawstring trousers and green blouse he'd set out on the bed in the guest room, her feet bare on the travertine floor. Her blonde hair -- darker after being washed -- fell around her shoulders in damp waves. For a split second, he forgot to breathe. Her emerald eyes pierced the darkness of the living room, and he had the sudden and powerful urge to close the distance between them and take her delicate face in his hands, claim her lips with his own.

"Hello," he said.

She didn't anything.

"Please," he said, "make yourself at home." He came around to the living room and turned on the table lamps flanking the couch. "Are you hungry?"

"Bringing me here doesn't change anything," she said, crossing her arms over her chest. "I'm not going to eat."

Her defiance lit a spark of anger inside him, but there was something else too. Something he was forced to acknowledge was excitement. No one defied him. Ever. She was physically in his possession, but she was making it clear that he couldn't bend her to his will. Not voluntarily anyway.

He thought about calling Luca, having him come and get her. Nico was trying to make things easier for her. If she didn't want his help, so be it. Let her rot in the basement until he got what he wanted.

But he knew almost as soon as he thought it that he wouldn't send her away. Not yet. His curiosity had gotten the better of him. And why shouldn't it? He had a professional interest in her. He needed to understand Carlo's next move and where he might be hiding. Angelica knew these things and more about her father. It was worth a little inconvenience to find out what he could about the other man. He ignored the voice in his head that called him a liar and made his way back to the kitchen.

"I admire your ingenuity, but starving yourself isn't going to improve the situation."

She stood straighter, and he recognized the jut of her chin from the altercation in the basement. "You need me for something. You wouldn't be keeping me alive otherwise."

He couldn't help the smile that touched his lips. "It will take you at least three months to starve to death. It's a very painful way to go." He heaped pasta onto two plates. "And the truth is, I don't need you alive."

Uncertainty flashed in her eyes. It was gone a moment later. "Then why haven't you killed me?"

He spooned food onto the plates. "It will be easier in the long run to keep you alive, and more in line with my business principles. But sometimes I don't have the luxury of standing on principle." He let his gaze settle on her eyes. "This is one of those times."

He brought the plates around to the dining table that was part of the apartment's open floor plan. Then he went back to the kitchen for a box of matches and lit the candles at the center of the table.

"Eating or not eating has no bearing on my actions. I've set my course. Nothing you do will change it, but taking advantage of a chance to eat a home-cooked meal will make things more pleasant for you." He walked around the table and pulled out one of the chairs. "Either way, you will sit."

Her gaze drifted from him to the table and back again. "If I eat, you answer my questions."

He tamped down his annoyance. "I already told you I don't care whether you eat or not."

"I think you're lying," she said.

The girl had balls. "I'm not. However, I am a bit curious, so I'll accept your terms -- as long as you meet me question for question."

She narrowed her eyes. "What do you mean?"

"I answer one of your questions, you answer one of mine. We both eat."

She chewed her thumbnail, and for a moment, he wondered what it would be like to slip his finger inside her mouth, to feel her lips close around his flesh, enveloping him in warmth.

She pushed off the wall and walked toward him. "Fine."

11

She sat down, catching Nico's scent as he stood behind her. The pure
maleness of it sent a rush of adrenaline through her body, and a bolt
of heat shot like an arrow to the core of her body. He leaned down as
he helped push in her chair, and for one crazy moment, she had to
resist the urge to turn and press her cheek against his face.

Then he stood and walked to his chair across the table.

She put her napkin in her lap, her heart beating too rapidly in
her chest. It was hard to catch her breath. She told herself it was
because she was afraid. As far as she knew, there was no one else in
the apartment. He could be planning to drug and rape her. She
looked down at her food, suddenly suspicious.

Nico sighed, his amber eyes surveying her from across the
table. A moment later, he stood and walked toward her with his plate
in one hand, wine glass in the other. She was wondering if she'd
finally reached the end of his patience when he swapped his plate
and glass for hers and made his way back to his seat across the table.

"Now can we eat?" he asked, his voice tight.

She picked up her fork and took a bite of the pasta. It took
effort not to groan with pleasure. After days with no food, the
spaghetti with clam sauce was pure heaven, and she had to force
herself to chew slowly, both because she didn't want to make herself

sick and because she didn't want to give Nico the satisfaction of watching her scarf down her food. When she'd had a couple more bites and taken a small sip of wine, she spoke.

"Why am I here?"

He met her eyes across the table. "I already told you; because I want you here."

"Why do you want me here?"

He shook his head. "You asked, I answered. It's my turn."

She wanted to protest, but she knew it would only sound childish. "Fine."

"What was your childhood like -- in three sentences?"

She paused with her fork halfway to her mouth, then set it back down on the plate. "In three sentences?"

He shrugged. "I'm making good use of my question."

He was good. She was going to have to be on her game.

She took a deep breath, formulating an answer that would tell him as little as possible while still meeting his requirement. "It was quiet. It was safe. It was..."

He raised his eyebrows, a smirk playing at the corner of his mouth. He'd stumped her, and he knew it. How did she sum up her childhood beyond safe and quiet in short sentences?

"I'm waiting," he said. "Don't make me institute a time limit."

"I went to boarding school when I was twelve," she finally said. "My turn."

He nodded, but he didn't seem overly concerned.

"Why do you want me here?" she asked, cursing herself for using two questions instead of one to get an answer.

He wiped the corners of his mouth with his napkin and dropped it into his lap. She tried not to look at the patch of bare skin visible in the "V" of his T-shirt.

"It will be better for my business if I keep you comfortable, and I'm under no delusion that the basement room is comfortable. Plus, I imagine you're used to better food than you've been getting."

She tried to hide her surprise. Unlike her, he didn't seem concerned with giving away too much.

"What was your mother like?" Nico asked.

Alarm clanged through her. "How do you know about my mother?"

He took another drink of his wine. "Do you want me to advance you the next question?"

She shook her head.

"Then I hope you'll be as generous in your answer as I've been, although I can always revert to my earlier format if it's the only way to get you to play fair."

She thought about that while she finished chewing. He was throwing her off balance. Being generous. Being nice. Looking at her with his jungle cat eyes.

She started speaking, as much to distract her from his gaze as to move the game along. "She was... warm. Kind. My father was always larger than life, but it was my mother who made me feel safe."

His nod was thoughtful. What was she doing? Why would she tell him something so personal? She glanced at the wine. She'd only had two drinks of it, but obviously the hunger strike had lowered her tolerance. She would have to be careful.

She took a sip from her water glass before asking her next question.

"What are you trying to accomplish by holding me hostage?"

He leaned back in his chair, studying her, and she suddenly felt self-conscious, like he could see right through the clothes he'd left for her.

"There's something I need," he finally said. "Something very important, very... personal. Holding you as collateral is the only way I can get it."

So it was something from her father. Although was money personal?

"Money?" she asked.

"Is that your next question?"

She sighed. "Okay, yes. That's my next question. Do you want money from my father?"

"No."

She puzzled over his answer while he took another bite. If not money, then what? What else could Nico Vitale possibly want from a man who developed property in Boston? Her mind paged through the possibilities. Help getting permission to build something? A better price on a piece of available land, or a building under development?

"I get two questions now," he said, interrupting her thoughts.

She nodded, still trying to figure out what was going on.

"Tell me about your relationship with your father."

"That's not a question." She wondered if he'd object to the sharpness of her tone.

"You're right," he said. "Let me rephrase; How would you describe your relationship with your father?"

Same question. Although making him rephrase it had bought her a little time.

"Complicated," she said.

If he was annoyed by her short response, he didn't show it. She took another bite of the pasta, ravenous now that she had the feeling of food in her stomach again. She would never admit it, but the pasta was good. Better than good. Amazing.

"Why is it complicated?" he asked, setting down his fork and wiping his mouth.

She thought about the question while she chewed. Why was it complicated? She knew her father loved her. David, too. And they loved him back. Still, nothing had been the same since her mother's death.

"After my mother died..." She felt Nico's eyes on her as she stared at her plate, searching for the words she needed. "He just didn't know what to do with David and me. He sent us to boarding school right after her funeral. Separate boarding schools. We only saw him a couple times a year when he was in the area or when we took vacations, and on the rare occasions we were allowed home to Boston for Christmas or summer break."

He seemed surprised. "You weren't allowed home for holidays?"

She almost answered, then caught herself. "It's my turn."

He nodded. "You're absolutely right."

Why was he being so nice? Had she misread the danger she'd sensed in him the first time they'd met? But no, that didn't make sense. He was part of the mob. Danger was an understatement.

"Will you kill me?" she asked suddenly.

He toyed with the stem of his wine glass. "That's not currently the plan."

Her stomach tightened. "That's not what I asked."

He nodded, then met her eyes. "As long as your father gives me what I want, you'll be released unharmed."

Some of the tension left her body. If her survival depended on her father coming through, she would be fine.

"What do you want from him?" she blurted. "He's..." She shrugged. "He's just a business man."

It was the only time he'd seemed off balance, and she thought she caught confusion in his eyes before his expression turned placid. She wondered if she'd imagined it.

"That's between your father and me," he said. "Would you like some more food?"

She looked down at her plate. Somehow during their conversation, she'd eaten every bite. "No, thank you."

"I hope you enjoyed it," he said.

"It was very good." The compliment wasn't really for him, which was the only reason she could offer it. She had no doubt he was hiding a housekeeper, and probably someone else responsible for the cooking.

He nodded, holding her gaze, and for a minute she felt like she couldn't breathe. Felt like she didn't need to breathe. Like the light in Nico Vitale's eyes was the only thing necessary to her survival.

Which was ridiculous and stupid. Not to mention dangerous. Very, very dangerous.

She stood, anxious to break eye contact with him, and took her plate to the kitchen. She rinsed it off and left it in the sink, forcing herself not to look at Nico as he came into the kitchen. If she just avoided his eyes, she would be okay. She would be back in the basement room that was her prison, a place that felt oddly safe compared to being alone with this man.

She jumped a little as his arms snaked around her, and she felt the press of his body as he rinsed off his plate and set it in the sink. His back was as sturdy as a giant oak, his thighs strong on the back of hers.

She froze, afraid to move, afraid to do anything that would allow her to feel his body more fully. Not because she was afraid of him, although there was a part of her that was afraid -- a secret part she wanted to deny after four years surrounded by feminists at her liberal arts college. Because there was no way being scared of someone should be a turn on. No way she should desire the man responsible for her abduction and imprisonment.

But she did. And that was why she was really afraid. Because if Nico got any closer, she might not move to get away. She might turn in his arms instead. Might press against him and maybe even strip off his shirt so she could see the muscle she already knew lurked underneath it. She was willing herself to move, to get away from him while she still could, when she felt his hands on her hair.

He lifted it away from her neck, draping it over one shoulder so it tumbled down her chest. She struggled to keep her breathing calm, not wanting him to know the effect he was having on her.

His breath was a whisper as he lowered his head to the sensitive skin of her neck. When he pressed his mouth to the edge of her collarbone, her head fell back against his shoulder. A sigh escaped her lips, but she didn't have the strength to care. Not while his mouth was on her, as soft as satin, the flick of his tongue hot against her bare skin.

She was hardly aware of the water running in the sink as he placed his hands on her hips and pulled her back against his erection. She moved without thinking, rotating against the hard length of him. There was a voice somewhere in the depths of her mind calling for her to stop. But it was so small, so faint, compared to the roar building inside her body as waves of desire crashed over her.

A moment later she felt the heat of his hands on the flat plane of her stomach as he moved them under her shirt. When they reached the lace of her bra, he groaned and spun her to face him. She didn't have time to think before his mouth covered hers. There was nothing gentle in the kiss. It was angry and demanding, his hands tangled in her hair, tipping her head so he could devour her, his tongue sweeping her mouth.

She didn't even try to resist when he lifted her onto the edge of the granite counter. He spread her legs, pressing his hard on against the hot softness at her center. She braced herself on the counter with her arms, closing her eyes as he lifted her shirt.

He peeled back the lace of her bra. The cold air hit her already erect nipples, and a moment later she felt the hot stroke of his tongue on one sensitive bud while he lightly pinched the other one.

She was coming apart, the feel of his cock between her legs and his mouth on her breasts spinning her into a universe where there was no rhyme, no reason. He left a trail of hot kisses from her breasts to her stomach. His tongue dipped below the waist band of her trousers, and she thought she might die from the crystalline torture of it.

"Angelica..." He breathed her name, and in it she heard something else.

Angelica, her father.

Ange, her brother.

What was she doing? What was she thinking?

"Wait," she gasped, struggling against the passion that threatened to pull her back under the surface of her reason. "Nico... stop."

He went still. For a moment, neither of them moved. Then he straightened, his eyes on fire. With desire? Anger? She couldn't tell.

She swallowed hard, forcing herself to say the words she didn't quite believe she wanted to say. "I'd like to go now."

She thought he might be mad, but his lips turned up into a faint smile instead. He traced a line down her cheek.

"Angelica," he whispered, his eyes still on hers. And then, "Angel."

She wanted to push him away from her, but she was rendered immobile by the power of his gaze. And then he was fixing her bra, pulling up the lacy fabric to cover her, gently lowering her shirt.

He stepped away, nodding like they had just concluded some kind of business meeting. "I'll call Luca."

12

She was still shaking when she stepped into the elevator. Not because of what had happened, but because of what she'd wanted to happen. Because even as the elevator doors closed, she wanted to step back into the apartment. To feel Nico's hands on her body.

Instead, she'd averted her gaze, refusing to look at him as the doors closed between them.

She took a deep breath when the elevator started to descend, the fog lifting from her desire-addled brain. She watched the numbers on the display in their countdown from the fortieth floor and realized something; she was completely alone.

She started pushing buttons on the control panel. Twenty-first floor, sixteenth floor, fourth floor; anything but the basement signified by the lit "B" that had somehow already been pressed when she stepped into the elevator.

But none of the other buttons seemed to work, and she was forced to acknowledge that Nico's all-consuming power extended even to the elevator. It must be exclusive to the penthouse and controlled from the apartment.

She leaned back against the mirrored interior and pushed away the memory of Nico's lips on her neck, her breasts. She needed to get away from him for good. She was losing it.

She was almost looking forward to seeing Luca -- calm, reliable Luca -- when the elevator doors finally opened. But it wasn't Luca who stood waiting for her.

It was Dante, a mixture of pleasure and hatred in his eyes.

"Well, well, well," he said. "I guess the boss is all done with you."

She froze, pinned to the floor of the elevator like a dead butterfly on display.

"Are you stupid?" he said. "Let's go."

He reached into the elevator and grabbed her arm, twisting as he pulled her into the basement. She cried out against her will.

He pulled her down the hall so fast she had to trot to keep up, her arm bent at an unnatural angle, feeling like it was on the verge of snapping.

The black SUV was waiting when they crashed out of the basement doors. Fear turned her blood to ice when she saw that it was was empty. Dante opened the door and shoved her into the back seat.

"Where's Luca?" she asked, rubbing her aching arm.

"Don't you worry about Luca," Dante said. He leaned into the backseat and grabbed her breast, squeezing so hard it brought tears to her eyes. "I'm not usually into sloppy seconds, but I'm going to take real good care of you now that the boss is finished."

She was weighing her chances of gouging out his eyes and making a run for it when something came down over her head. She was plunged into darkness, and she fought against the return of her panic as the door closed with a resolute thud.

Think, Angelica. Don't panic. Think.

She frantically felt along the door, looking for the unlock button or the door handle, anything that would get her away from Dante. A second later, she heard him slide into the front seat and start the car. She sensed him watching her in the silence.

"There are no handles back there," he finally said. "No locks either."

She wondered if she was imagining the satisfaction in his voice, but she didn't have a chance to analyze it further. The car started, and then they were in motion.

"Just sit back and enjoy the ride." He laughed like it was some kind of joke.

She tried to think of another way to escape, but it didn't take long to admit to herself that it was futile. She would have to stay alert, look for an opportunity when they got back to the building where they were keeping her. Maybe Luca would be there. She hung onto the possibility like a life boat in a stormy sea.

They twisted and turned through the streets of New York City. The pasta she'd eaten at Nico's had turned sour in her stomach, and she was fighting motion sickness when the car finally slowed down, then stopped altogether.

"Home, sweet home," Dante said.

She heard him get out of the car and braced herself for another assault. He grabbed her already-sore arm, then dragged her from the car.

She thought he would remove the pillowcase, but it remained on her head even after she heard a lock turn, felt the warm rush of air as he shoved her inside. He moved her roughly down a set of stairs, and then she was being pushed forward, too grateful for the distance opening up between them to care that she stumbled and fell to the ground.

Her hands went instinctively to the pillowcase. She pulled it from her head, hoping Dante would be gone. But he wasn't. He was in the room with her, the door closed.

He advanced on her, and she scrambled to her feet, determined to maintain as much control over the situation as possible. She might not be able to stop whatever was coming, but she wouldn't be cowering from him when it came.

He stopped in front of her, his eyes dropping to her breasts. She was still wondering what was coming when he reached up and ripped open her blouse, as easy as if it were made of paper.

Her hands went up, instinctively trying to cover her body by holding together the two pieces of green silk. But it was no use. He was fast, and he grabbed her wrists and held them together, crushing them in one of his hands and backing her up against the wall.

He lifted her arms over her head and pressed his body into hers. His excitement was obvious through his jeans, and she turned her head, wanting to deny this was happening. She tried to get away, but his hands might have been made of steel for all the progress she made.

"You were with the boss awhile," he said, grinding his hips into hers. "Must be good."

Her stomach turned as his words echoed in her head.

The boss...

The boss...

Nico was Dante's boss. Didn't that mean something -- something important -- in the mafia?

"Nico won't like this," she gasped as he lowered his head to her breasts.

He looked up. "What did you say?"

"I said..." Would mentioning Nico make her situation worse? It didn't matter. It was all she had. "Nico won't like this."

He hesitated. "What? You think your father makes you *special?*"

"I don't know, but Nico said it would hurt his business if something happened to me."

Dante straightened, dragging his eyes from her chest to her face. "He said that?"

"Yes."

"But he had you."

She shook her head. "He didn't."

"Then why did he bring you to his apartment?" he asked.

"I... I don't know. He just wanted to talk to me, I think." She licked her lips. This was working. "He said he has to keep me safe to get what he wants."

It was a white lie, but the stakes were too high to stand on principle. Maybe Nico had insinuated that keeping her alive only mattered as long as he got what he wanted from her father. But he would get it, and he *had* said that it was better for his business to keep her alive.

The seconds seemed to tick into infinity. Dante's eyes glazed over as he thought about what she said. She sensed a reprieve, and her heart threatened to beat out of her chest while she waited for him to speak.

Finally, he let go of her hands and stepped back. The confusion cleared from his eyes, replaced by disgust as he looked at her.

"You better hope Daddy comes through. And if he doesn't, you better hope Nico doesn't ask me to deal with you."

He took one last look at her chest, covered only by her white lace bra. Then he left, locking the door behind him.

She stumbled to the bed, tears of relief stinging her eyes. It had been a close call. Too close. She'd been lured into a sense of safety -- physical safety anyway, let's not talk about the danger her body had been getting her into -- at Nico's apartment. Now she felt her vulnerability all over again.

She was at their mercy. All of them.

Where are you, Dad? Get me out of here.

When her breathing had returned to normal, she dug through her purse for the two small safety pins she kept in the change compartment of her wallet. They wouldn't make up for the loss of her buttons, but they were better than nothing. She pinned her blouse closed and took inventory of her injuries.

The arm hurt, but she could move it. She'd have a nasty bruise, but at least it wasn't broken. She carefully touched her wrists, still feeling the sting of Dante's iron grip. Maybe a bruise there, too. But she was alive, and she hadn't been raped. She would make it to see another day. At this point, it felt like a gift.

She curled up on the bed, hugging her purse to her chest, breathing in the scent of her old life. She thought of David, of his warmth and kindness, his pain over the fact that their father couldn't accept him. She thought of her father's stubborn strength, his refusal to let either of them in after their mother's death. She had been the glue that held them together. Without her, they were puzzle pieces that didn't quite fit. Angelica had always assumed they'd have the time to figure it out. Now she couldn't help wondering if that was true.

But it wasn't her family that drifted through her mind in the moment before she finally fell into sleep. It was Nico. She remembered his arms around her at the apartment and realized something; she hadn't been afraid. Not once had she believed he would take her by force. Instead he'd looked at her with his amber eyes, and she would have sworn he would never hurt her.

And that he wouldn't let anyone else hurt her either.

13

Nico sat in the chair behind his desk, silently rolling the rosary beads through his fingers. His mother would be offended that he never said the rosary prayer. His complicated relationship with his faith wouldn't allow for the hypocrisy of it, but he enjoyed the feel of the cool beads between his fingers. It was a kind of meditation, and he kept a rosary stashed in his desk at home, at the office, even in his cars.

He was ashamed at the turn of his thoughts. Not because of the infamous guilt wielded by the Catholic church to keep its members in line, but because his preoccupation defied every ounce of his business acumen.

He should not be thinking about Angelica — Angel — right now.

Not the way he was thinking about her.

But he couldn't seem to help himself. The creaminess of her skin still glowed in his mind like a pearl, the perfect heaviness of her breast in his hand, the point of her nipple rising to a peak under his tongue. It was all there whether he wanted it to be or not.

He'd prowled his apartment in the dark after she left, feeling like he would jump out of his skin if he didn't have her. He'd taken a cold shower, even watched TV, something he hadn't done in at least a year. Still she'd been front and center in his mind, and he'd finally gone to bed, tossing and turning until the sunrise started to sweep the horizon pale orange. Then he'd gone for a run along the river, hoping the pounding of the pavement under his feet would banish her from his mind.

None of it had done a damn bit of good.

"You need to get laid, Nico," he whispered to the empty room.

Saying it made him feel better. That was the source of the problem. A man with his appetites needed release on a regular basis. A very regular basis. It had been too long. He would call his favorite escort service tonight, let off some steam.

He stood, dropping the beads into the top drawer of his desk. He walked to the window and looked out over the leafy suburban street lined with brownstones.

Carlo's daughter was just like everything else he did — all business. Learning about her last night had been an interesting diversion, but it was time for something more substantial. Nico had put the word out that he had something belonging to Carlo. He'd made it known that if Carlo wished its safe return, he would contact Nico within the week.

And yet they still hadn't heard from the bastard.

Word on the street was that he was in hiding, and no one seemed to know where the man was holed up. Nico was tired of waiting. And he was doubly tired of babysitting Carlo's daughter.

He turned to grab his suit jacket. He was slipping it on when he met Luca in the stairwell, holding a paper bag and heading for the basement.

"Morning," Nico said. "What are you up to?"

"Taking breakfast to Angelica."

Nico raised his eyebrows. "Angelica?"

Luca shrugged. "It doesn't seem right to keep calling her 'the girl'."

Was Luca Cassano blushing? Nico didn't know whether to be impressed or annoyed by Angel's ability to incite protectiveness in one of his most trusted men.

When they got to the basement, Nico put a hand on Luca's shoulder. "Why don't you give that to me?"

Luca hesitated, before handing over the bag of food.

Nico clapped the other man's shoulder. "I'm not going to hurt her," he said. "For now."

"It's nothing to me," Luca said.

Nico didn't make a big deal of the lie. Luca could hold his own with any man in Nico's army, but unlike some, he had a conscience. Hurting people was something he only did out of necessity, and he'd been one of the fiercest advocates for Nico's sweeping changes of the family.

Nico appreciated Luca's moral restraint. Violence was best administered by those who truly understood its consequences.

"We still haven't heard anything from Carlo. I'm going to put some heat on Angel — Angelica. See if she might know where he's hiding."

"Got it." If Luca noticed Nico's slip, he didn't say anything about it. "Want help?"

"I can handle it."

"I'm going to get in a workout then," Luca said. "Unless you need me for something else."

"I'm good," Nico said, already turning to make his way down the hall.

He continued to the closed door and withdrew a set of keys from his jacket pocket, then unlocked the door and stepped inside. Angel bolted up from the bed. He'd obviously woken her up.

He shut the door behind him. No need to lock it; Angel wasn't going anywhere he didn't want her to go.

"Good morning," he said, putting the food on the desk. "I've brought you breakfast."

Keeping his voice professional wasn't easy. She was sleepy and rumpled, her hair a mass of tousled waves around her delicate face. Sex hair. He banished the thought as soon as it hit him, but it was too late. He already felt the stirring of desire in his blood.

She didn't say anything, and when he stepped closer, he knew immediately that something was wrong. There were purple smudges under her eyes, and she was at least two shades paler than she'd been in his apartment. Then he saw her blouse, the one he'd left for her last night, and the two safety pins barely keeping it closed.

He was taking in the rest of her, trying to stop the tide of rage building inside him, when his gaze stopped on her arm. It was ringed with deep violet, clearly left by someone's hand.

"What happened?"

She flinched, and he realized his voice had gone cold. It was the voice he used for the worst of his business associates, the ones Nico didn't think twice about hurting. He hadn't meant to use it with Angel, but the sight of her scared, wounded, caused a visceral reaction in him, and he had to fight the urge to put his fist through one of the walls.

She turned her face away. "Nothing."

He stepped closer and took her chin in his hand, gently tipping her face up until she was looking at him. "Tell me."

"I guess your friends expect you to share." She spat the words at him, her eyes defiant.

"I don't know what you're talking about," he said. "Please elaborate."

"Let's just say Dante wanted in on the action after I left your apartment last night."

Her voice was calm and steady, but he saw the shimmer of tears in her eyes. It made him admire her all over again. It was one thing to be too stupid to be scared. It was something else to be terrified and keep your head up anyway.

"Did he touch you?"

She glanced down at her arm. "You could say that."

"You know what I mean."

"He didn't rape me, if that's what you're getting at. But only because I lied."

"How so?"

"I told him you wouldn't like it if he did," she said.

"That's an understatement." Nico thought he might snap from the fury flooding his body. He took a deep breath and stepped back from her. "Are you alright?"

"Am I alright?" There was a hint of hysteria in her laughter. "I'm as alright as I can be imprisoned in this room, wondering if every day is the day I'm going to die. Or worse."

He nodded. "I'll have Luca bring you some clothes. You have my word that you'll never see Dante here again."

He left the bag of food on the desk and headed for the door, anxious to reach the hall before his temper got the best of him.

Stepping outside the room, he locked the door and strode to the stairwell. His mind cleared as he took the steps two at a time, the anger that had made him feel hot and out of control receding to make room for cold, hard fury as he headed for the gym.

He burst through the doors and stopped, taking inventory of the bodies occupying the space. Luca was beating on a heavy bag while Marco worked with the Judo coach nearby. In the boxing ring, Gideon and Anthony circled each other, taking jabs when they could get one in.

He turned his eyes to the free weights, his gaze coming to rest on Dante, laying mid-press on one of the benches.

Peeling off his jacket, Nico tossed it aside as he strode across the floor. His soldiers were starting to notice his arrival, but he ignored their greetings, homing in on Dante like a heat-seeking missile, then grabbing hold of his right leg and pulling him out from under the bar in one smooth motion.

Dante lost his grip on the bar, and it crashed to the bench, narrowly missing his head, on its way to the floor.

"Whoa, whoa, whoa! What the fuck..." It was all he had time to say before Nico threw him to the ground, silencing him with a series of punishing punches to the face.

Nico felt none of the rage he had felt in the basement with Angel. Now the stormy sea of his mind was dead calm, nothing in it but the satisfaction of hearing the bones in Dante's face crunch under his fists. He punched and punched. He punched until Dante stopped moving, until his eyes were closed and he thought Dante might be dead.

Finally, the pace of his punches slowed, then stopped. The room was as quiet as a church. No one moved.

He waited until his breathing was under control to stand. Luca handed him his jacket.

"Take out this trash," Nico said, slipping his arms into the jacket. "Confiscate his keys and revoke his permissions immediately. Make sure everyone on the street knows that he is no longer affiliated with the Vitale family."

Luca nodded, his face impassive. "You got it, boss."

Nico walked past the shocked faces in the gym. He had meetings all day.

14

"Brought you some Thai food this time," Luca said, entering the room. "I hope that's okay."

He shut the door, but this time he didn't lock it. Did they believe she was too scared to make a run for it? Somehow she didn't think so. She heard Nico's voice in his apartment.

Do you think I need a gun to make you do what I want you to do?

The gun had never been necessary. She understood that now. Luca had used it because it was a show of force she could understand. But he didn't need it. None of them did.

She threw her legs over the side of the bed. "Fine."

She'd given up her hunger strike. In the face of Dante's assault the day before, it seemed childish and ineffectual. Nico was right; starving herself wouldn't change anything. She needed to be smart, keep up her strength in case an opportunity to escape presented itself.

Luca set the food on the desk and glanced at her. "Clothes fit okay?"

She nodded. He had brought her two shopping bags full of clothes yesterday, and she'd been surprised to find not only a new blouse, but jeans, a long skirt, two t-shirts, socks, a pair of ballet flats, and even underclothes. She'd felt embarrassed by the bra and panties until she realized some assistant had probably bought them. She couldn't imagine Luca doing it — even though Luca seemed to be in charge of bringing her things — and she didn't want to think about Nico choosing the lacy garments with her in mind. It was too personal. Too reminiscent of their moment in his kitchen.

He couldn't know how desperate she was to ditch the clothes she'd been wearing when Dante put his hands on her, but she was still grateful.

"I'm glad." He pulled a book out of his back pocket and handed it to her.

She looked down at the cover. "*To the Lighthouse?*"

He shrugged. "The lady at the bookstore said you can't go wrong with Virginia Woolf. Nico thought it might help you pass the time."

She looked up at him. "Nico knows about this?"

"He's the one who suggested it." Luca stuck his hands in the pocket of his slacks. "He's not a bad guy, you know."

"You care about him," she said.

"Love him like a brother. Would take a bullet for him without a second thought."

His voice had gone hard, and she had no doubt that he meant every word. What kind of history did the two men share to breed that kind of loyalty? Or was it just a mob thing?

"It's kind of hard to see him as a good guy when he's responsible for the fact that I've been locked in this room for the last week," she finally said.

He nodded. "I understand. I just want you to know there's more there than meets the eye."

"Why?" she asked. "Why do you care what I think of Nico?"

"Because he does." He turned around. "Enjoy your lunch."

He closed the door behind him, and this time he locked it.

She dropped onto the bed, still holding the book in her hands. Nico cared what she thought of him? Hard to believe under the circumstances. He'd been angry when he saw what Dante had done to her — when he'd heard what Dante had almost done. But Nico was keeping her prisoner to further his business interests. If he was angry at Dante, it was only because he had violated orders, not because Nico cared. It would take a lot more than a book and some clothes to make her believe otherwise. This was probably some kind of mind fuck designed to get her to trust them.

She dug into the Thai food and opened the book, feeling as close to content as she'd come since the day she'd been kidnapped. She ached to talk to her brother, to know what was going on with her father and why he hadn't given into Nico's demands — whatever they were. But she had food and a good book. It was enough for now.

She had just finished eating when the key rattled in the lock. She looked up, her heart picking up its pace. Nico had said Dante wouldn't be back, but she still felt a jolt of fear when she thought of him.

A moment later the door opened, and Nico stepped into the room.

He avoided her gaze as he made his way to the desk. Spinning the chair around, he placed it a couple of feet away and sat down. She lowered her eyes as the silence stretched between them. The knuckles of his right hand were scraped and bruised. She wondered if he was a boxer.

"How are you feeling today?" he asked.

"I'm fine."

He nodded. "I'm sorry about yesterday. That's not the way I do business."

"I'm glad to hear that." She couldn't keep the note of sarcasm from her voice. He might not be a rapist, but he was still keeping her hostage. If not raping someone was the measuring stick for being a good guy, it was a pretty low bar.

"We need to talk," he said. "I'm trying to make you comfortable, but this can't continue for much longer. I need information."

His voice was steely. Where was the Nico she'd met in his apartment? The one with the gentle voice? The tender but passionate touch?

She pushed the thought from her mind. She couldn't afford to think about him like that.

"I don't know what I could possibly tell you," she said.

"I need information about your father."

Was her father in danger? Would giving Nico the information he wanted put her father at risk? On the other hand, hearing what Nico wanted to know might give her some leverage, or at least help her understand what he he was hoping to gain.

"It seems like you already know a lot about him," she said.

Nico studied her face, and she felt her cheeks grow hot with the intensity of his stare. "He hasn't contacted us. We need to know where he might be hiding."

"Maybe he doesn't know I'm missing," she said.

"He knows." There was an ominous kind of certainty in his voice.

"We aren't very close." She was surprised to hear her voice crack. Like admitting it out loud somehow made it more true. "We don't talk very often."

"He knows," Nico repeated coldly. "We're aware of the house in Boston, the apartment on the West Side, and the house in Miami. We need to know where else he might be hiding."

"I... I don't know," she said.

She jumped as he slammed a hand down on the desk at his side. "You're only hurting yourself, Angel."

She was torn between relief at his use of the nickname (it had to mean something, didn't it?) and fear at his frustration. She'd only seen him a couple of times before this, but he'd always been in perfect control. Even the first day when he'd been angry that she wasn't eating.

She covered her face with her hands. "I don't know what you want from me!"

"I want you to make it possible for me to let you go without hurting you."

She looked up at him and felt desire roll through her body. She was more fucked up than she realized if she could still want this man while he was threatening her. How could she ever have thought he wouldn't hurt her? Stupid.

"I already told you; we aren't close. I see him a couple times a year when he's upstate. We used to take vacations, but since I graduated, we don't even do that." It sounded pathetic, and she suddenly hated Nico for making her say it all out loud.

"Where do you spend holidays?" he asked.

"I spent last Christmas with my brother in my apartment." Her voice had become as cold as his.

"Where did your father spend the holiday?"

"In Boston, as far as I know," she said.

He stood and paced the room. "Where did you used to go on vacation?" He continued without waiting for her to answer. "Who are his closest friends? Come on, Angel! Help yourself."

She threw up her hands, standing as her anger built. "We went to different resorts in Hawaii, the Bahamas. We went to Tahiti once. I don't remember the names of the places we stayed. You're asking for information I don't have. My father was obsessed with his business. It was all he thought about. He didn't have time for walks on the beach or long phone conversations." She stepped closer to him as she continued ranting. "And you know what? He may not be a great father, but he's a decent man! Whatever you want with him, he doesn't deserve to be hunted like an animal!"

It had been a mistake to get close to him. His scent enveloped her, his raw power filling the space between them, pulling her in like a predator luring its prey.

"A decent man?" he said softly. "Is that what you think?"

It wasn't what she expected. "It's what I know."

"What you know?"

She swallowed hard, dread pulling her under like quicksand. "Yes."

He held her gaze, and she had to resist the urge to lift her hand to his neck, push her fingers into his hair, dark as a raven, pull his mouth to hers.

"Luca!" he shouted.

It startled her, and she let her eyes skip to the door as Luca stepped through it. He was carrying something in his arms, but it wasn't until he got closer that she realized they were newspapers.

"Set them on the desk," Nico ordered.

Luca put them down, glancing at her as he headed for the door. She thought she saw an apology in his eyes, although she couldn't imagine why Luca would be sorry. He was the only person who'd been decent to her since this whole mess began.

Nico picked up the newspaper on top, letting it unfold. He put it between them, forcing her to look at it.

"CARLO ROSSI INDICTED FOR RACKETEERING," the headline screamed.

She lifted her eyes from the paper to look at Nico. "So?"

"So," he said, "this is your father."

She shook her head, relief lighting like a flame in the darkness inside her. Nico had the wrong man. The wrong daughter. "My father's last name is Bondesan, like mine. Like my brother's."

He pushed the paper at her. "Look at the picture."

She took it, forcing herself to lower her eyes to the paper. A man was stepping from a limousine outside a courthouse. He was tall and distinguished looking even in the black and white photo. It was weird to see her father in the newspaper, but it was undoubtedly him.

She read the caption; *Carlo Rossi arrives at New York District Court to face twelve counts of racketeering.*

"It looks like him," she finally said. "But it's not. I don't know what's going on, but my father's name is Carlo Bondesan."

Nico shook his head. "That's his mother's maiden name. He must have given it to you and David to protect you."

"Don't say my brother's name," she shouted. She took a deep breath, forcing her voice steady. "Don't you say my brother's name."

He took a deep breath. "Your father is Carlo Rossi, head of the Boston Syndicate."

"What Syndicate?"

"The Syndicate is the organization that oversees organized crime around the world."

"That's impossible." And it was. It had to be. Because if it wasn't, it meant everything she believed about her father, about her life, was a lie. "My father owns a real estate development company."

"You're absolutely right. Like many of the families in the Syndicate — myself included — your father owns a legal business that acts as a front for a lot of illegal businesses."

"So you're admitting to being a criminal?" Her voice was bitter. It was somehow easier to focus on Nico than to think about her father.

"I think it's safe to say you're not wearing a wire," he said. "So yes. I suppose you can call me a criminal — of a sort."

"That's not hard to believe," she said. "I've seen your name in the news. My father has never been in the news."

"Have you ever done a search under Carlo Rossi?" He continued when she didn't answer. "Listen, your father has chosen to manage his interests by making himself scarce. I've chosen a more... transparent approach. My hunch is that your father kept a low profile as much to prevent you and your brother from discovering his affiliation with the Syndicate as it was to stay under the radar of law enforcement." He inhaled deeply, then looked at the ceiling, like he might find the words he was looking for there. When he returned his gaze to her face, his expression was perfectly composed. "I know this must be difficult for you, but it's absolutely imperative to your well-being that we find your father. I'll give you some time to think about that."

He turned away, leaving the newspapers on the desk, and left the room. A moment later, the lock turned with a quiet click.

15

"Again."

Nico ordered another punch to Bill Molten's face before Vincent's massive arm had fully retreated from the last one. Vincent punched again, and the bones in Bill's face yielded with a wet slap.

"We don't do business with child molesters," Nico said.

"I never touched them, I swear!" Bill muttered through his broken teeth.

Nico shoved Vincent aside and grabbed Bill by the lapels of his jacket. After twenty minutes under Vincent's fists, he was dead weight, his eyes almost entirely swollen shut.

"Do you think that matters?" Nico asked. He'd meant to keep his voice even, but it had lowered to a growl in spite of his efforts. Bill cringed, trying to move away from him. "You took pictures, made videos, sold them. You're as guilty as anyone."

Before he knew what was happening, Nico's fist was connecting to Bill's face again and again. The man had lost consciousness by the time Nico shoved him away, letting him fall to the ground.

He held out his hand, and Luca gave him a handkerchief. Nico wiped the blood off his knuckles.

"Wait until he regains consciousness," Nico ordered Vincent as he put on his jacket. "Tell him our business is concluded. Permanently. And if I ever hear that he's resumed his activities, I'll have him dumped into the East River with his cock in his mouth and a concrete block around his neck."

"Yes, boss," Vincent said.

Nico walked across the concrete floor of the old warehouse with Luca by his side. Some people had no limit to their depravity. He was still teaching them that he had no limit when it came to punishing them for it.

"How did it go with Gianni?" Nico asked as they approached the car.

"Fine," Luca said, opening the door for him. "He thanked you for your consideration. Said he'll start making payments again as soon as his wife's out of the hospital."

Nico stepped into the back seat. "Good."

Luca started the car, and Nico sat back, trying to clear his mind.

Bill Molten was a holdover from Nico's father who had been running a sanctioned skim off the profits from an underground poker ring. He'd also been taking naked pictures of little kids, and that was something Nico wouldn't allow. He didn't prey on the weak, and he didn't allow others in his family to do it either. The soldier who'd taken a cut of Bill's earnings to keep the pornography ring from Nico was already gone. Nico's father had been a good man, but he'd been out of touch. There had been too many people on the payroll, too few conscionable men keeping tabs. Nico was still cleaning up the mess.

He sighed, a bone-deep weariness snaking through his body. His mind went unbidden to Angelica.

Angel.

He'd been surprised to realize she didn't know about her father's illegal business. Carlo Rossi had been head of the Rossi family for over a decade. How had he kept such a secret from his daughter? Was his son equally in the dark?

Nico tried to imagine being so cut off from his family. Shipped off to boarding school, discouraged from coming home for holidays, attending college upstate... If Angel hadn't been overly curious, if she'd been wrapped up in her own life like most young people were, it was possible that she had no idea, especially given her father's business use of the name Rossi while Angel and her brother went by Bondesan.

He flashed back to her face in the basement, the shock giving way to horror, then denial, as she looked at the newspaper. He'd done that to her, and he hated himself for it. Fuck Carlo Rossi. Anything could have happened to Angel. She could have been kidnapped — or worse — by someone far less conscientious than Nico, and she wouldn't even know why.

The thought of someone hurting her caused an unfamiliar surge of protectiveness. She'd been sheltered from his world, and he was surprised to find he wanted to keep it that way.

Too late, he thought bitterly.

And finding out about her father wasn't the worst thing that could happen to her. Carlo still hadn't shown himself, and Angel didn't seem to know much about where her father might be hiding. Nico would have to force Carlo's hand — and soon — to draw him out of hiding.

The thought made him want to punch something.

Could he hurt her? He saw her as she had been in the kitchen, head tipped back as he'd taken her pink nipple in his mouth, the mound between her legs hot even through the silky fabric of her pants. He'd wanted to pull them off, taste her, devour her, own her. But it was more than that. He wanted to cloak himself in her innocence. Wanted to ease the loneliness in her eyes that was a mirror to his own.

But that could never happen. He needed Carlo to come forward, give him the tape. Then he could let Angel go. She would never forgive him for what he would have to do to her father after he relinquished the tape, but at least she'd be safe. And free.

"How's the girl?' Nico asked Luca as they turned onto the parkway leaving Queens. He avoided her name, hoping to hide his feelings from Luca.

"She didn't eat tonight, but I don't think it's some kind of statement." Luca said, pointing the car toward Brooklyn. "I think she's in shock."

"Is she reading the newspapers?"

"Looks like it," Luca asked. "Any word from Rossi?"

"None," Nico said.

"What a bastard."

Nico nodded. He had a reputation for having a higher moral ground than many of the families in the Syndicate, but he wasn't above violence, and Carlo knew it. Which meant that Carlo was leaving his daughter to Nico and his men, knowingly forcing Nico to commit an act of violence against his daughter to prove a point.

Bastard was an understatement.

He wished he could talk to Angel, ask if she was okay. Nico had been told about the family business when he started college, and he still remembered how hard it had been to reconcile what he knew about the mob with his father, a man he loved and respected like no other. It was true that Carlo Rossi was a different brand of criminal from Raphael Vitale, but Nico was still hoping to shield Angel from that particularly ugly truth.

"Bring her to the gardens tomorrow at eight am," Nico said from the back seat. "I'll have Jenna clear the park."

"No problem," Luca said.

If he had questions about Nico's plans, he didn't voice them. One of many reasons Nico trusted the other man so much.

They exited on Fulton and made their way to Headquarters. Nico wanted to get in a workout before he headed home. He needed to regain control — of his desire and the unfamiliar emotions Carlo Rossi's daughter brought out in him.

16

She woke up the next morning surrounded by newspapers. She'd read and reread until her eyes burned, until there was absolutely no way to deny that what Nico had said was true.

Her father wasn't a commercial real estate developer. Not really. He was one of the most violent and dangerous men in the country. He'd been lying to her and David all their lives.

And not just him.

She sat up and sifted through the newspapers on the bed. When she found what she was looking for, she reread the caption.

Frances (Frank) Morra, alleged member of the Boston mafia, is escorted by bailiffs from the Massachusetts District Court.

It was her Uncle Frank. The man who was her godfather, who had been a fixture at every birthday and graduation, who had given her a thick stack of cash to mark the passage of every important occasion of her life. In the photo, he was flanked by uniformed men guiding him through a door at the side of the courtroom. The date on the paper was three years earlier.

She thought back to her senior year of college. Her relationship with her father had already been distant, but she remembered him saying something about an extended business trip to Tokyo for Uncle Frank. Had her father created the story as a way to explain a prison stay for the man who was her godfather? And how many other people who had been a fixture in Angel's childhood were part of her father's real business? Had her mother known?

If what the papers said was true, her whole life had been financed by organized crime. The private school she and David attended as kids. The boarding schools they'd gone to as teenagers. Their college education. The houses and cars and vacations.

All bought with money from cheating and stealing and killing and who knew what else.

She'd been so self-righteous with Nico when all along they came from the same kind of people. And now she knew why he hadn't been worried about keeping her here, about bringing her to his apartment. The pillowcase over her head had just been part of the game. They knew she wouldn't be able to go to the police if — and it was a bigger if now than it had been yesterday — she made it out alive. If she turned in Nico and his men, she'd be outing her father, too.

She swept the newspapers to the ground in one angry motion. How dare her father put her and David at risk this way.

Oh, god… David. Did he suspect? Did he know? She would give anything to pick up the phone and talk to him. To tell him everything that happened. Was he safe? Would Nico and his men go after David next if they didn't get what they wanted from her father?

The questions just kept coming. Too bad there weren't any answers. And she didn't have any for Nico either. Knowing the truth about her father didn't change the fact that she had no idea where he might be hiding, or why he hadn't come forward to save her. The reality of it twisted in her stomach. Maybe something had happened to him. Would Nico let her know if it had?

His face flashed in her mind. He hadn't enjoyed telling her about her father. That had been obvious. Was it because he actually cared? Or because it was yet another thing that ran counter to his business interests? She didn't know, but she thought she'd seen regret in his eyes. She didn't know what was worse — being kept prisoner by Nico Vitale, being pitied by him, or wanting him the way she had in his apartment.

And how she had wanted him. She remembered his hands on her breasts, his fingers gentle but demanding, his tongue teasing her nipples until the warmth smoldering between her legs had burst into a full fledged inferno. She'd almost felt him inside her then, imagined him sliding into her heat, filling her, completing her.

She stood up, her face hot, and hurried into the bathroom. She took a shower and brushed her teeth, then stared at her reflection. She almost didn't recognize herself. Outwardly, not much had changed. Her skin was a little paler, and she'd lost weight she hadn't needed or wanted to lose. But it was her eyes that made her seem changed. Still green, but there was something else there now, too. Something haunted and sad.

She shook her head. This was temporary. Her father would give in to Nico's demands. She would be set free. Then she and David would figure things out with their father.

She threw on the long skirt and one of the t-shirts sent by Nico, then combed through her hair. She was stepping back into the bedroom when Luca walked through the door. She hadn't heard the key in the lock from the bathroom.

"Good morning," Luca said.

"Morning."

"I need you to put on your shoes. We have somewhere to be," he said.

She didn't know whether to be scared or relieved. "Where are we going?"

"Nico's asked to see you," Luca said. "That's all I can say."

She thought about pressing for details about their destination, but there didn't seem to be a point. At least she'd get to leave the room for awhile. She ignored the voice inside her head that wondered if she would get to be alone with Nico again. It didn't matter. What happened in his apartment couldn't happen again.

She slipped her feet into the ballet flats. They fit perfectly, just like everything else Nico had sent. Luca handed her a leather jacket.

"You might need this. It's getting cold."

"Thank you." The jacket was too big, but it would keep her warm. She thought she caught Nico's scent when she put it on, but it was gone a moment later.

He took the gun from his belt. "Let's go."

She lowered her eyes to the weapon. "You don't really need that, do you?"

He seemed to think about it. "Not really, no," he finally admitted.

"Noted," she said. "And now I know that I can't out your little operation here without outing my father, so I don't think we need the pillowcase either. I'd rather not play games from now on, if it's alright with you."

He hesitated before stuffing the gun back under his belt. He covered it with his jacket. "Don't make me regret it, Angelica." He leveled his significantly intense blue eyes at her. "Okay?"

"Okay."

He held open the door, and she stepped through it. They made their way to the stairwell at the end of the hall and walked up the narrow flight of stairs. They emerged on the second floor, right outside the mysterious double doors. A grunt emerged from inside the room, and the floor shook as something crashed from behind the closed doors.

"What is that?" she asked Luca.

He opened a door that led to an alley behind the building. "Gym."

"A gym?"

He nodded.

It was the last thing she had expected him to say. "Like… a gym where you workout and stuff?"

"That's the one," he said. "Come on. We're going to be late."

She stepped out into the alley and was relieved to find the waiting SUV empty. No Dante. Just like Nico had promised.

She headed for the back door, but Luca opened the passenger side instead.

"I guess I've moved up in the world," she said drily.

Luca shrugged. "You're one of us."

"I will never be one of you," she snapped, slamming the door closed.

He came around to the driver's side and started the car, and then they were moving out of the alley and into traffic. It didn't take long to realize they were in Brooklyn. Interesting. Brooklyn had become a haven for hipsters. Not the location she would have expected as headquarters for one of the country's most notorious mobsters. Then again, maybe that was the point.

Luca drove around Prospect Park, pulling to a stop in front of a granite and brick archway on Flatbush Avenue. BROOKLYN BOTANIC GARDENS was etched into the top of the archway.

"The Botanical Gardens?" Angel asked, looking out the window.

Luca nodded. "Nico's inside. I'll be waiting right here."

"But… how will I find him?" She didn't say the other thing she was saying; why are you trusting me? What makes you think I won't scream for help? Tell someone what you're doing to me?

"The park's been cleared until ten," Luca said, as if reading her mind. "He'll find you. Just go through the door there."

He'll find you.

As certain as the sun rising in the east and setting in the west. She didn't want to think about the thrill that coursed through her body at the idea of Nico finding her. At the implication that he would always find her.

She stepped from the car, and for a minute, she was giddy with the freedom of it. She was outside. The sky was blue, so blue, and the air was sharp with the perfect crispness of fall.

She heard a hum behind her. When she turned, Luca was watching her through the open passenger window.

"I'm going," she said, stepping through the archway.

Sidewalks marked a path in either direction, and lush green spaces sprawled like giant carpets dotted with splashes of color. But it was the silence that got her attention. The traffic of the city was muffled in the distance, but the gardens were deserted. It was early November — not exactly prime garden season — but the quiet was still startling.

She looked around for Nico but didn't see him.

He'll find you.

She started walking. She had just passed a large open field on her left when she came to the buildings that were used for food service and restrooms. A large INFORMATION sign stood above a closed window. Luca hadn't been kidding. The whole park had been cleared, and she felt a thrill at the realization of Nico's authoritative reach. What had it taken?

A bribe? A favor? A threat?

She immediately scolded herself. None of those things should impress her.

She stepped into shade as she neared the end of the low slung buildings that served tourists. A pale yellow building rose into the sky on her left, it's circular, multi-paned windows staring back at her like giant eyes. She craned her neck as she looked up, following the line of the building to a turret-like structure that seemed to pierce the autumn sky. When she lowered her gaze, Nico was standing in front of her.

Her breath caught in her throat, and her earlier resolve to keep her distance seemed to drift away on the fragrant air of the gardens. He was back in casual clothes, although she wasn't sure anything really looked casual on Nico Vitale. His gray slacks fit his body like they'd been made for him. Who knows? Maybe they had.

He wore a long sleeve sweater under a black leather jacket, and she suddenly wondered if the one Luca had given her was on loan from Nico. She had to fight the urge to bury her face in it, try to catch his scent again.

For a split second, she was happy to see him. Then she reminded herself that he wasn't her friend. He was her captor. A criminal of the worst sort.

Like your father.

"Hello," he said. The greeting seemed all wrong for the way he was looking at her. Like he wanted to eat her whole.

Or maybe that was wishful thinking.

"Hello," she said.

"Are you warm enough?" he asked.

She nodded.

He shoved his hands in his jacket pockets. "Let's walk then."

17

They continued on the path in silence at first. She was acutely aware of him next to her, his presence so commanding she had to fight not to lean against him. She kept her eyes forward, reminding herself with every step that she didn't care about Nico. Wanting him was something different.

Biology. Chemistry. Whatever.

But it didn't mean anything, and she needed to focus on getting out of the situation alive. That meant finding out all she could about what Nico wanted with her father, about whether he was still alive and what would happen to her if he didn't come forward.

"You really didn't know," he finally said.

"No, I really didn't." She felt ashamed saying it aloud. Her ignorance placed her squarely within a group of her peers that she had no desire to be part of; rich kids who never gave a thought to what their parents did for a living as long as the money kept flowing their way. It's not the way she'd seen herself.

"I trust you understand why it became necessary to tell you." He didn't look at her as he spoke.

"Not really. It doesn't change anything. I have no idea where my father might be hiding. Clearly I don't know much about him at all." She sighed. "But that doesn't mean I wish you hadn't told me."

"Yes," he said. "I suppose it's good you know, although I wish there had been another way for you to find out."

"That would have been nice," she said bitterly.

"Does your brother know?" he asked as they rounded a bend in the walkway.

A circle of hedges ringed in stone lay beyond the pathway. The lawn in the center of the circle had turned brown, the long grass brittle and yellow with the impending winter.

"I don't know. He's never said anything." She looked up at him and forced herself to ask the next question. "Are you going to hurt him?"

"I don't think that would be very productive."

For the first time she thought she caught shadows under his eyes. It didn't make her happy like she would have expected. Instead she wondered if the situation was taking as much a toll on him as it was on her. Whatever he wanted from her father, he must want it badly to hold her hostage. The realization brought to mind another question.

"Isn't this against the rules?"

He looked down at her, and she felt the same jolt of chemistry flow between them that had been present in his apartment. "What rules?"

"I don't know… the mob rules?" She laughed a little, even though there was nothing funny about the situation. "Isn't there some kind of rule against messing with members of someone's family?"

For a split second, pain flashed across his usually calm features, and she saw such naked loneliness in his eyes that she wanted to cry. It was gone a moment later.

He looked away. "There used to be."

"Not anymore?" she prodded.

"Not anymore." He said it softly, and she had the sudden desire to reach out, lay her hand against his cheek.

They came to a wood sign that read SHAKESPEARE GARDEN. Nico stopped, tipping his head at the brick walkway that led to the hidden space.

"Shall we?"

She nodded, and they stepped onto the path. It wound away from the main walkway, leading them into a sheltered garden filled with dead or dying shrubs and flowers. She tried to see it as it must look in the spring and summer, when everything was blooming and fragrant. She'd never been here, and she promised herself that if she got out of this alive, she would take more time to appreciate all the magical things that existed in plain sight but which she'd never bothered to explore.

He stopped walking and plucked something from a nearby bush. When he held it up, she saw that it was a tiny pink flower. A miracle blooming amid the seasonal death and destruction in the rest of the garden.

"I don't think you're supposed to pick those," she said.

He tucked a piece of hair behind her ear and placed the flower there. "I do a lot of things I'm not supposed to do," he said, his voice gruff.

He held her gaze, and her breath seemed to catch somewhere between her lungs and her mouth. He was violent. Dangerous. But beautiful, too. She couldn't deny it. It took effort to form the question that had been burning in her mind.

"What exactly do you want from my father?"

He dropped his hand, and an indulgent smile touched the corners of his mouth. It was devastating, and she had to work not to look away. Letting him know how much he affected her was a losing strategy, maybe even a deadly one.

"That's between us."

He took her hand, leading her deeper into the garden. She didn't pull away. She told herself it had nothing to do with the feel of his slightly rough palm against the smoothness of her skin, with the false sense of protection it gave her. She just wanted to keep him in a conciliatory mood, try to draw him out.

They wound around the path. A fountain, dry and scattered with dead leaves, stood to the side. They continued deeper into the garden, farther from the main walkway. The distant sound of traffic had grown almost silent. Everything else seemed very far away.

"Maybe I can help," she said, trying to keep the conversation focused on her father, on the things she needed to do to get out alive. "I might know something about what you want from him."

He stopped walking. "Somehow I doubt that."

"You can't have it both ways, Nico." Using his name felt oddly intimate, and she felt a flush of something like pleasure as she said it. "You let me in on this big secret, tell me I'm one of you, but you won't tell me what you want so I can do something to help myself. You tell me I'm in danger, that you'll hurt me if my father doesn't come through, and then I have no choice but to feel scared and helpless, because you won't tell me anything else." She was angry now, but she couldn't seem to help herself. It felt good to unload all of her pent up anger and frustration. "What do you want from me?"

"I told you; I need to find your father. That's all you need to know." His voice was laced with steel, and she had a glimpse of how formidable he must be in his business.

"It isn't all I need to know! Tell me why you want to find him. Tell me what you want from him."

"It's personal," he said, crossing his arms over his chest.

"Yeah? Well, it's personal to me now, too," she said.

She regretted the words as soon as she said them. She'd been talking about her father. But Nico was right there, his body looming over hers, his chest close enough to touch, and the words suddenly seemed to imply something more.

He reached out, tracing a line from her temple to her chin, his eyes never leaving hers. Rubbing his thumb along her lower lip, his own mouth parted. She wanted to stand on her tip-toes, press her mouth to his, slip her tongue through the opening he had given her.

She didn't have a chance. A moment later his big hands were on either side of her face. He tipped up her head and lowered his own, covering her lips with his. There was still no tenderness in his kiss. It was all passion.

She still didn't care.

His tongue probed her mouth, sliding against her own, exploring every recess until she didn't know where he ended and she began. She moaned in protest as he pulled back, and he nibbled at her bottom lip and went in for more, his hands working their way into her hair as he pulled her closer.

His erection pressed against her stomach, hard as stone, sending a lick of need to her core. She felt herself grow wet as a primal pulse began beating between her legs, calling for him to fill her.

He kissed his way up her jaw and took her earlobe in his mouth, nibbling and sucking until she moaned. His lips trailed down her neck, across her collarbone. He was mapping her, charting a course from which she would never return. Her legs would barely support her weight. She wanted to lay with him right there on the walkway, take the length of him in her hand, guide him inside her.

As if he'd heard her thoughts, he pulled back long enough to lift her into his arms. It hurt not to have his mouth on her, and when his lips founds hers again she sighed into his mouth as he started walking.

He met her sigh with a groan and deposited her on the bench. Then he knelt between her legs and hooked his hands behind her knees. He pulled her down so her ass was at the edge of the bench. She closed her eyes as his hands found her bare ankles, and he slid his palms up her calves, lifting her skirt inch by inch.

"Nico." She gasped his name, the chilly autumn air an erotic counterpoint to the heat of his mouth working its way up her calves to her thighs.

"I'll die if I don't taste you." His voice was hoarse, and when she opened her eyes, she saw a fire burning in them that matched the one building in her body.

She let her head fall back against the bench, letting go of everything as he kissed his way up her inner thighs, his tongue working the sensitive skin until she thought she would come before he ever reached his destination.

He slid his hands through the folds of her skirt and slid off her lace panties.

"My god, you're beautiful." It was a whisper. A prayer.

He spread her legs, growling as he leaned in. His tongue swept her silken folds, closing his mouth over her clit. He sucked and lapped, and just when she thought she would die from the pleasure of it, he slid his finger into her.

"Oh, god…" She slid farther down on the bench, wanting him to take all of her, taste all of her.

He groaned. "You're so wet."

He ran his tongue the length of her, burying his face in her heat. He darted around her clit, slow at first, excruciatingly slow, then gradually picked up the pace, working the sensitive bundle with his tongue while his fingers slid in and out of her.

She was moving with him now, reaching for the climax that was undeniable, irreversible. Losing herself to his hands and his mouth. He closed his mouth around her sucked, sending her over the edge, breaking her into a million pieces as she cried out, coming with a force that shook her whole body, that threatened to destroy her.

She was still trembling when she reached for him. There was an empty place inside her, and only Nico could fill it. She leaned forward and reached mindlessly for him, desperate for him to slide into her.

He kissed her deeply while she undid his belt buckle. The taste of her on his mouth was erotic, and she felt another orgasm build between her legs as she reached into his pants, taking his cock into her hand. He was massive, heavy with his desire, and she moaned as she imagined him thrusting into her.

"Angel…" Her name emerged in a shudder from his mouth. "Say you want me, Angel."

She was too intent on exploring his mouth, on the feel of his desire in her hand.

He pulled away, and she looked at him as if through a fog, her need for him still beating between her legs.

"You have to say you want me, Angel." He looked like he was in pain as he said it. "I can't… I have to know that you want this."

The shock of cold air between them forced her into semi-lucidity. She looked at him, his eyes glazed with desire.

Nico.

Now something else was beating in her. Knowledge she wanted to deny. A reality she wanted to ignore in order to feel his hands on her again, to make it okay for him to take her.

Nico.

What was she doing?

She sat up, rummaging around in the folds of her skirt until she could smooth it over her bare legs. Her bare everything.

"I... oh, my god..." she said. "I don't know what... I'm sorry."

She slid away from him, her legs shaky as she tried to put some distance between them. Between her and what she had done, what she had almost done.

He stood, turning his back to her as he zipped his pants. When he turned around, his face was composed.

"I apologize." The sincerity of his apology was written all over his face.

She swallowed hard. Part of her —- the crazy part — wanted to close the distance between them, put her hands on his face, tell him it wasn't his fault.

And it wasn't. Not really. She hadn't wanted him to stop. If he hadn't paused to ask her permission, it would be a done deal.

"It wasn't your fault," she said. "I... I don't know what I was thinking."

His eyes darkened. "I have a pretty good idea."

Her cheeks grew hot. "I got carried away. I'm sorry. But you have to know why it's a bad idea."

His nod was tight. "The bad idea to end all bad ideas."

She had no idea why the words stung. "Exactly."

He bent to pick up her panties and held them out to her. She put them in the pocket of his jacket.

"Thank you."

"Shall we go?" His voice was distant, polite. "Luca will be waiting."

She nodded.

They retraced their steps in silence. She was careful to keep some space between them. Clearly she couldn't be trusted to think straight when he was around. It was only smart to minimize their contact as much as the circumstances allowed.

They passed the concessions stands and headed for the gated archway. When they stepped onto the street, she slid the leather jacket from her arms.

"I think this is yours," she said, handing it to him. "Thank you."

She turned to open the car door, then paused and looked back at him.

"Why did you bring me here?"

"I wanted to see you." He met her eyes. "That's all."

She pushed away the longing that made her want to step away from the car, to step back into Nico's arms. She wasn't thinking clearly. It was that simple.

She got into the car and shut the door, then faced forward, staring out the windshield as Luca pulled away from the curb.

18

Nico sat in the backseat while the limo idled at the curb. His time with Angel lingered like a dream, and if he turned his head just right, he could still smell her on the jacket he'd loaned her earlier that day.

He put his hand in one of the pockets, closing his fingers around the scrap of lace she'd forgotten there. He was immediately taken back to the moment he'd pulled the underwear from her hips, the smell of her desire hitting him like a tropical storm. He'd been ravenous for her, had barely been able to keep himself from driving into her then and there. It was only the image of her, spread out for him in broad daylight, that had stopped him. He'd needed to taste her then, needed to run his tongue along the soft crease at her center.

He felt himself grow hard. He had just removed his hand from his pocket when the back door opened. A second later, Carmine slid into the seat next to him. Luca shut the door but stood in front of it, keeping lookout.

"Nico." Carmine reached over and kissed Nico's cheeks. "How are you?"

"I'm fine, Carmine. How are you?" Nico asked.

"Doing well, doing well," Carmine said. "Busy, but that's always good for the family."

Carmine Alfiero had been Underboss to Nico's father. It had been assumed that Carmine would take over the Vitale family business if anything happened to Raphael Vitale. But that was before Nico's father appointed Carmine as his Consigliere and made Nico his Underboss. It had sent shockwaves through the family, and it had taken some getting used to for Nico, too. He loved his Uncle Carmine. He'd been worried there would be bad blood. But Carmine was more than happy to be appointed as Consigliere, a position that made him a trusted advisor to Nico's father — and one that also kept him largely out of the line of fire. Now he was Nico's Consigliere, and there was no one Nico trusted more.

"True," Nico said. "So what's the problem?"

Carmine smiled, his round face cherubic under the wisps of hair he had left. "There's no problem, Nico. I'm just checking in on the Carlo situation."

"There's not much to report," Nico said. "We've put out the word, but there's no sign of him."

Carmine leaned forward and poured himself a drink from the bar. "And you still have the girl?"

"I do."

Carmine took a drink, then stared down into the amber liquid. "How long do you intend to keep her?"

Forever.

"Until Carlo shows himself."

"And if he never shows himself?" Carmine asked.

"He'll have to," Nico said. "Frank Morra can't run Boston forever."

Frank was Carlo's Underboss, and while Frank was every bit as ruthless, he wasn't quite as bright. Things would start to fall apart eventually.

"That may be true," Carmine said. "But you can't keep the girl forever either. Especially when it's against the rules."

"It doesn't seem like we're playing by the rules anymore." *In more ways than one,* Nico thought.

Carmine sighed. "I understand. I do. But no one can farm scorched earth."

Nico turned his face to the window, watched people hurrying along the sidewalks. They didn't have a clue how complicated things could be.

"I'm not planning on lighting anything on fire."

"How long will you be able to keep the girl before you have to hurt her? Before you send a finger — or something else — to Carlo's family to prove your threats aren't empty?"

Fury rose in Nico's gut like a tempest. He forced it down, forced himself to think rationally. "Not much longer," he admitted.

Carmine studied his face. "You don't want to do it."

"Of course, I don't want to do it."

"And yet you've backed yourself into a corner by taking the girl in the first place. Now you have to follow through, or every threat the Vitale family makes will seem empty."

Nico pressed his fingers to his forehead, trying to rub out the headache that was starting to hammer at his brain. "I know."

Carmine put a hand on Nico's leg. "Good. You've had her over a week now?"

Nico nodded.

"Then I'd say you have another two days. I'll leak it to Frank. Maybe he can get word to Carlo, wherever he is."

"Sounds good." Nico had to choke out the words. The thought of hurting Angel, of damaging her perfection, made him sick. "Thank you."

Carmine wrapped a hand around Nico's neck and kissed his forehead. "No thanks necessary. I'm watching your back. You know that, don't you?"

"I do," Nico said. "And I appreciate it."

"We'll talk soon," Carmine said. "Maybe get some food?"

Nico forced a smile.

Carmine knocked on the window and Luca opened the door. Nico sat in silence, Carmine's words ringing in his ears as Luca came around to the driver's side and started the car. He looked at Nico in the rearview mirror.

"Where to?"

Nico pulled his phone out of his pocket. "The Plaza."

He made the call while Luca worked his way through the city. By the time they got to the hotel, Nico was feeling better. Angel was just a woman, like any other. The fact that she was Carlo's daughter had brought out some twisted sense of retribution in him. It was understandable, but he couldn't let his personal vendetta cloud his judgement. Angel was a pawn in a very complicated chessboard. She could be sacrificed, but it would have to be clean, the same way he'd sacrifice any pawn.

Starting with her fingers.

He met the concierge in the lobby and picked up his key. It wouldn't do to be seen checking in at the front desk in the middle of the day in his home town.

He made his way up to the tenth floor and let himself into the suite. Then he loosened his tie and headed for the mini-bar. He poured himself a drink, downed it in one swallow, and poured another before crossing to the big windows overlooking the park.

It had been helpful to meet with Carmine. The older man had been part of the business for a long time, and he could always be counted on to see the big picture when Nico's mind became clouded with rage. Raneiro served the same purpose, but he was headquartered in Rome, and Nico didn't often get to spend time with the man he thought of as a second father. Carmine was right here, and this wasn't the first time he'd given Nico some much needed perspective.

A knock at the door pulled him from his thoughts. He put down his drink and opened the door to a curvaceous brunette in a designer dress. Classy, the way he liked them.

"Come in," Nico said.

She smiled. "Thank you."

"Can I get you a drink?" Nico asked.

She set her purse on one of the end tables. "No, thank you."

He wasn't surprised. Escorts at this level were professionals. Nico suspected they were told not to get drunk.

He sat on the sofa, and she came to sit next to him. Carefully, and not too close.

Good. He liked it when they let him set the pace.

She traced a line down his arm with one manicured hand, and he caught the scent of her perfume, expensive, probably french. Nothing at all like Angel, who smelled like fresh air and clean water and an undercurrent of desire.

Even better. This woman didn't remind him of Angel at all.

"What do you want to do?" she asked, her voice sly.

"Straddle me," he said.

She climbed over him and hiked up her dress, then sat purposefully on top of him. His cock always had a mind of its own, and it didn't let him down this time, arising immediately to the occasion.

He slipped his hands under her dress and realized she wasn't wearing underwear. He held onto her hips as she moved back and forth, rubbing her bare pussy against his hard on.

This was good. This was working.

She lowered her mouth to his, her hair falling on either side of his head, and kissed him deeply. For a few seconds, his tongue did the work for him. But she didn't taste right, didn't feel right.

She didn't taste like Angel, didn't feel like Angel.

His eyes flew open, and before he realized what he was doing, he'd shoved the woman off him.

"What the…" She got up and put her hands on her hips. "What's going on?"

He stood and ran a hand through his hair. "I'm sorry. You need to leave."

She smoothed her dress. "Did I do something wrong?"

"No. I'll make sure you're paid, and I'll make sure the agency knows you did your job." He walked to the window and turned his back on her. "Now please go."

He heard the sounds of her moving around the room, picking up her purse, closing the door behind her. When she was gone, he closed his eyes, remembering the taste of Angel in his mouth, the feel of her moving under his hands, the sound of her coming for him. When he had banished all trace of the other woman, he opened his eyes.

Fuck. He was in deep shit.

19

Angel tossed and turned, unable to get comfortable in the small bed. The room wasn't hot, but her skin was clammy, and she threw off the sheet as she rolled onto her back.

She had spent the day pacing her room after Luca brought her home from the garden. She'd been ashamed, barely able to look Luca in the eyes. Would Nico tell him what had happened between them? Would it be a story to tell the men who worked for him?

Somehow she didn't think so. She flashed back to the moment before he'd lowered his mouth to hers. What she'd seen in his eyes had been more complicated than ambition or simple lust.

Then again, maybe she was just rationalizing what she'd done. And she needed to rationalize. Otherwise she would have to live with the fact that she'd allowed Nico Vitale — the criminal responsible for her captivity — to bring her to an orgasm in broad daylight. Worse, that she'd wanted him to take her then and there. That only his own chivalry — for lack of a better word — had prevented it.

She turned the pillow over to the cold side. What was wrong with her? She was romanticizing him. Assigning him qualities he didn't have to make her desire for him more palatable. It wasn't like her to be dishonest with herself.

She almost laughed aloud. She'd been dishonest with herself all along. Her father was a criminal every bit as violent as Nico, and she hadn't looked close enough to ask a single question. Denial was practically her middle name. She had wanted Nico, plain and simple. She still wanted him.

The thought of him brought a flash of memory; his dark head between her legs, the feel of his tongue, hot and insistent, against the petals of her sex.

A surge of desire rolled through her. She was already — or maybe the most appropriate word was *still* - wet for him. She imagined him prowling the halls of the building that was obviously his headquarters. He could be right on the other side of the door for all she knew, thinking about her like she was thinking about him.

There was a vibration between her legs now, and she punched the pillow and rolled over, willing herself not to think about his mouth on her inner thigh, the look in his eyes when he'd spread her legs and called her beautiful.

There was nowhere for this to go. The fact that her father was in the same business as Nico didn't make his profession acceptable. She would have to cut ties with her father if it were true, and she would definitely have to cut ties with the man who had kidnapped her. She didn't want to be part of their world, and that meant Nico could never be part of hers, assuming he wanted to.

Which was a pretty big assumption.

She closed her eyes and took a deep breath, sinking deeper into the pillow. A moment later she heard a bang from somewhere outside her room. She opened her eyes just as the sound of breaking glass crashed through the building.

She bolted upright, her heart picking up its pace in her chest. A series of thuds sounded in quick succession, and then there was no doubt.

It was gunfire. Somewhere in the building, someone was shooting.

She heard the sound of men shouting and jumped out of bed, walking cautiously to the door as a cacophony of gunfire, breaking glass, and splintered wood exploded from elsewhere in the building.

It was reflex to look for a way out. Stupid. She'd already looked a thousand times. But something was going on outside, and she was locked up in this stupid room, completely helpless.

A burst of noise, closer now, came from outside her room. She stepped back from the door, not wanting to get hit by a stray bullet, and tried to stay calm around the adrenaline flooding her brains.

Fight or flight. Except there was no flight.

Tuning her ears to the sounds outside the room, she tried to determine what was going on from the shouting and exchange of gunfire. She jumped as a series of staccato bursts rang from the hall. Whoever it was would reach her in seconds.

She scanned the room, desperate for a weapon. It was pointless. Nico hadn't given her anything but clothes and toiletries. There wasn't even an object heavy enough to hit someone over the head.

The shouting was just outside her door now, the pop of gunfire nearly continuous as she backed up against the wall. Seconds later, something smashed against the door in three sharp cracks.

She jumped, watching the door splinter as the banging continued. She barely had time to register what was happening when the door crashed inward.

Two black-clad figures in masks strode into the room and headed right for her.

She shook her head. "What are you doing? Who are - "

One of the men grabbed her roughly by the arm. "Move," he ordered, propelling her toward the door.

The other man stood in front of them, covering them with his gun as Angel was shoved forward.

She struggled, kicking and screaming, trying to wrench her arm free from the man's steely grasp. There was a voice inside her asking what she was doing — she wanted to escape, didn't she? — but it was drowned out by the panic of being dragged kicking and screaming from the place that had sheltered her for the last week.

"Stop it," the man ordered. "Your father sent us. We're trying to get you out of here."

She stopped fighting and moved with them to the door. The man still had ahold of her arm, but she wasn't resisting anymore. She was finally going to get out of here.

Nico.

She ignored the voice inside her head and moved.

20

He'd been in his office, trying to concentrate on work instead of the dilemma with Angel, when the first round of gunfire erupted from downstairs.

He jumped up, reflex kicking in as he grabbed his gun. He flattened himself against the wall next to the door and listened, trying to get a handle on how many shooters were in the building and what they were up against.

It took him less than a minute to determine there were at least three gunmen, maybe as many as five. He hurried to his desk, grabbed extra ammo, and stuffed it in his pockets. Then he threw open the door and eased into the quiet third floor hall.

He was working his way carefully toward the stairs when Luca burst out of the stairwell with his own gun in hand.

Nico lowered his weapon. "What the fuck is going on?"

Luca ran toward him. "Five gunmen, three of them heading for the basement."

"Then what the fuck are you doing up here?" Nico roared, running for the stairs.

"Marco and Vincent are going for her," he said, following Nico into the stairwell.

"I don't need a babysitter." He was screaming inside, the placidity he'd learned to count on abandoning him at the thought of Carlo's thugs going for Angel. Carlo might be her father, but Nico didn't trust him or his soldiers.

He stood against the wall, listening for sounds in the stairwell, then took a careful look down the stairs.

Clear.

He hurried down, half-expecting someone to burst into the stairwell from one of the other floors.

"I've got to get you out of here," Luca said, descending behind him. "If they're Carlo's men, they're going to take Angelica and then come for you."

"I can take care of myself," Nico said. "Angel won't stand a chance in a gunfight."

Luca's hand came down on Nico's arms. "If they were sent by her father, they're not going to hurt her."

Nico shook off Luca's hand. "Take your hand off me."

Luca removed his hand.

"Do you think Carlo gives a fuck about her?" Anger fought its way through the adrenaline pumping in Nico's veins. "He's left her with us for over a week. She's better off with us at this point." He leveled his gaze at Luca. "Now you can either come with me or go help someone else, but I'm not going to debate it with you."

He hurried down the stairs with Luca's footsteps behind him. He passed the door to the second floor without a thought. His men were trained to take care of themselves and each other, and the soldiers in the computer lab knew how to protect their data.

It was Angel who needed his help.

A series of gunshots came from the basement, reverberating through the stairwell. Nico didn't want to to think about what it meant that his heart was in his throat, that he was having trouble concentrating when all he could see was Angel in the hands of Carlo's men. Old school hoodlums who had no sense of honor, just like Carlo.

They reached the door leading to the basement hall. Nico flattened himself against the wall as Luca did the same on the opposite side of the door. Nico tipped his head at the door. He pointed first to himself, then to Luca, indicating that Luca should follow him into the hall.

Luca shook his head. He pointed to himself, then the door.

Nico understood. It was Luca's job to protect him. Letting Nico run first into a gunfight with members of an opposing family was the opposite of what Luca was supposed to do.

But this wasn't about Nico. It was about Angel, and Nico would be damned if he'd trust her safety to anyone but him, regardless of how much he trusted Luca with everything else.

He reached for the knob and eased open the door before Luca could say anything.

He glanced into the hall and made a quick assessment of the situation; two of his men at the other end of the hall, blocking the second stairwell, one masked figure in the doorway to Angel's room.

A muffled thud and shout from the open door to Angel's room told him that at least one man was in there with her.

He made eye contact with his men at the end of the hall and gestured toward Angel's room, hoping they got the message to cover him. He slid into the hall, relieved when a burst of gunfire was directed at the man covering Angel's room.

Nico thought the man would retreat back into the room, putting him — and whoever was with Angel — on the defensive. Instead, he stepped into the hallway and leveled a steady stream of gunfire at Nico's men.

They retreated into the stairwell, and two more men stepped into the hall from Angel's room. But they weren't the ones who got his attention — it was Angel, held close to the side of one of the men as the other two surrounded them in a protective formation. Nico wanted to roar when he saw the gun aimed at Angel's temple.

He forced his mind clear. He still had the element of surprise. Carlo's men were busy getting into the hall. They had their eyes on the soldiers at the other end and hadn't noticed that Nico and Luca were approaching from the opposite side.

Nico steadied his weapon, aiming for the guy in back. When he had his shot, he took it. The man fell with a heavy thud as the bullet entered the back of his head. The other men spun to face him with Angel between them. The one who had ahold of her faced Nico and Luca. The other faced Nico's soldiers across the hall.

"I've got the guy in back," Luca whispered.

"Only if it's clean," Nico said softly. "I don't want her hurt."

"You better clear one of these stairwells or we're going to start shooting," the guy holding Angel said.

Nico's gaze slid to Angel, her eyes wide with terror. He forced his eyes back to the man holding her. He couldn't afford to be distracted by his fear — and Angel couldn't afford for him to be distracted either.

"Unless you have men hiding in the walls, I'd say you're probably on the losing end of that deal," Nico said.

"You can't shoot us without risking the girl," the man said.

Nico tuned his ear to the voice, trying to match it to someone he might know in the Rossi family. God help the man who was behind that mask. The man who had Angel.

"And you'll have to answer for it if we start shooting and something happens to Carlo Rossi's daughter — if you make it out alive," Nico said.

He was watching the man's body language, looking for a clue to his next move, when the guy shoved Angel in front of him.

"Do you think I care what happens to this bitch?"

Nico hesitated. Why was one of Carlo's men using Carlo's daughter as a human shield?

"Drop your weapons," the guy said. "All of you."

"Do it," Nico called to his men on the other side of the hall.

They leaned down, dropping the guns slowly. Nico could only hope that Luca knew him as well as he thought he did.

Nico waited until the moment before the guns hit the floor. Then he lifted his weapon and took the shot that had been teasing him since the man had thrust Angel in front of him. The man released his hold on Angel and fell to the floor. A split second later, Luca's bullet whizzed past Nico's head in a ferocious blast of gunfire. The other man dropped to the floor next to the one who had been holding Angel.

They stood in the deafening silence for a good five seconds before his men scrambled for their weapons.

"Secure the rest of the house," Nico ordered, hurrying toward Angel. "I want a casualty report in an hour with details on loss of life and possible data breaches."

They hurried up the stairs as Nico stopped in front of Angel. She was shaking, and there was blood on the side of her face. He reached up, wanting to make sure it wasn't hers.

The palm of her hand cracked against his face. "They were coming to get me out of here," she said bitterly.

He licked a trickle of blood where his tooth had cut his lip, then turned to Luca. "Get her things and take her to my office. Lock the door."

He strode to the stairs, leaving Luca and Angel alone in the hall.

21

She wanted to fight Luca as he led her up the stairs. She'd been so close to escape. She almost couldn't believe she was still here.

But all of the fight had gone out of her after the shootout in the basement hall. Now she was crashing, and all she wanted to do was cry and sleep. And not necessarily in that order.

Luca left her in the center of the room and headed for the door. He turned back to her. "You're not as smart as you look, you know that?"

The words stung, especially coming from him. "Because I wanted to take my shot at getting out of here?"

He shook his head. "I'm not sure I've ever met anyone so blind."

He stepped into the hall and closed the door behind him. A second later she heard him lock it.

She paced the room a couple of times before sinking onto the leather couch against one wall. The office was nice, homier than she would have expected after seeing Nico's apartment. The big sofa faced a rough-hewn coffee table made out of what looked like oak. There was a flat screen TV on the wall and a row of DVDs, plus a state of the art sound system. On the far side of the room, a massive desk stood in front of the window. The antique clock on Nico's desk said it was two in the morning.

She leaned back against the couch and took a deep breath. The whole incident in the basement couldn't have taken more than fifteen minutes, but it felt like a lifetime had passed since she'd been tossing and turning in bed.

Her father had come through. Maybe not the way she'd expected — by giving Nico what he wanted, whatever that was — but he'd come for her. Now his men were dead and she was right back where she started.

Do you think I care what happens to this bitch?

She shook her head against the words. The man who'd held her at gunpoint had been bluffing. He knew Nico wouldn't risk her life.

But… why *wouldn't* Nico risk her life? She was nothing but a hostage to him. And on the off chance that she was wrong, that their time together had meant something to him, there was no way her father's men could know that. How could they be sure Nico wouldn't hurt her?

The questions ran together in her mind like paint bleeding across canvas. She pushed them away. She couldn't deal right now. She was both amped and exhausted, and her mind was running in circles.

She spotted a half open door across the room and discovered a well-appointed bathroom. She took a clean hand towel off a stack of them and washed her face, trying not to think about the wet slap of blood that had hit her temple when the man holding her was shot in the head. When she was done, she felt a little bit better, and she spent some time fishing around in Nico's medicine cabinet. She didn't know what she was looking for — any hope of fighting her way out of her captivity had ended when she'd been witness to the overwhelming show of force against her father's men. It's not like she was going to fight her way out with a men's razor. Even if Nico had a fancy straight-edged one, and she wouldn't be surprised if he did, she had no doubt that she'd be disarmed in under five seconds.

She would have to be smarter than that.

And there wasn't anything unusual there anyway. Aspirin (she took two), shaving cream, a brush, cologne. She reached for the blue bottle and pulled off the cap, then held it under her nose. Her eyes closed involuntarily as the scent of him enveloped her.

Nico.

She returned the cologne to the shelf and was closing the medicine cabinet when a voice spoke from behind her.

"Can I help you with something?"

She looked in the mirror and saw Nico standing in the open doorway.

She met his eyes in the reflection. "I think you've done enough."

Silence lengthened between them. He held out a bag. "Here are your things. Let's go."

She turned to face him and took the bag from his hands. "Go where?"

"You'll find out when we get there."

She followed him into the office. He'd said "we". Did that mean he was going with her? The idea should have been repugnant after what he'd done in the basement. Instead, relief swept through her, although she couldn't have said why.

He pulled a duffel bag out of a large cabinet and walked to the closet. He packed some clothes and moved to the bathroom. She heard him rattling around in the medicine cabinet while she clutched the bag to her chest. Less than five minutes later, he put his hand on the door knob.

"Do I need to use a gun to get you to the car?" His expression softened. Or maybe he was just tired. "Because I'd rather not."

She wanted to fire off some kind of smart-ass reply, but the words stuck in her throat. She shook her head.

"Good." He opened the door. "Let's go."

She followed him down the stairs and onto the second floor. People were scurrying back and forth, running into the hall from a large space at the front of the house, hurrying in and out of the offices on either side of the hallway. There was a smear of blood on one of the walls, and Angel wondered if it belonged to one of Nico's men or one of the men who worked for her father. What had happened to the men killed in the basement? There was no ambulance, no police. Just the hum of people in crisis mode, doing what people do when something unexpected has happened.

They started down the hall, past the computer lab she'd seen before. Several people were hunched over the monitors, typing and comparing notes, muttering and arguing.

"You're freaking out over nothing," one woman said. "They weren't here for our data."

"Run the check anyway," an older man said.

When they got to the end of the hall, Angel saw that for once, the double doors were open. Luca hadn't been kidding; it was a gym. And not a little one either.

A boxing ring and several bags hung from the ceiling, plus enough equipment to fill a weight room in any modern fitness club. Treadmills lined one wall, and white karate jackets with black belts hung in a row on a metal rack.

Nico held the door open for her. She hesitated, then stepped outside. Her father's men were gone. Who knew if he'd send more. Nico had proven that he would keep her alive, at least.

It was something.

This time a car, black and low to the ground, lurked outside. It reminded her of Nico, all sleek darkness and mystery.

He held the door open, and she climbed inside. He took her bag and tucked it into the small space behind the front seats. Then he leaned over her, his hands working near her hip. She wanted to ask him what he was doing, but his nearness made it impossible to speak. Her nerves were already raw, and it was all she could to keep breathing with him so close to her.

He pulled her seat belt across her lap, his hands brushing her stomach as he slid the buckle into place. His touch was like a fuse, the heat racing to every secret corner of her body.

"All set." His face was inches from hers, his mouth close enough to kiss.

He stood and closed the door, and she sank back into the plush leather seat and tried to catch her breath.

A moment later he slid behind the wheel. The car started with a low growl, and they pulled out of the alley. Brooklyn was deserted this time of night, the street lights casting yellow circles on the pavement.

"Now can you tell me where we're going?" she asked softly, more for something to say than because she expected him to answer.

"Someplace no one will find us," he said without looking at her.

She should have been scared. She wasn't.

22

She thought he might be taking her home, but they continued past Boston, following signs pointing to Manchester and Portland. By the time the sun started to rise, they'd veered off the highway in favor of the coast. The early morning light cast a blanket of diamonds over the Atlantic, and gulls swept low over the sea, diving for fish. They stopped once for gas, coffee, and restrooms. Nico stayed close, but the truth is, she was in no condition to run. Not now. She was still reeling from the night's events, still shaking off the memory of the blood on her face from the man who worked for her father. And then there was the failed rescue.

Do you think I care what happens to this bitch?

She stuffed the memory down. The man had been trying to make it out of Nico's alive. He'd been bluffing, trying to force Nico's hand so he could return Angel to her father. She'd almost gotten out, and she was still recovering from the close call, the sharp burst of hope that the nightmare was over before the sting of disappointment when she'd been escorted to Nico's office.

They continued into Maine and up the coast, past Freeport and Bath, Rockland and Camden. She thought they might just keep going to Nova Scotia. She looked over at Nico, his powerful arms on the wheel of the car, dark hair tousled from the breeze coming in the open window, and for one traitorous minute she felt exhilarated at the thought of leaving it all behind. Of hiding out and starting over with Nico.

Finally, Nico pulled off the main road and followed back streets to a town called Bass Harbor. When they got there, Angel saw that it wasn't so much a town as a little fishing village with a harbor full of boats. Nico parked in a tiny lot and turned off the car. Then he got out, removed their bags from the back, and came around to open her door.

He handed her a bundle of leather, and she saw that it was the same jacket Luca had given her before she met Nico at the Botanical Garden.

"Put this on," he said.

She slipped her arms into the sleeves, trying to ignore the sensual rush of pleasure as his musky scent enveloped her.

"Let's go."

She followed him toward the water. He didn't seem at all concerned that she might run. She thought of David and her old bitterness returned. Of course, Nico didn't think she'd run. He'd said it wouldn't be productive to hurt David, but he had to know she wouldn't bank on it. Wouldn't take even the smallest risk with David's life. All of which forced her to travel more as Nico's companion than his prisoner.

A lie that would be all too easy to believe if she wasn't careful.

Several people were boarding a ferry in the harbor, but before they reached it, Nico turned left and walked parallel to the water.

They continued for about a half a mile until they came to a small dock nestled on the shoreline. He took her arm and guided her down the wooden planks to a boat tied at the end. They were almost there when an older man emerged from the cabin.

"Hello, there." His face was like the craggy shoreline that surrounded them, etched as if the wind and sea itself had worn away at it. Blue eyes sparkled from under a stained baseball cap, and when he smiled, Angel saw that he was missing a tooth.

Definitely not one of Nico's regular men. They were really off reservation now.

"Ed," Nico said, reaching out to grasp his hand. "Thanks for coming on such short notice."

"It's not a problem, Mr. Vitale. You know that." His eyes skittered to Angel's face. "Hello."

"Hello," she said.

Nico stepped on board without introducing them, then reached for her hand to help her into the boat. It rocked with the motion of the water, and she stumbled a little before catching her balance.

Nico pointed to a bench at the back of the boat. "You can sit if you'd like."

She did, and Nico turned his attention to Ed.

"How's the weather?" he asked.

"Same as always this time of year." Ed turned a key and the boat's engine roared to life. He shouted over his shoulder at Nico. "Rough. Cold."

Nico nodded.

"Mind untying us?" Ed said.

Nico untied the rope and pushed off the dock. The boat moved forward, and Angel grabbed onto the bench as they headed out of the harbor. When they cleared the last ring of buoys, Ed shifted and the boat surged ahead, the wind whipping Angel's hair back as they sped toward open water.

She turned around, watching the harbor recede behind them, the final falling away of her old life. She faced forward, trying not to panic. Her gaze settled on Nico, as steady on his feet next to Ed as he was everyplace else. How had she come to a place where Nico Vitale was the most familiar thing to her? Where his presence somehow brought her comfort even as she remained his prisoner?

They left the mainland behind, but instead of the open water she'd expected, the glimmer of the Atlantic was broken up by countless islands. Some of them were large enough that they almost looked like part of the mainland. Others were emerald jewels nestled in the fabric of the sea. They passed the ones closest to the harbor and continued out into the ocean, the sky gray and cold above them.

She settled into the rocking of the boat. By the time Ed downshifted, she had been lulled into a kind of trance by the sting of the wind on her face, the bouncing of the bow against the waves.

She walked carefully toward Nico as the boat slowed even further. They were approaching a small island rimmed with a rocky shoreline. There was no harbor here. No restaurants or markets or tourists. In fact, the place looked deserted, and she marveled again at Nico's ability to find — or create — so much isolation.

Ed steered the boat toward a rickety looking dock on a small beach.

"Had Martha stock the fridge and cupboards for you," he said to Nico. "There's a storm coming in, so we won't be able to get back out here for at least a couple days."

"I understand," Nico said.

Ed cut the engine and they coasted the rest of the way to the dock.

Nico jumped out of the boat and tied on, then held out his hand for Angel. She waited while Ed and Nico exchanged a few more words. Then Nico was throwing the ropes back into the boat, and Ed was heading away from the island. The boat's motor was just a hum in the distance when Nico finally turned to her.

"Ready?"

She nodded, which was stupid. She hadn't been ready for anything that had happened in the past week and a half.

He lifted both their bags off the dock and started walking.

They made their way up the dock and onto the sandy beach, then continued into a dense copse of trees. There was no traffic, no planes overhead, no construction equipment or people talking. It was like being at the end of the world.

The wind blew sharp and cold, and Angel pulled Nico's jacket tightly around her as they moved through the woods. The sun was nowhere to be found, the little light that managed to make it through the trees casting the forest into a kind of twilight even though it couldn't be much past noon.

Finally they emerged into a clearing with a dirt road leading up a small hill.

"Are you all right?" Nico asked her.

She nodded.

"We're almost there."

She followed him up the dirt road. When they got to the top of the hill, she spotted a house in the clearing below them. She tried to take advantage of the view by scanning the surrounding area, wanting to to get a feel for how many other houses were on the island. But all she could see were trees, and the ocean unfurling like cold steel on every side.

She followed Nico toward the house. It was bigger than it had looked from a distance, with a peaked roof and walls of glass that opened to decks and porches on every side.

Nico led her up a walkway to the front door and pulled a key from his pocket. He unlocked the door and stepped inside. She heard the electronic beep of buttons being pressed from inside the foyer. A soft chirp emitted from the control panel, and he held the door open wider.

"Come in."

She stepped into a vaulted foyer with polished wood floors and stone walls on either side. Nico shut the door, picked up their bags, and headed further into the house.

At first it seemed small, but then they cleared the foyer, and it was like emerging from a cave onto a cliff. The room was huge, with a wall of glass that looked out over a wild beach enclosed with rock.

The water seemed close enough to touch, the roar of the waves audible even with the doors closed. It was dizzying, all that sea and sky, and she reached down to touch an overstuffed chair for balance.

Nico strode toward the glass and Angel saw that they weren't windows at all; the entire wall was made of doors. He slid one open, and it disappeared behind the rest of the glass. The briny scent of the sea instantly invaded the room, the sound of the water crashing against the rocks on either side of the private beach.

She took a deep breath almost against her will. The sense of calm that settled over her felt like a betrayal. This wasn't some kind of romantic getaway. She was still being held against her will.

Nico turned back to her. "I'll show you to your room while the house airs out."

He led her up a set of open stairs to the second floor and a large hallway. They passed one closed door before coming to a stop at another.

"There's a deck, and a private bath," Nico said, leading her into an airy space that seemed to hover over the sea. "No cable, I'm afraid, although there are some DVDs downstairs."

She stepped into the room. What was the expected etiquette when you were being shown first class accommodations by your captor?

"Thank you," she said. Absurd.

"You should feel free to make yourself at home while we're here."

She folded her arms over chest. "How long will that be?"

"I don't know," he said. "I need to regroup. Think about what happened back at Headquarters. We'll ride out the storm here at least. Then we'll see."

She nodded.

"There's food in the kitchen. Have a rest and I'll see you for dinner."

He shut the door behind him.

A quick look around revealed a well appointed bedroom and luxury bathroom, complete with a soaking tub overlooking the water. She unpacked her few belongings, undressed, and climbed into the tub.

The sea was mesmerizing, and the glass wall made her feel like she was suspended between the sky and the ocean. She refilled the water twice when it got cold. When her fingers started to prune, she wrapped herself in a towel and squeezed the water out of her hair with another one. Then she climbed naked into the massive bed and pulled the heavy covers over her body. She fell asleep with the sound of the water crashing against the rocks below her window.

23

He poured himself a drink and walked to the window overlooking the ocean. It was too cold to keep the doors open to the deck, but he made no move to close them. He was exhausted from the sleepless night and the long drive, but he wanted to call Luca for an update. Then he'd need to unpack and shower, make dinner. The icy air woke him up, made him feel alive.

The waves were already bigger than they'd been when Ed had brought them over, and Nico could almost taste the impending storm. There was a tang to the air, like electricity gathering force. The reality of it gave him a kind of peace. There was nothing he could do now about Carlo and what had happened at Headquarters. He was surprised to realize he didn't mind the imposed distance from the situation, although he was beginning to suspect it had more to do with the fact that he was with Angel than any desire to leave it all behind.

Angel.

He didn't believe in love at first sight. In fact, if he hadn't seen it for himself in his parents, he might not believe in love at all. But her name had been like an echo in his mind since that first night in his apartment. He saw her face when he slept, when he ran in the first light of early morning. He hadn't scheduled another appointment with the escort service, because he couldn't imagine touching another woman after tasting Angel.

And this. This was the biggest mistake of all.

No one knew about the island in Maine. Not Luca. Not Carmine. No one.

It had been his father's idea; a place to hide. A place no one could find him if he found himself under attack — or simply in need of an escape. Nico had bought the island with some of the money left to him by his parents. The deed was listed in the name of one of many offshore corporations Nico had set up for just this kind of purpose.

No one would ever find him and Angel here, and he had the sudden desire to leave it all behind. To keep her with him and start over with nothing but the two of them and the sky and the endless sea.

But that was ridiculous. Angel despised him. Maybe she wanted him. Sometimes. But that was just lust. She was the daughter of his sworn enemy. And he had brought her here.

He closed the doors and turned away from the window, then climbed the stairs to the second floor. His room was next to the one he'd given Angel, and he could hear the water running in her bath. A minute later, it shut off, and he had to forcibly banish the thought of her naked body, water lapping at her perfect pink nipples, working its way between her legs.

It was too late. His cock was already hard, and he turned the shower on cold, then stripped and stepped in. He stood there for a long time, letting his skin grow icy as penance for being stupid. When he couldn't stand it any longer, he toweled off and put on a pair of loose sweatpants and a T-shirt.

He pulled a rosary from the nightstand and sat in the chair in front of the big window. The beads eased through this fingers as he went through the sequence of events at Headquarters. How had Carlo known that's where Nico was keeping Angel? Or had it been a lucky guess? He hadn't been surprised by their attempt to rescue Angel. It was their willingness to give her up that worried him.

Do you think I care what happens to this bitch?

Angel hadn't said anything about it, but she had been in survival mode, had probably gone into shock after Nico killed the man holding her. Did she even remember it?

He wasn't surprised. Not exactly. Carlo was the worst kind of criminal; an old-school thug hiding behind a facade of normalcy. He had been one of the biggest critics of Nico's business plan, and Nico remained convinced it wasn't the plan Carlo objected to — it was the lack of violence.

Nico had done his research, had run the numbers. If it was all about profit, every family in the Syndicate would be making the same changes. No, Carlo just liked to hurt people with all the stuff Nico made off limits — human trafficking, child porn, sending drugs into schools, issuing high-interest loans to desperate people who couldn't pay them back, forcing small business owners to pay for protection. Nico had banished them all in favor of cyber theft from corrupt corporations and individuals, loans for small businesses that were vetted by his underwriters, and protection for companies that could afford to pay for the Vitale influence. Bookmaking was still a legitimate enterprise, but gamblers were carefully screened and cut off before they could do too much damage to themselves or their families. There were bribes — for building permits and liquor licenses and a thousand other petty things that businesses needed to do business. But as organized crime went, it was somewhat civilized, and Nico was proud of the fact that violence and death had become increasingly rare within his organization.

But what had happened at Headquarters wasn't civilized. Because if those had really been Carlo's men, they weren't there to rescue Angel at all. They were there to send a message to Nico. To make it clear that Carlo would sacrifice his daughter rather than give in to Nico's demands.

Nico had already known Carlo didn't care about the honor code that protected the families of Syndicate members; he just hadn't realized the bastard didn't care about his own daughter either.

He set down the rosary beads and ran a hand through his damp hair. He didn't want to be the one to tell Angel about her father. It had been bad enough to tell her Carlo was part of the Syndicate. How would she feel when she found out the rest?

He picked up the phone next to the bed and called Luca. Everything was under control, thanks to a couple of their friends at NYPD, and Luca insisted that it was best for Nico to be out of sight while everything settled down. There had been no data breach, and none of Nico's men had lost their lives, although Vincent's head had been grazed by a bullet in the basement firefight. Luca had already put out the word that Carlo's men had failed. Nico gave him a few last minute instructions, then hung up.

He knew he should call Carmine, too, but exhaustion was pulling at his eyelids. Carmine would only remind him that taking Angel had been ill-advised, and while Nico counted on his Consigliere for advice, he really wasn't up for an "I told you so", however sensitively it might be phrased.

He stretched out in the chair, not wanting to sleep too deeply in case Angel woke up.

It seemed like only a few minutes later that he opened his eyes to the sound of footsteps. The room was dark, the ocean invisible beyond the windows. He walked to the door and peered into the hall. Angel was there, standing at the top of the stairs with her back to him.

"Angel?"

She turned. "I think I heard thunder," she said.

"Probably."

The wind had kicked up, whistling outside the windows as the ocean beat fast and frantic against the rocks. She jumped as a bolt of lightning cracked the sky, spilling blue light into the house.

"Are you all right?" he asked.

She crossed her arms over her chest. "A little disoriented."

"A lot's happened." He hesitated. "Come here."

She regarded him with suspicion. "Where?"

"My room." She narrowed her eyes, and he smiled. "There's a phone. I thought you might like to call your brother before the storm knocks out phone service."

"David?"

He hated himself for the light in her eyes. All of his phone lines were blocked for anonymity. He could have given her this at any time and he hadn't.

"Yes. Come on." She followed him into his room, and he turned on the light next to the bed and handed her the house phone. He didn't let go when she closed her hand around it. "Things are... volatile between our families right now, as I'm sure you know. Can I trust you to keep David out of it?"

She ripped the phone from his grasp. "I would never do anything to put my brother in danger."

He nodded, the ferocity of her words taking him by surprise. "Go ahead."

She dialed then turned her back on him.

She breathed his name a moment later. "David. It's me." She paused, then let out a strangled laugh. "I know. I'm sorry to worry you."

Nico felt like an intruder, but he didn't dare leave her alone. She had promised not to endanger her brother, but he had to make sure she didn't let anything slip about their location.

He shouldn't have worried. She was a pro, telling David how she'd decided to make a last minute trip to Cancun, how she and her friend, Rachel, were drinking margaritas and dancing and sleeping before winter really set in in New York. She asked about David's midterms, about a guy he was interested in, and about his roommate who was apparently a slob. She was so calm, Nico almost bought it himself.

A couple minutes into the call, after the initial rush of conversation, she sank onto Nico's bed with the phone still cradled against her ear.

"I haven't heard from him either," she said into the phone. "But I'm sure he's fine. You know how he is." She sighed and lowered her voice. "He'll come around, David. He loves you." A pause. "Because I *know.*"

They exchanged a few more words before Angel said she had to go.

"I love you, too," she said. Her eyes flickered to Nico, leaning against the wall. "I can't wait either. Okay. See you soon."

She disconnected the call, but didn't immediately give up the phone. He waited, wanting to give her time. Finally she set the phone back on the receiver and stood.

"Thank you."

It was cold, and Nico knew she resented having to be grateful for something as simple as making a phone call. He didn't blame her.

"I should have done it sooner," he said. "I'm sorry."

Her shoulders seemed to soften.

"Hungry?" he asked.

She nodded. "Very."

"Good. Let's go downstairs. I'll make dinner."

24

She sat on a stool while Nico cooked. She thought about offering to help, then felt stupid. It wasn't her job to help Nico Vitale keep her prisoner.

They didn't speak while he moved around the kitchen, marinating steaks and making salad. Her feelings for him were increasingly complicated. How could she hate him so much and still notice how defined his arms were under the sleeves of his T-shirt? How could she want to get away from him at the same time she wanted to press her body against his, reach inside the waistband of his sweats and take him in her hand, feel his mouth on her breasts?

She was grateful he'd let her call David — she'd almost wept with relief at the sound of his voice, so even, so normal — but she was also pissed at herself for being grateful, and at Nico for putting her in a position to appreciate so small a favor.

This was supposed to be simple. Nico had kidnapped her, was keeping her prisoner. She should hate him.

He'd cooked the meat on an indoor grill and took everything to the table. The first splatter of rain hit the windows as they sat down to eat. It was disorienting, sitting in the house with nothing but darkness and the raging storm outside. Like she and Nico were floating calmly through space in the middle of a hurricane.

The steak was perfect, rare and tender. She hadn't eaten since the snacks they'd grabbed at the gas station early that morning, and she had to force herself not to inhale the food in front of her.

"You don't like the wine?" Nico asked, eyeing her untouched glass.

She couldn't tell him that she didn't trust herself to be even remotely drunk around him. "Just not in the drinking mood."

"Can I get you something else?"

"The water's fine." She took a bite of salad. "How long have you had this place?" She told herself it was to ease the tension of their silence, but the truth is, she was curious. From a penthouse apartment in New York City that must have cost millions to a house that was both sleek and rustic on an island in the Atlantic. Nico was an enigma. Just when she thought she had a handle on him, he threw her another curve ball.

"A couple years," he said, looking at the wineglass in his fingertips. "I bought it after my parents died."

"Why?" she asked. "I mean, it's beautiful, but it doesn't seem..." She shook her head.

"What?" he prompted.

"It doesn't seem like you."

He seemed to consider his words. "I like this place better than the apartment in the city."

"Really?"

"It's more personal."

"Like your business with my father."

"Yes. Like that."

Another crack of thunder sounded, followed by a flash of lightning that lit up the sky in a wicked zig-zag. The lights flickered, then went out.

Nico stood. "I'll get some candles."

She heard him moving around in the kitchen, and a moment later he appeared with two candles. He put them on the table and sat down.

She pushed her salad around with her fork before letting it fall to her plate with a clatter. "Why can't you tell me what you want from him?"

At first he didn't say anything. Just looked at her across the candle lit table. Then his gaze seemed to soften. "Because I don't want to hurt you."

"You don't want to hurt me?" She choked out a laugh. "Right. That's why you kidnapped me, threatened my brother, brought me to the middle of nowhere where no one will ever be able to find me."

"I'm sorry about that," he said. "All of it."

She was feeling belligerent now, annoyed by her attraction to him in spite of everything he'd done, angered that he sometimes made her *like* him. It was all a lie. He was a criminal. The polished exterior was all artifice.

"I don't believe you."

"I understand," he said evenly.

It only made her more angry.

"I think it's all a lie," she said. "Every bit of it. I think you're just like every other criminal. You want money from my father, but you don't want to cop to it, so you're going to make it seem like he did something horrible, something that would make what you've done to me all right when there's nothing my father could have done that - "

He pounded the table with his fist. "He killed my parents!"

Everything ceased to exist in the vacuum left by his words. There was only the rain beating against the windows, the waves seeming to crash right against the house as another bolt of thunder shook the ground.

She stared at him. "You're a liar."

"I'm not."

There was none of his usual bravado, none of the satisfaction she would have expected from such a revelation.

He took a deep breath. "My parents were killed in an execution style hit two years ago. You're father is one of the men who pulled the trigger."

"I don't believe you."

"But he wasn't alone," Nico continued. "Someone helped him. Someone inside my organization."

"I feel sorry for you," she said.

"Your father has the security tape from outside the restaurant that night," he said as if she hadn't spoken.

"You want to kill him, and you're making this up to justify it."

The Nico who'd kissed her in his apartment, who'd made her come on the bench at the garden, disappeared behind cold eyes. "You're right; I do want to kill him. But that's not what this is about. I need that tape. Need to know who's a traitor in my family. I'll let the Syndicate deal with your father."

"My father..." She started off strong, but the words seemed to leave her. She tried again. "My father is not a perfect man, but he's no murderer."

"I'm afraid he is, Angel."

"Stop calling me that!" she shouted. She stood, pacing to the window. "It's not my name."

She felt him behind her — his chest against her back, his hands on her shoulders. "I'm sorry. I didn't expect..."

She spun to face him, forgetting that he was so close, that if she turned she would be facing him, forced to look into his eyes, to feel the chiseled planes of his body.

"You didn't expect what? That I wouldn't believe my father is a cold blooded killer?" She shoved him away from her, but he only stepped forward again.

"I knew you wouldn't believe it. I just didn't expect to care."

She turned her face from him as another bolt of lightning ripped the sky in two. "Another lie."

"I care, Angel." He put his hands on either side of her face, forcing her to look into his eyes. "So much more than I wish I did."

She wanted to walk away. To block out the words that had to be lies. To ignore the feelings rushing through her like a tidal wave. But she couldn't. His eyes bound her as sure as any chain.

"I hate you." She'd meant for it to come out with some force, but it sounded more like resignation.

He stepped closer. He was only inches away, close enough that she could see the rise and fall of his chest. "I know."

"I really, really hate you."

He slid a hand into the hair at the back of her neck. "I know."

"Nothing that happens between us will change that."

He lowered his head, stopping when she could feel his breath on her lips. "I know, I know."

The moment seemed to freeze, the air crackling with electricity to rival the storm outside. They were both breathing too fast, the tension between them rising like an unstoppable tide. She barely had time to register him closing the distance before his mouth was on hers.

Then there was no room for doubt or regrets. There was just his tongue sparring with her own, pillaging her mouth as his hands tipped her head so he could taste more of her. She molded herself to his body, wanting to feel every inch of him against her while he claimed her with his mouth.

He kissed the corner of her lips, continuing along her jaw until he reached the tender spot near her ear. She gasped as his hot tongue flicked against her skin. He took her earlobe in his mouth and sucked, then nipped at it with his teeth while his hands slid across her shoulders and down to her breasts.

She gasped. "I still hate you."

"I know."

She was pressed against the glass now, her legs weak and rubbery as he left a trail of kisses down her neck and across her collarbone. Her body was hot and wet, already screaming for him.

He cupped her breasts through her T-shirt, then growled as he raised his head. "Not this way. Not this time."

Her skin clamored for the feel of his mouth, his hands. "Please…"

He took her face in his hand, rubbed his thumb across her lower lip. "Tell me."

"I… I can't."

She wanted his mouth on her naked skin, his body sliding against hers with nothing between them. Most of all she wanted him inside her. Needed him to fill the empty places in her body that were meant for him. But she couldn't make herself say any of it.

He put her hand on him, and his hard length sent another rush of moisture between her legs.

His voice was low and dangerous. "You have to tell me you want it. That you want me."

She didn't have the willpower to second guess it. There was only need.

Desire.

Desperation.

She wrapped her arms around his neck and pressed against him.

"I want it," she said against his mouth. "I want you."

He pulled back, forcing her to look at him. "Look at me when you tell me you want me."

She couldn't have looked away if she tried. "I want you."

He let out another growl and swept her into his arms like she weighed no more than a feather.

He carried her across the darkened room, the candles still flickering low on the table. By the time they got to the stairs, his mouth was on hers again, his tongue moving with more force, challenging her, taking everything she would give him and more.

She was barely aware of crossing the threshold of his bedroom. He kicked the door closed even though they were the only ones in the house, then set her down next to the bed and kissed her again while he reached for the bottom of her T-shirt.

He lifted it over her head and bent his head to her neck, working his way down to the hollow of her throat, flicking his tongue over the sensitive skin while he unhooked her bra. Then he cupped her breasts, teasing the nipples to hard points before letting his hand continue down her stomach.

He kept his eyes on hers as he slipped one hand into her lace panties, his fingers sliding between the hot folds of her sex. Her head dropped back as a moan escaped from her lips, and his fingers retreated. He slid the lacy garment from her hips.

"Fuck, you're beautiful, Angel."

She could see the outline of his erection and knew that he believed it. Then she was back in his arms as he lowered her gently to the bed. He bent over her all too briefly, his tongue invading her mouth just long enough to make the throbbing start between her legs.

She reached for him. "Please…"

She watched as he stripped off his T-shirt and had to resist the urge to gasp in appreciation. His biceps were big — bigger than they looked under the expensive fabric of his suit. His pecs were muscled and defined, tapering to a narrow waist and defined abs that begged to be touched, a trail of dark hair winding its way beneath the waistband of his sweats. She pressed her legs together against the pulse of an orgasm she could already feel building there.

He slid off his sweats, and the beat between her legs grew more insistent at the sight of him standing hard and ready for her.

A perfect specimen of man. A god.

He lowered himself onto the bed and pulled her against the length of him. She gasped at their first skin to skin contact; her breasts pressed against his well-formed chest, the insistent demand of his cock on her stomach. For a moment, he held her just like that while he looked into her eyes. Then his lips found hers, his tongue invading her mouth, sending a shock of desire straight to her center.

His kisses grew deeper and deeper. She met his demands and made more of her own, arching her back, wanting to be closer to him, to make it easier for him to reach every secret crevice of her body.

His hands roamed her breasts and arms, her back and ass, all the way down the length of her thighs to her feet. He explored her like he wanted to memorize every curve, every recess. Finally she couldn't take it anymore, and he groaned as she closed her hand around him.

"Angel... what are you doing to me?"

He pulsed in her hand, and she felt an answering wetness between her legs. She stroked him while he kissed his way down her neck. She could almost feel him inside her, imagine the rigid length of him pressing into her hot slickness.

He moved to her breasts and was suddenly out of reach. She grasped blindly for him, desperate to feel him in her hand again.

"Not yet, baby," he murmured. "Just lay back. Let me taste you."

His mouth closed on one of her breasts, and she had no choice but to obey his command. His took her nipple in his mouth and sucked, gently at first, then harder. She arched her back, overcome by a storm of sensation; his hot mouth on her skin, his cock sliding against her inner thigh while he worked her nipple, the occasional brush against her already-swollen clit.

When she thought she would die from the pleasure of it, he moved lower, working his way down her stomach. He bent between her legs and spread her thighs, sighing with pleasure as he looked at her. She squirmed, and he lowered his head and licked the length of her, running his tongue back and forth over her dewy folds before working his way to her clit. He slipped a finger inside her while he closed his mouth around the tiny bundle of nerves.

"Oh my god... Nico..." She reached for his head, twining her fingers into his dark hair, pressing against his mouth.

He slipped a second finger inside her, sliding in and out while he mercilessly worked her clit, lapping and sucking until she was almost out of her mind, delirious with pleasure.

The climax had been there all along, lurking at her core from the first moment he'd kissed her downstairs. Now it built with the force of a desert wind, and she moved her hips in time to his fingers and his mouth, reaching for the cliff, letting herself go in the moment that it became inevitable, stepping off the edge as the orgasm rocked her body, clenching around his fingers as she came and came.

When the last shudder had moved through her body, he lifted his head and moved between her legs. She already wanted more. Wanted to feel him inside her, fulfilling the promise he'd made when he pressed her hand against him in the living room.

He reached for the nightstand and tore open a condom. She sat up between his legs and took it from his hand, kissed his satiny tip, and slid her mouth down the length of him.

"Fuck, Angel." He pulled her head away. "I need to be inside of you."

She rolled the condom onto his shaft and he pushed her gently back onto the bed, lifting her knees, spreading her wider for him. She could feel the tip of him balanced against her opening. All she had to do was lift her hips.

He looked into her eyes. "I'm going to own you tonight, baby."

She gasped as he drove into her. He filled and stretched her, pushing all the way inside until she could feel him everywhere. She matched him thrust for thrust, her whole body throbbing as lightning burst through the room.

Angel looked down at their joined bodies, the sight of Nico's olive complexion against her pale skin making her even wetter as he slid almost all the way out before pushing into her again. He pushed until there was nowhere else to go, until the continuous brushes against her clit started another climax building inside her. It was a sweet kind of torture, and she grabbed onto his rock hard ass and drove him into her.

"Come for me, baby."

His words only made her hotter, wetter.

He was moving faster now, his shaft bigger and harder, growing with his own climax. She moved with him, and he lowered his head to hers, thrusting his tongue into her mouth while he owned her, just like he said he would. There was nothing else in the world. Just Nico inside her, his mouth claiming hers, their bodies one and the same as she rocked toward her orgasm, coming in a rush that sent a burst of white light through her brain, eclipsing every other thought, every other sensation as he came with her.

He shuddered inside her with his last few thrusts, and she reached up and ran a hand through his dark hair, her mind suspended in a kind of pleasant white noise. When their breathing returned to normal, he stretched out and pulled her into his arms, kissing her gently but passionately on the mouth before nestling her in the crook of his arm.

She lay her head on his chest, listening to the slowing of his heartbeat as waves crashed outside the bedroom.

"I still hate you," she said softly.

He kissed the top of her head. "I know."

25

She woke on her side, Nico's arm flung over her waist. The rain was still lashing the windows, the light weak and gray. She lay there for awhile, listening to the waves crash under the window, feeling the soft exhalation of Nico's breath behind her. Finally, she slid out from under his arm.

She picked her clothes off the floor and went into her bedroom where she dressed in her jeans and a sweater that had been in the stuff Luca brought to her after the altercation with Dante. Had it been less than a week earlier? She couldn't believe it.

Creeping pass Nico's room and down the stairs, she made her way to the wall of windows where Nico has kissed her. She tipped her head against the glass, letting it cool her forehead while images from the night before filled her mind; Nico's hands on her, his head between her legs, his body joining hers.

Stepping outside, she closed the doors quietly behind her. The storm didn't seem to be receding, and the waves were still rolling fast and angry onto the private beach below the house. She crossed her arms over her chest and made her way down the stairs to the sand.

The wind blew her hair around, the sting of it numbing her face as she walked down to the water. She relished the cold. It drove everything else out of her mind, made it hard to think about what Nico had said about her father, what she had done with Nico afterwards. There was the vague feeling that she should feel guilty, that she might even be crazy to sleep with the man who'd kept her prisoner for the last two weeks. But it was so distant. So easy to ignore.

The ocean stretched endless and wide in front of her, blending in with the steely sky above it. Most of the trees on the shoreline were evergreens, standing out in sharp relief against the white and gray. She imagined what it looked like in the winter, the rocky shore covered with snow, the waves rolling in just like they always did, season after season. There was a kind of comfort in the certainty of it.

She felt hands on her shoulders, and Nico pulled back her wild hair and touched his mouth to her neck. His lips were hot against her cold skin.

"You're freezing," he said softly.

She didn't say anything, didn't move. As long as she stared at the sea, as long as she didn't take her eyes off it, she wouldn't have to think about anything else.

He turned her to face him and wrapped his big arms around her, swallowing her in the warmth of his embrace. He looked down at her.

"We don't have to talk about this," he said. "Not yet." His eyes had turned a shade darker in the gray light, and he looked out over the water before returning his gaze to her. "I just want to be with you, Angel." He sighed. "Can we do that until this storm breaks?"

She reached up to touch his face, then nodded. There was nothing to say.

He took her face in his hands and kissed her gently. "Come on. Let's get you warm."

He led her inside, up the stairs and into his bathroom where he started the shower. Then he carefully peeled off her wet clothes while she stood shivering and silent. When she was naked, he stripped and led her into the shower, moving her so that she was fully under the warm spray of water.

He shampooed her hair, starting at the top just like she did, careful not to let it get too tangled. Tipping her head back into the water, he worked the shampoo from her hair, then started on her body, soaping her gently like a child. At first, she could feel nothing beyond the warmth of the water. But little by little, his hands brought her alive. They moved over her shoulders and down to her breasts, slippery with soap, Her nipples hardened of their own accord, and a fire built in her belly as he soaped her hips, washed between her legs.

By the time the water sluiced the soap off her body, she was humming for him again, begging for more of his touch. She thought he might take her then, but instead he turned off the water and stepped from the shower.

He wrapped a towel around his waist and returned with one for her. The towel was soft and thick, and he moved it gently across her arms and breasts, down her stomach and in the space between her thighs, behind her knees. When he was done with her body, he squeezed the excess water out of her hair.

She followed him into the bedroom and watched as he removed a shirt from the dresser. He slipped it over her arms and buttoned it while she stood perfectly still, her body coming alive like a tuning fork to lightning as his hands brushed against her belly.

He put on a fresh pair of black lounge pants. "Sit down," he said softly. "I'll be right back."

She sat on the edge of the bed while he went into the bathroom. He returned with a hairbrush and positioned himself behind her where he began at the bottom, tenderly brushing the tangles from her hair. The storm seemed to be ripping the world apart on the other side of the windows, but they didn't speak. She lost track of time, relaxing into the gentle motion of the brush in her hair, Nico's occasional touch on the top of her head, against her shoulder. She didn't know what was between them, but she didn't want to analyze it anymore. Not right now.

Finally, he set the brush aside. She felt the soft sweep of his breath as he dropped a kiss on her neck. Then he stood and took her hand, pulling her up off the bed.

"Come on. I'll make you breakfast."

26

He tried not to stare at her across the table, but it wasn't easy. He'd thought possessing her physically would kill the emotional connection he had felt to her almost since the beginning. That's how it usually worked. Instead their night together had only solidified it.

He'd sensed their loneliness merge along with their bodies, felt the same disconnection in her that existed in himself. Once she'd let go, she hadn't been at all hesitant. It had been the opening of a floodgate, and she had been as hungry for him as he'd been for her. He had never wanted to possess someone so completely. Had never felt so totally the futility of the desire.

He sensed in her a deep goodness, a stubborn innocence in spite of everything that had happened. She was the only thing he'd never wanted to remake. The only thing he'd ever found perfect, just as it was. He knew instinctively that she wasn't someone he would possess easily, but it only made him want her more.

"What?"

He blinked, realizing she'd caught him staring. "You're beautiful. It's hard not to stare."

She shook her head little. "This isn't that kind of thing."

"What do you mean?" he asked.

"This…" She looked at her empty plate. He'd made eggs and bacon and toast. "This thing between us. It's not an emotional kind of thing. You don't have to say nice things to me."

"Are you speaking for yourself or for me?"

She shrugged. "Both."

"Well, don't," he said. "I don't know what this is yet, but I can assure you that it's not nothing."

"I don't see how it can be anything more than that," she said.

Her words fell like a stone between them, and the potential loss of her moved through him like a brushfire. He stood and walked toward her, then gently pulled her to her feet.

He tucked a piece of golden hair behind her ear. "I don't have it figured out," he said. "But I'm not going to make light of it while I have you."

She seemed to hesitate, then nodded.

"Come on," he said. "The rain seems to be letting up a little. Let's go for a walk."

They changed into warm clothes, and Nico dug out an extra pair of galoshes for Angel. It was strangely intimate, getting ready in the same room, dressing, watching her brush her teeth. He wanted to memorize her movements, the way she looked at herself in the mirror while she pulled her hair back into a ponytail, the line of her back when she bent to pull on the boots.

He gave her his biggest coat and pulled up the hood, looking into her eyes as he tied it around her face. Then he bent his head, unable to resist tasting her lips. He swept them gently with his tongue, then pulled back, studying her face. She smiled a little, and he felt the corners of his mouth lift in response.

He took her hand and led her outside. The wind was still coming in strong off the water, but it wasn't quite as bad as it had been the night before, and the rain was noticeably less violent.

He led her away from the house, back the way they'd come from the boat the day before. The island had been his secret, and he suddenly wanted her to see it all.

They picked their way along the rocky shoreline, traveling away from the place where Ed had dropped them off. He hadn't walked the perimeter of the island since he'd first bought it. He'd been alone then, pondering the merits of the place as it related to his need for privacy.

This was different, and he stopped to point out the meadow that stood beyond the beach on the west end of the island, the way the waves crashed against the breakers that jutted out into the ocean. There was a lighthouse barely visible on an adjacent island, and they stood atop one of the highest peaks, watching the light make a slow circle toward them again and again.

They were making their way back when thunder rocked the ground. A few seconds later, lightning tore through the sky, and Nico pulled Angel under a rocky outcropping.

"We should wait a few minutes," he said.

She nodded.

Water dripped from her hood, and her cheeks were pink from the cold. A piece of hair had escaped from her ponytail. It hung in a loose curl, and he reached out, wrapping it around his finger. He was torn between wanting to feel her naked body against his — now — and wanting to protect her from anything and everything that might hurt her.

"What are you doing to me, Angel?" he murmured.

"Nothing," she whispered.

He took her hand, pressing it against his chest, hoping she could feel his rapidly beating heart. "This isn't nothing." He moved her hand lower, pressing it against the erection already straining against his jeans. "And whatever you might think, this isn't nothing either."

Her lips parted at the contact, and he was surprised to feel her palm rub against the swollen flesh in his pants. She stepped closer, snaking her free arm around his neck, pulling his head to hers.

"I know." She pressed her lips to his, slipping her tongue, hot and urgent, inside his mouth.

He held her face in his hands, deepening their kiss, wanting all of her. Even here, even now. She met the thrusts of his tongue, pushing her body against his until he could feel the warmth of her even through the layers of their clothes. His cock responded, growing harder and more persistent. He could feel her now, could imagine sliding into her wetness, letting her heat milk him until he poured himself into her.

He pulled back. "Not here." He was barely able to get out the words, but he wasn't going to take her outside in the cold. Not Angel. Not like that. "It's too cold."

She reached up, slipping a hand into his hood and twining it into the hair at the back of his head. "Then take me to bed."

He was riveted on her eyes, on the need there that matched his own. Finally, he took her hand and hurriedly headed for the house.

They stripped in the entryway, her fingers hurried and demanding on his clothes while he tried to undress her without removing his mouth from hers. When they were naked, she pulled him down on the staircase, her hands roaming his body, closing around his shaft until he drove into her, his tongue plundering her mouth.

She lifted her hips to meet him, her pussy hot and tight, panting as she grasped for the orgasm he could feel building at the center of her body.

"Do it, baby," he urged her. "Come for me."

The words seemed to send her over the edge, and she cried out as she tumbled over the precipice. It set him off, releasing his last vestige of control. He let go, his body shuddering as he emptied himself into her.

Later, they lay in the bath, candles flickering, the rain falling softly against the roof. Her head was tipped back against the tub, her eyes closed, and her long blond hair was swept away from her face in a loose bun. Some of the loose strands curled around her face.

He took her foot in his hand and rubbed, marveling at the softness of her skin, the delicate lift of her arch. "Tell me about your brother," he said softly.

Her eyes snapped open, and she regarded him with the first hint of suspicion he'd seen since he'd taken her the night before.

"I just want to hear about something good in your life." It stung to think that she was still afraid of him, but he couldn't really blame her.

She seemed to relax. Her expression turned pensive as she started to speak.

"He's the best person I know," she said simply. "Just… good and decent. We were close, even before my mother died. Being sent to separate schools almost killed me."

Nico felt an irrational surge of jealousy. Not because Angel loved her brother. She deserved to love and be loved, and he was glad she had that in her life. But she would never talk about him like that. Never talk about how good and decent he was. He had made that impossible, and he suddenly found that he wanted nothing more than for Angel to think those things about him.

"Did you stay close?" he asked, lifting her other foot.

She nodded. "We talked on the phone, Skyped… But I don't know if I'll ever be able to forgive my father for separating us when we needed each other the most."

"I can understand that." It wasn't easy to keep his voice calm. Carlo had sacrificed the happiness of his children for his own gain — either because he was too selfish to think about what was best for them or because he was so desperate to keep his secrets.

"What about you?" she asked. "Any siblings?"

"No, it's just me." He spoke carefully, not wanting to disrupt the seemingly normal conversation with any of the anger and bitterness he'd been carrying around since his parent's death.

"Must be lonely," she said softly.

He looked into her eyes across the tub. "I've never thought so until now."

She held his gaze before looking around the luxurious bathroom. "Why did you chose this place? It's so… isolated. "

"I bought it on the suggestion of my father before he died. He thought I might need a place to escape."

"And have you?" she asked.

"At various times for various reasons," he said. "But never because I felt physically threatened."

"Why do you feel threatened now?" she asked softly. "They were after me."

He looked away. "There are things you don't know."

Silence stretched between them.

"Tell me," she finally said.

"No."

"Why?" she asked. "If what you say is true, I'm as involved in this as you. I deserve to know."

He sighed. "I don't dispute that, Angel. But I'm not going to be the one to hurt you if I can help it."

"And telling me the things I don't know will hurt me?"

"Yes," he said.

He didn't say the other thing; that she had already started to feel essential to him. He didn't know what would happen to them when they were forced to rejoin the real world, but if he told her everything, she would hate him all over again, even if it was just because he was the messenger.

"If they're out there, they have the power to hurt me anyway," she said. "Wouldn't it be better for me to know what I'm up against?"

The argument was valid, but it didn't change anything. He stood, his body dripping. "I'm not discussing this with you, Angel."

He stepped from the tub and headed for the bedroom. He was looking out over the storm-tossed beach when he felt her hands wrap around his waist, her naked body pressed to his back.

"I'm not sorry for asking," she said. "I deserve to know."

"You do," he said hoarsely.

The stood in silence before she spoke again. "Let's not talk about my father. I just want to be with you."

He turned to face her. "Good."

27

She was careful to avoid conversation about their families after the incident in the tub. It was a stupid kind of denial, but she didn't have the energy to fight it. Something had shifted in the two days since they'd left New York. Maybe it was the way Nico took her, without inhibition, his need for her as raw and visible as an open wound. Or maybe it was the way he looked at her, like he would pluck the moon from the sky if she wanted it.

Or maybe she was just being stupid.

She didn't know how to explain it, but she felt safe with him against all reason. More than that, she felt a connection to him she couldn't explain. She tried telling herself it was just sex. She'd never been claimed so completely, never lost control of herself like she did in Nico's arms. He did more than take her — he occupied her, took up residence under her skin. When his hands were on her, there was nothing but the two of them. Nothing but Nico's mouth and hands, his hardness sliding exquisitely inside her. There was nothing but light then. For the first time that she could remember, there was light.

Whatever it was, she felt sick at the thought of losing it, and she blocked out the past and the future, determined to live in the moment with Nico, whatever waited for them on the other side of it.

She sat on the counter in his shirt and let him feed her succulent pieces of fish and tender fingerling potatoes while he cooked. He dipped her fingers in the cream sauce simmering on the stove, then put them in his mouth, sucking until she was wet for him all over again. They listened to music while he worked, talking about their childhoods and their adolescence, steering clear of anything that would take them too close to the forbidden territory of Angel's father.

They sat close at dinner. Nico touched her wrist, his bare feet next to hers under the table. She thrilled with every stroke of his skin, had to resist the urge to touch her lips to his, strip off his shirt, run her hands over his perfectly sculpted body.

They loaded the dishwasher, then moved to the couch where Angel sat cradled between his denim-clad legs. His chest was solid against her back, and she leaned into him, resting her head in the space between his collarbone and chest. He stroked her hair while he told her about his parents, about the business he'd remade after their death. She wanted to ask him details; did he hurt people? Kill them? Somehow she couldn't imagine it, despite the power he emanated. But she didn't ask. She didn't know what waited for them beyond the sanctity of the island, but tonight belonged to them.

The candles were flickering low in their holders when the lights over the dining room table flickered on. Angel looked up silently, fighting the despair that unwound in her body. How much longer would they be able to justify staying here now that the storm was coming to an end?

Nico kissed the top of her head. "I need to see if the phones are back up."

She leaned forward so he could get out, then sat back, watching him prowl to the phone on the kitchen island.

He picked up the receiver. "It's working."

She nodded, not trusting herself to speak.

"I'm going to make a quick call," he said. "Sit tight."

He turned off the dining room light before heading for a closed door off the living room. She tried to make out his end of the conversation through the half-open door, but he spoke quietly, raising his voice only once; "I'm not taking her anywhere until I know it's safe."

It went quiet again in the moments before he came back into the room, still holding the phone. He leaned in the doorway, watching her.

"Everything okay?" she asked softly.

His eyes darkened. "It is now."

She smiled a little.

"We have to go back tomorrow." Regret shaded his voice.

"I know." She held out a hand for him. "Come here."

He set the phone on the mantel and came toward her.

She pulled him down, stretching out against his body, fitting herself to him. He held her close, kissed her hair, his tenderness quickly turning to passion as her skin came alive under his fingers. He undressed her in front of the fireplace, sucking in his breath at the sight of her like he hadn't already seen her without clothes at least five times. She knew the feeling. She was breathless in the face of his naked form, his chiseled body glowing in the firelight. They started slowly, drawing out their pleasure, but it wasn't long before she guided him inside her, meeting his thrusts with her hips, urging him on with words, begging him to fuck her, to take her, to come with her. Wanted all of him, everywhere.

Hours later, they were still naked on the sofa. The flames had burned low in the grate, and the candles had long since burned out.

"We should go to bed," Nico said,

"Hmmm...." Angel nestled into him, draping an arm across his chest.

He didn't say anything at first, and she thought he might have fallen asleep.

"We'll have to talk in the morning," he finally said. "About everything."

"I know." She closed her eyes, listened to the muffled rhythm of his heartbeat. "But it's not morning."

He tightened his arms around her. "Fair enough."

She let herself drift, carried on waves of contentment and something too powerful to name. Tomorrow she would have to ask questions, and she would have to deal with the answers — and with Nico if he didn't want to give them to her.

But not tonight.

28

She woke to the sun streaming in through the windows, the sound of rain strangely absent after two days of of torrential downpour. The waves rushed softly up the beach below the house, breaking more gently on the rocks than they had in the previous two days.

She turned on the couch, grasping in vain for Nico's warm body.

"Morning." He sat down on the edge of the couch with a steaming cup in his hand. "Thought you could use this."

The smell of coffee coaxed her to a sitting position, and she looked down, realizing she was still naked. He handed her the shirt she'd been wearing the night before, and she put it on, leaving it unbuttoned, before taking the cup from his hands.

"Thank you." She took a sip of the coffee. Heavenly. Then she noticed that he was wearing black slacks and a dark blue button down. "You're already dressed."

"I wanted to let you sleep, so I took a shower and packed."

He was obviously waiting, trying to find the right moment to begin the conversation they both knew they had to have. She took a long drink of the coffee to fortify herself, then held it between her two hands.

"You said my father killed your parents."

"I'd rather not talk about that," he said. "Let's talk about us."

"I can't do that. Not until we talk about my father."

He nodded. "Okay, yes. Your father killed my parents."

"I thought targeting family was against the rules." She felt vaguely ridiculous saying it. The only thing she knew about the mob was what she'd read in the papers or seen in movies.

"It was," he said. "It is."

"You took me," she reminded him.

"But I didn't put a gun to your head and kill you. I didn't kill your brother. I just want justice for my parents."

She swallowed hard. "Do you have proof?" she asked softly.

"I can get it." His voice turned flinty around the words.

"But you don't have it now," she said.

"I can get it."

She forced herself to meet his eyes. "It's not enough. It's hard enough to believe that my father is a member of the mob. Now you want me to accept that he's a murderer without any proof?"

"It's true," Nico insisted. "I wish it wasn't. But it is."

She put the mug down on the table and stood, the shirt falling open as she stalked to the fireplace. "Says you."

"It was him," he said through gritted teeth. "The thing I want... the thing I wanted when I took you, it will prove it beyond a shadow of a doubt."

Her stomach twisted at the thought. He was sure. She could hear it in his voice. Nico wasn't the kind of man to posture, and he wasn't the kind of man to lie. She felt crazy even thinking it. He was a criminal. Why would she think lying was beneath him?

And yet, she did. She knew it with a certainty she would have bet her life on.

Which meant what? That her father was a murderer. A cold blooded murderer. Or that Nico was simply mistaken.

"Let me go," she said. "I'll talk to him, and then I'll know."

He ran his hands through his hair. She wanted to go to him, to pull his face to her stomach, let him wrap his arms around her waist while she stood half naked before him. But this moment wasn't about that.

"He's not going to tell you the truth," Nico said. "He wouldn't even come clean to Raneiro. That's why I need the evidence in your father's possession."

She crossed her arms over her chest. "Who is Raneiro?"

He sighed, then stood and walked to the windows. "He runs the Syndicate. It's up to him to mete out punishment when members violate our honor code." He gazed out over the beach in silence before turning to her, his eyes full of pain. "But I need proof."

She heard the apology in his voice. He didn't like this. The evidence that would avenge his parents would also be the thing to prove her father a murderer. She thought about her brother. What would he say when they found out — *if* they found out — that it was true?

She tried to focus on something practical to avoid screaming out loud. "How do you know one of your men was part of it?"

"Witnesses said there were two gunmen. And my father was careful when he went out with my mother — even more so right before he died. He didn't advertise their movements, and he kept a bodyguard near them at all times. Only someone in our family could have known where they were going that night, and the guard was conveniently absent when the shooting occurred."

His voice had turned clinical, as if he was trying to distance himself from the details of his parent's death.

"Okay, but if it's true, why would my father keep proof of his crime? It sounds stupid, and whatever you may think about him, he isn't stupid. Wouldn't he have gotten rid of the evidence by now?"

"Not if he wanted to hold it over the head of whoever was helping him," he said.

"Then let me go," she said. "I'll talk to him, find out if it's true."

"He almost killed you!"

She jumped at the sound of his raised voice. "What are you talking about?"

"Those men..." He took a deep breath, like he was trying to compose himself. "They almost got you killed."

"They were there to rescue me," she said stubbornly.

"Rescue you?" His laugh was bitter. "Is that why they used you as human shield? Why the man who was holding you said he didn't care if you lived or died?"

"That wasn't my father's fault," she said, fighting to keep Nico's words from piercing her heart. "His men must have… gone rogue or something. Maybe they were scared."

He shook his head. "They would be as good as dead if they purposefully violated an order to get you out alive."

"So what are you saying?" she demanded. "That my father told them to have me killed?"

"No," he said. "I'm saying he told them to get you out, but made it clear that it was okay if they couldn't get you out alive."

She tried to laugh to show him how ridiculous it was, but it sounded strangled in her throat. "Then why bother sending them in at all? They could have just left me to you, let you do their dirty work."

She saw the hurt on his face in the moment before he composed his features into a mask of indifference.

"In this business, you don't let your enemies have at your family — at anything that belongs to you. It's a show of weakness."

"So my father sent them after me not because he loves me, but because he didn't want to appear weak?"

"I"m not saying that, Angel. Just look at what happened. You were *there*. They treated you like a disposable commodity. Do you think I'm going to let you go to him? To risk something happening to you?"

"What do you care?" she hissed.

He stalked across the room until he was standing in front of her. He grabbed ahold of her shoulders. "Look at me." She didn't. Not at first. "Look at me, Angel."

She did then, but only because she wanted this to be over. Wanted to get away from him, from his scent and the powerful body that called to her like a siren even now when she thought she might really and truly despise him.

"You belong to me now," he said fiercely. "I won't put you in harm's way."

"So you won't let me go?" she asked quietly.

"You stay with me, where I know I can protect you until this is over." There was no room for argument in his voice.

She shook him off her, and headed for the stairs.

29

She would hate him now. That was inevitable. He glanced over at her as they drove, drinking in the long line of her neck, the slender arms that had only hours ago been wrapped around his naked body as he joined it to hers.

He'd called Ed after their argument, and the old man had picked them up in the boat a couple of hours later. Nico had stood in the doorway of the house a little longer than usual, wondering if he and Angel would ever be here together again. He would never be able to stand in the living room without picturing her naked in the light of the fire. Would never walk the beaches alone without wanting her with him. It had been a necessary escape, but now it was time to figure out what the fuck was going on.

She'd said less than ten words to him in the four hours they'd been on the road. It was fine with him. He had business to think about anyway. Namely, how to flush out Carlo Rossi so he could put his parent's murder to rest once and for all. He just wanted enough evidence to force the Syndicate to act. And then there was the issue of Angel. There was no future with this between them, and now he knew that he wanted one. He didn't know if they would be able to move past it once he proved her father was the person responsible for his parent's murder, but they would have to deal with that when the time came.

Just do the right thing, Nico. Nothing else is your business.

His father's words echoed in Nico's mind. This was the right thing. Justice. Not just for his parents, but for the rest of the Syndicate, too. Until Carlo murdered Nico's parents, there had been a kind of order to their world. Rules you could count on. Trust. All of that would be gone if this was allowed to stand. They couldn't go around killing each other, trying to take each other's territories by force. It would be a return to the gang wars that had seen hundreds of men killed by members of their own families. Worse, the violence had bled onto the streets, hurting innocent people who got in the way.

He couldn't afford to let this go. Not even for Angel. It wouldn't be the right thing in the long run. Angel would just have to understand that.

He replayed his conversation with Luca on the phone last night. Headquarters had been locked down, and there hadn't been any more trouble. But both Angel and Nico were wanted for different reasons by Carlo Rossi. They wouldn't be truly safe until the Syndicate dealt with him. Staying out of sight was the best they could do. Nico would have preferred to stay in Maine, but he needed access to his men. Carmine had put the word out that Nico was in hiding out of country, and only Nico's most trusted guards had been dispatched to his side as security.

The sun had sunk below the horizon by the time they reached the New York state line. Nico merged onto the Thruway heading north, away from the city.

"Where are we going?" Angel asked.

"Somewhere safe."

She returned her gaze to the window without saying anything.

They continued an hour north of the city, then got off the highway and headed toward the Hudson. The river glimmered beneath the Mid-Hudson Bridge, disappearing into inky darkness beyond the lights. He felt a fresh swell of guilt when he realized they weren't far from the town where Angel had been living when Luca and Dante had taken her. He pushed it aside. This was for her own good. Obviously she couldn't trust anybody on her father's side.

Nico steered the car into the foothills next to the river and came to a stop at an iron gate. A moment later, it swung smoothly and silently open.

"What is this place?" Angel asked.

"My home," he said.

"I thought you lived in the city."

"I have lots of homes." *Or none,* he thought. *Not without you. Not anymore.*

She glanced out the window, watching as they wound their way up the drive, sheltered on both sides by thick stands of trees. They emerged into a gravel courtyard outside the stone house that had been in his family since Roman, his great-great-grandfather, had emigrated to the US from Italy in the late 1800s.

The house rose three stories tall, the facade made of granite that had mellowed to a soft ivory. A portico stood to one side, overlooking the river, and the house was fronted with a small porch under the library's balcony. Four men lined the gravel driveway, all of them with weapons in their hands.

Good.

He parked the car and stepped out onto the courtyard, then walked around to open Angel's door. When he turned to face the house, he saw Luca coming down the porch's stairs.

"You made it," Luca said.

Nico reached out to clasp the other man on the shoulder. "We did."

"Good." Luca's eyes slid to Angel. "Hey."

"Hey," she said.

"How are you? How was... wherever you were?"

"It was fine." Nico clapped Luca on the back and guided him toward the house. His time with Angel in Maine had already taken on the quality of something sacred. He didn't want to talk about it. "Tell me how things are here."

He sensed Angel's absence and looked back to find her standing by the car.

"Our bags?" she asked.

"Someone will bring them in," Nico said.

He waited while she caught up, then headed inside with Luca.

"Security detail is in place, all vetted," Luca said.

"How well vetted?" Nico asked.

Luca held open the door. "Triple-checked. Don't worry. Word is you're out of the country. The only people who know you're here are the ones securing the property, and they're all under a communications embargo."

"Make sure to rotate them out," Nico said. "We can't keep them out of touch with their families indefinitely."

"Will do."

"I'm going to get Angel settled. I'll be down shortly."

"Where should we bring her bags?" Luca asked.

"My suite." A flicker of surprise passed over Luca's face. Nico turned to Angel, not wanting to give weight to Luca's reaction. He didn't owe anyone an explanation for anything he did. "Ready?"

She nodded, but she didn't look happy about it.

He ran his hand along the banister, relishing the smoothness of the mahogany under his palm as he led her up the stairs. He had memories of his parents here. Good ones. He wondered what they would have thought of Angel. If they could have welcomed her even though she was Carlo Rossi's daughter. He liked to think they would, that in some alternate universe his mother had gotten to cook with Angel in the big kitchen, that Angel had walked the manicured grounds while his father told her stories about the house when he was a boy.

They continued up the stairs to the second floor landing. The hall was carpeted with elaborate rugs from all over the world, the walls papered with a rich antique stripe chosen by his mother. She'd never wanted a decorator. Everything in the house was hand-picked by her, and he never felt her presence more strongly than he did here.

He stopped at a door near the end of the hall and removed a ring of keys from his pocket. He waved her in ahead of him. "Please."

She stepped inside, her arms crossed in front of her in a gesture he'd come to recognize as defensive. He shut the door while she looked around, her eyes coming to rest on the giant canopied bed in the center of the room.

"I can't stay here," she said.

He walked past her and dropped his keys on the nightstand. "The hell you can't."

"You can't just… order me around," she said. "Just because we slept together doesn't mean you own me."

Possessiveness took hold of him, and he stalked across the room and lowered his mouth to hers. At first, her lips were unyielding, but it only lasted a split second. Then she was opening herself to him, her hands grabbing the hair at the back of his head while her tongue ravished his mouth.

He waited to pull away until she was moaning in his mouth. He looked down at her, his cock hardening at the sight of her parted lips, her breasts rising in time with her breath. He could take her now and she wouldn't protest, could lift her into his arms and carry her to the bed, strip off her clothes, run his tongue over every inch of her perfect body before driving into her.

The only thing he wanted more was to make one thing clear.

"I do own you, Angel, whether you realize it or not." He paused. "But you own me, too." He lowered his mouth to hers again, kissing her tenderly this time, letting his tongue glide gently over hers while he held her face in his hands. When he pulled back, he looked at her a long time before speaking. "Take a bath. Sleep. I'll see you downstairs at nine for dinner."

He had his hand on the door when she spoke behind him. "My things are still in the car."

"I'll have them sent up," he said without turning around. "But I think you'll find plenty to work with in the closet and bureaus."

He stepped out into the hall and closed the door behind him, pausing to catch his breath. He needed to get his head together before this woman quite literally became the death of him.

30

Angel stared at the door, her heart thrashing in her chest. She wanted to deny that it was desire. Nico was still keeping her prisoner. She was back in another room, back under lock and key. Well, not technically. She hadn't heard Nico lock the door behind him, and he had told her to meet him downstairs for dinner. But the armed guards around the property said everything there was to say.

She wasn't supposed to leave. And she was staying with Nico in his room.

I do own you, Angel... but you own me, too.

This was the twenty-first century, dammit. People didn't own people anymore. But even as she tried to muster some indignation, she thrilled at the possessiveness she'd heard in his voice, his words hitting a primal nerve deep inside her.

She took a deep breath, trying to clear her head. When her heart was beating less erratically than a wounded bird trapped in a cage, she looked more closely at the room.

The bed was enormous, right in the middle of the room. Canopied with navy silk draperies, it was a bed you could sink into, a bed you could lose yourself in. An image of Nico, his magnificent body naked over her, flashed in her mind. She shook her head and continued her inventory of the room.

The room was at the back of the house, and the bed faced a picture window that looked out over a dark expanse that must have been the Hudson. In the distance, she could make out the bridge they'd passed on the way in, and across the darkness, more lights.

She poked her head into an adjacent room and found an extravagant bathroom, all of it tastefully designed to match the historical details of the home. The tub was deep and wide, with elaborate claw feet and a big bronze faucet.

She left the bathroom and spotted two large dressers across the room. What had Nico said? That there was plenty to work with in the bureaus?

She crossed the expansive room and opened the top drawer on one of the dressers. It was filled with rows of navy and black socks. A look at the second drawer revealed stacks of plain white T-shirts.

Nico's things.

She closed the drawer quickly and went to the other bureau, bracing for more of the same. But this time when she opened the top drawer, she was confronted with piles of silk and lace; pale pink, forest green, shimmering black, midnight blue…. panties and bras and bustiers and stockings and garters. She checked the tags, not as surprised as she should have been that they were all her size.

She closed the drawer, her face flushed, and opened the rest. There were silk pajamas and delicate nightgowns, lounge pants so soft she wanted to burrow her face in them, sweaters of every conceivable color and style.

How had he managed to purchase it all while they were in Maine? How had he known her size?

She thought she should be disturbed by the idea. Isn't that what the feminists at school would have said? That Nico had crossed boundaries? That his buying her clothes was creepy and controlling?

But that's not at all how she felt. Instead she imagined Nico ordering one of his men to do it — or maybe a female friend? She had to quash the jealousy that rose in her at the thought — to purchase these things for her. To make sure she had enough, that she would be comfortable.

She ran her hands over the comfortable lounge clothes. Of course, she couldn't lose sight of the fact that she wouldn't need any of it if Nico let her go. She shouldn't be grateful now that he'd bought her clothes. Still, she couldn't deny that this was infinitely more personal than the stuff Luca had handed her in shopping bags in the basement room. This felt like something Nico had done for her, and she was quickly beginning to realize that things weren't as black and white as she'd once believed. He was a complex alchemy of criminal and gentleman, animal and man.

She ran a bath in the enormous tub and stripped off her clothes. The water was hot, and she let it loosen the knots that had developed in the long car ride from Maine. Her mind tried to turn to the things Nico had said about her father, but she forced it back to emptiness. She was on overload. She needed to let it go for now. To regroup and reboot. She would face the future tomorrow.

She let her thoughts drift to Nico instead. To the Nico she'd known in Maine. She remembered the way his mouth, hot and urgent, had felt between her legs, the way his fingers had slid inside her while he tongued her clit. All of which was a very close second to the feel of him driving into her. She ran her hands over her body, imagining they were Nico's, then sunk lower into the tub with a groan.

The water was cooling off by the time she stepped from the tub. She dried off with one of the ultra-thick towels stacked in the bathroom and made her way into the bedroom where her bag had been set discreetly near the door.

The tension had been thick in the car, and she hadn't slept at all on the way back to New York. Now her eyelids were starting to feel heavy, her muscles languid from the bath. She was hoping for a nap, but a look at the old fashioned clock on the mantle told her it was eight-thirty. Plus, she was hungry. She needed food before she passed out anyway.

She hung the towel from a hook on the back of the bathroom door and crossed to the bureau full of clothes Nico had left for her. Lounge clothes and underwear. Not exactly appropriate dinner attire, especially with Luca in residence.

... I think you'll find plenty to work with in the closet and bureaus.

She looked at the closets flanking the bureaus against one wall. Had he meant there more were clothes there?

She tried the one on the right first, the light revealing a lavish walk-in. Rows of suits ran along one side, slacks and shirts on the others. Shoes were stacked on shelves in the middle, with special drawers labeled for ties and cufflinks, gloves and handkerchiefs.

Turning to the row of suits, she lifted a beautifully cut tuxedo jacket, rubbing the soft fabric against her face. Nico's scent unfurled from the fabric, that unique combination of leather and wool, the streets of New York and their beach in Maine. Her pulse quickened, and a thrumming started between her legs. But there was something else, too; a kind of reflexive urgency to find him, to be by his side.

Crazy.

She left the closet and made her way to the other one. A flick of the light switch left no doubt that this one was meant for her. For now, at least.

Dresses of every color lined one wall; there was red satin and gray tulle and black silk, pale yellow cotton and white linen. Beading and rhinestones glimmered from some of them. Others stood bare and beautiful in their simplicity.

She turned to the other wall and the rows of skirts and blouses that hung there. As with Nico's closet, shoes were stacked neatly at the back of the closet, the Jimmy Choo heels and Hermes flats lit up like jewels. A half hour suddenly didn't seem like nearly enough time to get dressed.

She stifled her panic and went to work, flipping through the hangars, looking for something that was nice, but not too formal. She had no idea how to dress for dinner here, but if the clothes were any indication, lounge pants probably wouldn't cut it.

After looking through everything twice, she finally settled on a diaphanous Jenny Packham gown. She took the dress off the hanger, then perused the underwear drawer until she found a pair of black lace panties and matching bustier with a french label she'd never heard of. Drawing the gown over her head, she let the midnight silk tulle fall over her head and slide down her body. She adjusted the criss-crossed neckline and ruched sleeves, then zipped up the back. She lingered over a pair of black satin Leboutin's before opting to keep her feet bare; the floors were warm despite the time of year, and it felt weird to wear heels for dinner at home.

At Nico's home, she silently corrected herself.

She touched her lips with her old pale pink gloss, and left her hair loose around her shoulders, then turned to the full length mirror. She sucked in her breath at the sight of the dress. She'd never worn anything like it, and she admired the way the slim black velvet band highlighted her waist, the skirt dripping to the ground in inky blue and black folds. The neckline accentuated her breasts without being tacky, the back dipping just low enough to show off her shoulder blades. It seemed wrong to feel so beautiful under the circumstances, but she was only human. She just hoped she wasn't overdressed.

It was nearly nine when she stepped out of the room. Nico hadn't given her directions to the dining room, but she retraced their earlier steps and made her way down the stairs. The banister was a work of intricately carved art, and the chandelier that hung over the grand foyer was somehow both impressive and intimate. There were a few modern touches — the warm floors that hinted at radiant heating, windows that mimicked those from a bygone era without letting in the cold like old windows would — but it was obvious that the house had been carefully and lovingly restored to maintain its historical character.

She paused in the two story entry, then followed muffled voices to the back of the house. She passed what looked like a library on one side and a large, paneled living area on the other. She continued into what must once have been a kind of ballroom, the wood floors polished like glass, the windows running from the floor all the way to the ceiling at least twenty feet overhead. It was empty, but she could imagine people talking as a small orchestra played in the corner, could almost see the formal gowns swishing against the parquet floor.

She heard the murmur of men's voices beyond the room and continued toward a set of double doors that stood open. The first thing she noticed was the extravagance of the room, but it only held her attention for a second before her eyes were drawn to Nico.

He sat at one end of an enormous table, his eyes hooded in the soft light cast from the fixture above and the candles flickering on the table. He was all dark grace in a smoky gray suit, his shirt partially unbuttoned as he leaned back in the chair. She had another flash of the panther, reclining lazily in the jungle, ready to pounce at a moment's notice.

She couldn't take her eyes of him, and she wasn't surprised when he turned his gaze on her as if he sensed her presence. It had been like that with them from the beginning. It was way too soon to feel so much synergy with him, but there it was.

"Angel." His voice was low as he stood. "Come."

She stepped into the room. She didn't think it was possible for his eyes to grow darker, but somehow they did when he looked at her, and memories flashed through her mind — Nico, naked, moving over her, his mouth closing over her breast....

"Hi, Angel," Luca said.

She turned with a start to realize Luca was standing on Nico's left. Why was it so hard to see anyone but Nico when she was around him? It was like there was no space for anyone else in her head when he was in front of her.

"Hello," she said.

"You're stunning," Nico said.

"Thank you."

He pulled out the chair to his right. "You must be hungry."

She sat, thrilling at the brush of his hands when he set them gently on her shoulders, bending to kiss her collarbone before returning to his seat. Her skin burned where his lips had been a moment before, and when she looked up, Luca was looking at her with something like awe. It was obvious the blatant show of affection had thrown him, but Nico seemed unconcerned. He poured some wine in her glass, then smiled slyly.

"Shall we switch?" he asked indicating his own glass.

"I'm good," she said, remembering their first dinner at his apartment in the city. If he'd wanted to kill her, he would have done it by now.

He nodded, and a moment later a large man entered through a set of doors at the back of the room. He wore a crisp white jacket, but that was where any resemblance to a professional chef ended. Tattoos snaked up his neck, and his dark hair was long and tied back in a ponytail. He set two silver trays on the table with a wink in Angel's direction.

"Thank you, Gideon," Nico said. "It smells wonderful."

"It's that duck with the cherry sauce you like." The man's voice was incongruously deep for someone talking about fancy food. "I'll get everything else."

Angel's stomach rumbled, and she realized she hadn't eaten since the tense lunch she and Nico had shared on the road. A moment later, the man named Gideon returned with two more platters.

"Sit with us," Nico said as Gideon set everything down.

"Can't do it this time," Gideon said. "I'm working on dessert. But thank you. Want me to serve?"

Nico waved him off. "Not necessary."

"You got it, boss." He retreated beyond the doors to the room Angel could only assume was the kitchen.

Nico removed the silver dome from one of the trays and served Angel slices of duck before serving himself. She was torn between pleasure at his solicitousness and annoyance that he was treating her like some kind of Victorian heroine who might have a fainting spell if she had to dish her own food.

Feminism meet chivalry, she thought.

"I can serve myself," she said, just to test him.

He nodded. "As you wish."

They passed the dishes, and Angel spooned wild rice and tender asparagus onto her plate while she looked around the room. It was as lavish as the rest of the house, with fabric covered walls the color of wine and lush velvet draperies tied back with tasseled cords. The fireplace was large enough to stand in, the flames burning soft and low, casting flickering light over the table. She glanced at Nico, as at ease in the old world surroundings as he had been in the sleek New York City apartment and the storm tossed beach in Maine.

"How is Vincent doing?" Nico asked Luca.

Luca finished chewing before wiping the corners of his mouth on the napkin in his lap. Who were these men? This was definitely not the mob immortalized in books and film.

"It's just a flesh wound," he said with a British accent.

Nico chuckled. "I'm glad to hear it. Any trouble with the department?"

"We were able to keep it pretty quiet," Luca said. "Morelli's uncle in the department squashed it."

"Good."

Hoping for some kind of information on her father, Angel tried to concentrate on the conversation, but after awhile the food and warmth started to lull her into a pleasant state of apathy. They were talking about logistics — shipments of computer processors made by the same factories that made them for Apple, a security breach that was allowed to happen because someone hadn't payed for their protection, a hacking job they'd done for an international company that wanted dirt on a competitor without having it traced back to them.

She realized idly that it was information that would probably interest the FBI, but none of it seemed deadly or violent, and she didn't have enough details to make sense of it. Plus, she had problems of her own. She needed to find a way to get to her father, find out the truth about everything Nico had said.

When they finished with dinner, Gideon brought out tiramisu and espresso, and they sat awhile longer over dessert. Conversation turned to safer territory, and Nico and Luca talked about a book Nico had read recently, and two new movies. They tried to engage Angel, but she was fighting to keep her eyes open and could only manage perfunctory responses. By the time Nico suggested they move to the library, she was ready to face plant in her empty dessert plate.

She thought about going to bed, but she was still hoping for some kind of slip on their part — something that would invalidate the things Nico had said about her father, or at least give her a hint about whether they were close to finding him.

"Can I get you something?" Nico asked, pouring drinks from a tray of decanters on top of a mahogany cabinet in the library.

She shook her head, sinking into one of the leather sofas and tucking her feet under her body. The dress billowed around her legs, and she fought the urge to sigh in contentment. This is not the way she was supposed to be feeling as Nico's prisoner. Like she was safe. Like she didn't want to leave.

She gazed into the fire and let her mind drift. Did Nico have someone whose job it was to light fires in every room of the house? Did he spend time in this room, choosing from the shelves lined with books? Had he ever brought a woman here? The idea made her throat tighten. She hoped not. He belonged to her, just like he said. The minuscule part of her mind that was still coherent and rational tried to fight against it, but it was no use. She let herself fall into the abyss of sleep.

It seemed like only moments later that she felt herself lifted into the air. She opened her eyes and realized Nico was carrying her out of the library, the fire burning low. Her head rested against the lapel of his jacket, and she inhaled, sinking into the smell and feel of him.

He dropped a kiss on her forehead. "Shhhh," he said. "I've got you."

The dress swished around her bare feet in a delicious swirl of silk as they headed for the stairs. She closed her eyes. She couldn't help the way she felt. And it was okay to feel safe for a minute, wasn't it?

They reached the second floor and continued to Nico's suite where flames crackled in the grate. He set her gently on the bed, and she wondered if they would make love. If he would make use of her exhaustion, her apathy, the passion that always rose in her body when they were together even when her mind tried to rebel.

But he only pulled the covers up around her and kissed her gently on the cheek.

"Sleep, my love," he whispered.

She did.

31

It was light out when she awoke, sun streaming in through the big windows. She looked at the other side of the bed to find that it was still made. Either Nico had slept somewhere else or he'd somehow managed to make the other side of the bed with her in it.

Doubtful.

She sat up and looked out over the Hudson, shimmering beyond trees just barely holding onto their red, gold, and orange leaves. Soon everything would look brown and white and grey, like an old photograph.

Looking down, she realized she was still in the dress she'd worn to dinner. There was no sign of Nico, so she showered and changed into a pair of silk lounge pants and a soft long sleeve T-shirt, then headed downstairs.

The house was quiet, and she stopped in a formal living room off the main hall to look out the big window. Luca stood talking to one of the guards that still lined the drive out front. They were evenly spaced, their posture alert behind seemingly bored expressions. She had no doubt they would be as responsive as Nico's men in the city during her father's failed rescue. She felt comforted by the fact even as she acknowledged that it was insane. She didn't need protection from her father.

She headed for the dining room where a pot of coffee sat on the sideboard along with fruit, croissants so golden she could almost feel them melt on her tongue, and three pots of jam. She filled a cup with coffee and grabbed one of the croissants, then made her way into the kitchen.

Gideon was there, whisking something in a large mixing bowl. He looked up as she stepped into the room. "Morning."

"Good morning," she said.

"Find everything you need in the dining room?"

She nodded. "Thank you."

"You're welcome." Her eyes drifted to a light filled room beyond the kitchen. "Can I...?"

He followed her gaze. "Feel free. It's pretty this time of day."

He returned his eyes to the mixture in front of him and Angel continued into the windowed room at the back of the house. It was a conservatory, furnished with sturdy wicker furniture, overstuffed cushions, and so many plants and miniature trees it might have been a greenhouse. An elaborate stone terrace extended from the doors to a vast lawn that stretched toward the river below.

She opened one of the doors, half expecting an alarm to sound. It didn't, and she closed the door behind her and sat on the stone steps.

She took a bite of the croissant and then a long drink of coffee, letting the hot liquid warm her against the chill. Had it only been a couple of weeks earlier that she'd been closing up after her shift at the Muddy Cup? Her whole world had turned upside down since then. She couldn't imagine being her old self, completely oblivious to her father's business activities. Completely oblivious to the fact that Nico Vitale existed in this world, that she could feel the way she did in spite of everything.

"Good morning, sleepyhead."

She turned to find Nico watching her from the doorway of the conservatory. "Good morning."

"Mind if I sit?"

"It's your terrace," she said, still looking out over the water.

"I'm happy to leave if you prefer it."

She sighed. She didn't want him to leave. It didn't mean she believed him about her father. But she trusted him, and god help her, she wanted him.

"No, sit," she said.

He lowered himself onto the step, and she could feel his eyes on her face.

"Hey," he said softly.

She turned her head and found herself being pulled back into his eyes. "Hey."

He leaned in, kissing her softly on the lips before taking her hand. "Sleep well?"

"Like the dead."

"I'm glad," he said.

"What about you?" she asked.

He hesitated. "I don't think I'll ever sleep well without you again."

She felt a smile touch her lips. He looked as sharp as ever, his slacks perfectly pressed, his cashmere sweater hugging every glorious muscle of his chest, arms, and back.

"Where did you sleep?" she asked, trying to distract herself from his beauty.

"One of the other rooms," he said. "I didn't want to disturb you."

She squeezed his hand and took another drink of coffee. She didn't know what to do in the face of so much contradiction. How could she want to get away from him at the same time she wanted to mold herself to his body? How could she feel something so much like affection when he had kidnapped her, held her prisoner, told her horrible things about her father? Most of all, how could she feel so much for someone who did the things Nico did for a living? How could he be so kind, so tender, and still be into something like organized crime where people got hurt and killed?

People will tell you who they are if you listen.

"You have questions," he said.

"Yes, but there's no point talking about my father anymore. I won't believe he killed your parents until I have proof. I can't. And you will believe he did it until it's proven otherwise. I think that's called a stalemate."

"I'm not talking about your father," he said. "You have questions about me. About what I do."

She turned to look at him. "You would answer them?"

"I'll never lie to you, Angel. Go ahead and ask your questions."

She took a deep breath. "You're in organized crime."

"Yes."

"Is it… I don't know. Is it what I think it is? Hurting people? Killing them? Forcing people to pay you to do business?"

He was quiet for a moment before answering. "My father and your father were part of the same generation. They were part of the old family, and the old family did things a certain way. To be honest, I didn't want any part of it for a long time."

"What changed?" she asked.

"My father started acting… scared."

"Scared?"

He nodded, and he suddenly seemed very far away. "It wasn't like him. He was the fiercest man I knew, and the strongest. But he got paranoid about my mother and me, and about a year before he died he asked me to be his Underboss when everyone expected the title to go to Dante's father."

Her blood ran cold. "Dante?"

"His father was a high ranking member of the family," Nico explained. "He was a natural choice."

She filed the information away to examine later. "But your father chose you?"

"He did," Nico said. "And I sensed that it mattered to him, that it was a kind of legacy. So I agreed, and I started learning from him, and as I learned, I also started to see where things could be different.

Where the family could move into the twenty-first century. Less killing, more business. Less risk, more profit."

"So you… don't kill people anymore?"

He looked into her eyes. "I've killed people, Angel. And I'll keep killing people if that's what it takes to protect what's mine." He let that sit between them before continuing. "But it's not a first line of defense. We have… other methods for making our point, and the vast majority of our business interests are every bit as ethical as the criminals on Wall Street."

"Sounds like a rationalization to me," she said, looking away from him.

"Maybe," he admitted. "But that doesn't mean it isn't true."

"What kinds of things do you do?" She needed to know the truth about him. Needed to be honest with herself about that much at least.

He shrugged. "Bookmaking is still a big part of it, although our clients are vetted to make sure they have the resources to play, and to make sure they don't have a history of addiction. Companies pay us for unconventional cyber protection, the same way mom and pop shops paid us for physical protection in the time of my father — and yours."

"Unconventional cyber protection? That sounds like code for illegal."

"It is," he said. "But hackers are vicious and inventive. Sometimes keeping them out requires measures that are equally vicious and inventive."

"What else?"

He sighed. "It would take me months to tell you everything, and while I'm happy to do so, I'm not sure now is the time. We do what we we have to do, but there are things the Vitale family doesn't touch; human trafficking, porn, drugs… All stuff that used to be standard and all stuff that's off the table for us now."

"Did the other families follow suit?" she asked.

"Each family is run by their own boss." His expression was pained. "The details are left to them as long as they follow the code laid down by the Syndicate."

She thought about her father. Had he run the Rossi family the old way? Had he been involved in all those hideous things that Nico claimed not to touch? It made her sick just thinking about it.

"I'm not a saint, Angel." He was back to looking out across the water, avoiding her eyes. "Some would even say I'm not a good man. But this is the man I am."

She didn't know what to say, so she didn't say anything. Assuming they could put the issue of her father to rest, could she accept Nico? Could she love him knowing what he did for a living, knowing about the world he was part of?

She didn't know. So much stood between them, she suddenly felt exhausted with the weight of trying to break through it all.

"Am I allowed to take a walk?" she asked, setting the empty coffee cup down on the terrace.

He nodded, and she knew he only agreed because his men were patrolling the perimeter. If she wanted to get away, to find her father and speak to him on her own terms, she'd have to be smarter than making a run for it while Nico's armed guards stood watch around the property.

"Thank you for trusting me," she said.

He stood next to her and took her hands in his. "I do trust you."

She looked up at him, bitterness and affection warring in her mind and body. "Is that why you won't let me leave?"

His face hardened. "We've discussed this. I'm not going to turn you lose with those animals out there. You're part of something bigger now."

"A pawn in your game, you mean."

"A pawn in the game your father started when he murdered my parents." He was angry, his voice hard. She looked away, not wanting to see how much he believed it. He took a deep breath and kissed her hand before dropping it. "You'll just have to trust me, Angel."

He had his hand on the door to the conservatory when she spoke. "What if I can't?"

He didn't turn to look at her. "You will. When I give you proof, you will."

She watched him disappear inside the house before stepping off the terrace onto the lawn.

32

Nico sat at the desk in his study, still thinking about his conversation with Angel. She'd spent most of the day wandering the grounds, and he'd tried to keep his distance. He was asking her to believe him — someone who had kidnapped and imprisoned her — over her father. It was a lot to expect. She needed space to figure it all out.

And he understood more than she realized. It hadn't been easy to accept the truth about his own father, and while Raphael Vitale had been a more compassionate breed of man from Carlo Rossi, Nico was under no illusions; his father had participated in some of vile parts of the business. Nico had only been able to forgive him through the lens of his death, and a generous allowance for the context of his generation.

Would Angel be able to do the same once she knew the dirty truth about her father? Once she realized that Carlo Rossi traded in the most disgusting aspects of the business — including all the things Nico mentioned were off the table for the Vitales? Drugs, porn, trafficking, assassinations, prostitution… they were all lynchpins of the Rossi family business. The thought of Angel being exposed to them — of having to face the truth about her father — made him want to punch something.

He settled for slamming his fist down on the antique cherry desk. The contents on the surface rattled.

"Boss?"

He looked up to see Luca standing in the doorway. "Yes."

"Everything okay?"

"Fine," Nico said, forcing his voice even. "What is it?"

"Carmine's here.'"

Nico sighed. "Send him up."

"Open the gates," Luca said into his headset. He turned his attention back to Nico. "You want me to bring him here?"

"Yes, and have Gideon send in some food."

"You got it."

Luca disappeared into the hall and Nico crossed to the window overlooking the lawn. He'd known the visit from Carmine was coming, and while he appreciated his Consigliere's advice — that was the point, after all — he didn't relish defending his stance regarding Angel. For Carmine, it was all business. To Nico, it had become something far more personal.

A few minutes later, Luca reappeared at the door with Carmine. Nico walked toward the stout, older man and kissed him on both cheeks.

"Carmine, welcome." He stepped back, leading Carmine into the room as Luca retreated. "How was the drive?"

Carmine waved away the question. "You know me. I'd never leave the city if I could help it."

Nico chuckled. "Can I get you something to drink?" he asked, pouring himself a Scotch.

"I'll have whatever you're having," Carmine said, settling on the small sofa in the middle of the room.

Gideon entered carrying a tray of salami, olives, bread, peppers, and cheese. "Evening, Carmine."

Carmine's eyes narrowed as he sized Gideon up.

"You remember Gideon Marconi," Nico said. "Arturo's son? Been working for me for years. Best chef in the Northeast."

Carmine nodded. "How's your father? He was sick for awhile, wasn't he?"

"He's in remission now," Gideon said.

Carmine reached for an olive. "Good, good. Give him my regards."

"Anything else, boss?" Gideon asked.

"That will be all," Nico said. "Thank you. And shut the door on your way out, will you?"

He handed Carmine a glass. "I take it this isn't a social call," Nico said when the door had closed.

Carmine set down his glass and rested his hands on his diminutive knees. "After the bloodbath at Headquarters?"

"It wasn't a bloodbath," Nico said. "Not for us anyway."

"That may be, but it was a breach of the code."

"Storming into my headquarters with weapons was a breach of code," Nico said, fighting to keep his voice respectful. He was in charge, but Carmine was his elder, and as his Consigliere, his most trusted advisor. More than that, he was a friend.

"Agreed, yet you instigated the invasion when you took the girl."

"Carlo Rossi instigated my taking of the girl by killing my parents and going underground," Nico said through gritted teeth.

"I'm on your side, Nico. But this isn't how things are done. I warned you that taking the girl was risky, and now that you've done it and Carlo hasn't met your demands, you must act."

He met Carmine's eyes. "I'll never hurt her, Carmine. And I won't let anyone else hurt her either."

Carmine studied him for a long moment. "So it's like that then," he said softly.

Nico nodded. "It is."

Carmine stood and paced the room. "That's... problematic."

"Maybe," Nico said. "But it's the way it is."

"What do you propose?" Carmine asked. "You can't keep her in good health indefinitely. You look more and more impotent with every passing day. Carlo's men invaded the sanctity of your headquarters, shot at your soldiers without approval from Raneiro and the Syndicate."

"Yet you say I have to follow the rules," Nico said angrily. "So which is it? Follow the rules or seek retribution?"

"You sought retribution the moment you took Carlo Rossi's daughter," Carmine said. "Now you can only minimize the damage."

"Only if doing so won't also compromise the justice my parents deserve."

"Raneiro isn't happy with these turn of events," Carmine said. He suddenly looked older and more tired than Nico remembered him.

"Then the Syndicate should have acted when I brought the charges to them two years ago."

Carmine opened his palms. "You had no proof. What did you expect them to do? Bring charges against one of the Syndicate's most important bosses with nothing but an accusation?" Carmine shook his head. "It doesn't work that way, Nico. The system is in place to protect everyone."

"Don't you defend them," Nico said, his voice low.

Carmine crossed the room and stood in front of him. "It's my job to advise you," Carmine said. "I've done that to the best of my ability. What you decide to do with that advice is up to you, but it seems you and Carlo are at an impasse."

Nico turned his back on Carmine and poured more Scotch into his glass. Carmine was right. He was walking a tightrope between Angel's safety, his feelings for her, and his need to bring her father to justice, to say nothing of the Syndicate's expectations and his responsibility to the people who worked for him.

When he'd calmed down, he turned to face Carmine. "I'm sorry."

Carmine nodded. "Think about what I said, will you?"

"I will," Nico said.

Carmine looked at his watch. "It's late. I should get on the road home."

"Why don't you stay?" Nico offered. "Head back in the morning."

"I wish I could, but Mary's expecting me. She worries when I'm out late."

Nico smiled. Mary, a voluptuous woman with a heart of gold, was Carmine's wife of forty-plus years. "Next time then."

Carmine patted Nico's cheek like he was still five years old. "Take care, Nico. And keep me posted. I'll talk to Frank, urge him to keep the Rossi family calm in Carlo's absence."

"Thank you," Nico said.

Carmine looked up at the soaring ceilings of the foyer as they made their way to the door. "Your mother loved this house."

"She did," Nico said. "It's part of why I love it, too. I can still feel her here."

Carmine looked into his eyes. "She would want you to be happy."

Nico tried to smile. "Maybe someday."

Carmine kissed him on both cheeks and walked out the door. Nico looked after him for a minute before returning to his study. He picked up his glass and realized it was already empty. He toyed with the idea of pouring another, then thought about Angel. He didn't want to be drunk and angry around her. There was already too much baggage between them. If only they could have met apart from the mess between their families. Of all the things he ever had to lose, she was the most valuable of all.

He was fucked. They all were.

He hurled the empty glass at the fireplace.

33

Angel stepped back into the shadows as the short man named Carmine strode from Nico's office.

I'll never hurt her, Carmine. And I won't let anyone else hurt her either.

She'd believed it even before she heard Nico's voice through the door, but now it felt even more true. She was debating the merit of checking on Nico versus giving him time alone when the sound of breaking glass erupted from behind the closed doors. She wasn't even aware of making the decision to enter the room.

Nico looked up, anguish visible on his face in the moment before he saw that it was her. A second later his features were smoothed over into the expression of calm assuredness he seemed to wear for everyone.

"I just… I wanted to make sure you're all right," she said, closing the door behind her.

"I'm fine," he said, turning to face the window. Turning away from her.

She crossed the room and stood behind him, sliding her arms around his waist and resting her head on his broad back. "Talk to me."

He turned to face her. His eyes burned into hers. "I don't want to talk."

She looked up at him and ran her hands over his chest, linking them behind his neck, pressing her body to his. "Then let's not talk."

She kissed him, gently at first, waiting for his lips to soften under hers before she slid her tongue inside. Finally, his arms came around her, pressing her more tightly against him as he dove into her mouth. But she didn't want him in control this time. It wasn't what he needed. And it wasn't what she needed either.

She pulled away and took his hand, pulling him toward the center of his office. She kissed him again, this time more forcefully, then pushed him so he was sitting on the sofa. He reached for her, and she lowered herself onto his lap where the hard length of him pressed between her legs.

She took his face in her hands and left soft kisses at the corners or his mouth before nibbling on his lower lip. His hands slipped into the hair at the back of her head. He tried to pull her closer, tried to deepen their kiss, but she moved her lips up his jaw and bit softly on his ear.

His hands came around her waist, sliding down to her ass. He pressed into her until she could feel every inch of his erection, could almost feel the exquisite push of him into her. This was going to be harder than she expected. She wanted him filling her, wanted him fucking her. But not yet. First she wanted him to forget everything but her. Everything but this moment.

Trying to distract herself, she unbuttoned his shirt and moved her lips down his neck to his chest. She took one of his nipples in her mouth, closing her teeth gently on it before sucking it to a peak.

He gasped. "Angel…"

He reached for the bottom of her shirt and lifted it over her head, then pulled down the pink lace of her bra so her breasts spilled out of the top. She let him close his mouth around one nipple while his hand worked the other one. His tongue flicked against the tiny bud, sending arrows of fire through her body, and she let her head fall back, losing herself in the moment.

"I want to be inside you," he said, his mouth moving to her other breast.

His words shook loose her purpose. This isn't how this was going to go.

She bent her head to kiss his lips. "No."

She rose off his lap and knelt between his legs, undoing the button on his slacks before rubbing her palm against the impressive bulge between his legs. He groaned, and she felt him thicken further under her hand.

She unzipped his pants and slid them off his body, releasing his magnificent cock. She took him in her hand, his flesh hot against her palm, and licked the smoothness of his tip before closing her mouth around it.

He drew in a ragged breath, and she pulled back, alternating between flicking her tongue against the head and sucking it until he became even bigger. Then she closed her lips around him and slid down his shaft until he was trapped in the moist heat of her mouth.

"Fuck, Angel," he gasped.

She waited a few seconds, feeling him pulse with desire in her mouth, then slid her mouth back up while she stroked the base of his shaft. She took him again, in and out of her mouth, circling the tip with her tongue when she reached the top, burying him when he was all the way inside her mouth. She got wetter as he got harder, her own desire building as she felt the evidence of her control over him. Her power. He wanted her as much as she wanted him.

"Let me taste you," he said, tugging at her arms.

She stroked him with her hand while she looked up at him. His eyes were glassy with desire. "No."

She stood, untying the drawstring on her pants and letting them fall to the floor.

"Condom?"

He gestured in the vicinity of his pants on the floor. "Wallet."

She found what she was looking for and stepped out of her lace panties before straddling his hips. A few seconds later she was poised over him, his tip straining at her entrance.

He looked at her with something like rapture. "Someday I'm going to come inside you, Angel. Then you'll really be mine."

She bent her head, dipping her tongue into his mouth, then lowered herself onto him with one slow movement.

He moaned in her mouth and grabbed ahold of her hips, thrusting upward. She was slick with need, and she met his movements instinctively, their bodies moving in perfect time while their tongues sparred in a frenzy. His body rubbed against her clit with every thrust, and she felt the orgasm mounting inside her, pushing her to the top of a peak from which there would be no return. No existence beyond the one she shared with Nico here and now.

"That's right," he murmured. "Come for me, baby."

His hands slid down, spreading her ass, opening her further as he drove harder into her. The movement sent a shockwave of pleasure through her body, and she came apart in his hands while he continued moving inside her, his thrusts increasingly frenzied as she came again.

Then he was calling out her name, burying himself in her warmth while he held her hips, forcing her to relinquish any idea of control she might have had as he made her his all over again.

She collapsed on top of him, her body coated with a fine sheen of sweat. They didn't say anything for a long time, the room seeming even more quiet as their breathing slowed. When she moved to get off him, he lowered her to the couch instead and stretched out next to her.

He stroked her hair back from her face while he looked into her eyes. "Do you know you're mine yet?"

Yes, she wanted to say. *I've always been yours.*

But she couldn't. It was nice to forget the things between them for awhile, but she wasn't stupid enough to think that meant they didn't exist.

She moved closer to him instead, then kissed him tenderly on the mouth before nestling into the crook of his arm, his heartbeat slow and steady under her ear.

This is Nico, she thought, drifting toward sleep. This man. This heartbeat.

34

The room was dark when Nico woke up with Angel, still naked, in his arms. He looked around, trying to orient himself. Then he heard something pop from outside, and he knew the noise was what had woken him.

He slid out from under Angel's body and pulled on his clothes, hoping he'd been wrong.

But then he heard it again; several muffled pops from somewhere outside the house. He was leaning down to wake Angel when Luca slid into the room with two duffel bags in his hand. He didn't wast any time getting to the point.

"The property's been breached." His voice was calm, but Nico saw his worry even through the darkness. "We have to get you and Angel out."

Nico drew a blanket from the back of the couch over Angel's naked form to shield her from Luca, then crossed the room.

"Which one of these is hers?" he asked Luca.

Luca handed him one of the bags and he hurried back the sofa.

"Angel," he said, placing a hand on her shoulder. "We have to go."

Shouting sounded from outside, followed by another series of muffled gunfire.

She sat up quickly. "What's happening?"

"Someone's here," Nico said. He rummaged through the bag and pulled out a pair of jeans, a turtleneck, and a pair of sneakers. "Get dressed."

She only hesitated a few seconds before she took the clothes from his hand.

Luca spoke from the shadows. "We have to hurry." Angel's eyes skipped to him, and she looked down at the blanket covering her body. "I'll turn around," he said.

She started pulling the clothes on as soon as his back was turned.

Nico hurried to his desk while she dressed, unlocking the drawer and pulling documents and cash from the false bottom. He took the other bag from Luca and stuffed everything inside. By the time he turned back to Angel, she was ready to go, duffel bag in hand.

Another round of gunfire sounded, closer this time, followed by a crash near the front of the house.

"Let's go," Luca said. "Car's ready."

Nico pulled his leather jacket off a chair and helped Angel put it on. Then he positioned her between him and Luca, who maintained point in front the way they'd rehearsed it in the drills Nico had forced on his men.

Luca handed Nico a gun and pulled another one out of a holster under his jacket.

Nico took one last look at Angel. "Stay between us."

She nodded, and he wondered if she knew what she was doing. If she was coming with him because she wanted to, because she had finally accepted the fact that she might not be safe with her father's men, or because everything was happening too fast to come up with a plan for escape. He didn't have time to come up with an answer.

Luca opened the door, listening for a second before sticking his head into the hall and looking both ways. He waved them forward, and Angel moved out behind him, Nico covering her back. They moved silently down the hall toward the back of the house just as the sound of splintering wood reached them from the front of the house.

Men shouted from the foyer, and Nico knew they'd been breached. Fuck. How the hell did Carl's flunkies get past his men? Men who were young, highly trained, and prepared to kill for him?

He filed the question away for another time and stepped into the darkened dining room after Angel. They were almost to the kitchen when gunfire broke out behind them. He looked back to see two men in black entering the dining room, the muzzles of their guns flaring as they fired.

Nico turned to Angel. "Go with Luca. I'm right behind you."

She shook her head, her eyes wide. "But you…"

"I'm right behind you," he said again, shoving his duffel at Luca. "Go!"

Luca took her arm, forcibly pulling her through the door to the kitchen as she shouted his name. "Nico!"

He ducked behind a sideboard just as a bullet tore through his thigh. It felt like he'd been shot with fire, then quickly turned numb. He peered out from under the cabinet's raised legs. Just the two men, one of them behind a dining chair and the other behind an old cabinet that stored his mother's silver.

It was doable.

He thought about Angel, worry thrumming through his body at the thought of something happening to her. She was with Luca. She would be okay. Nico would get her out of here, and the men who had compromised her safety would pay.

He marked the first man, his head visible between the open slats of the chair back. Then he sprayed the room with bullets, taking advantage of the brief moment when they sought cover to turn his gun on the man behind the chair. Wood splintered around his head as he fell back onto the carpet.

Nico forced himself to take a couple breaths as adrenaline surged through his body. Mistakes were made in the space between thought and action, especially when thought was colored by panic.

He took another glance at the guy behind the big cabinet, and wood splintered around his head. He crawled to the other end of the sideboard, tipping it on its front to give him more coverage. Silver and china spilled to the floor around him.

He leaned back against the sideboard and considered his options. Angel was waiting for him, and who knew how many men Luca was fighting off outside. Nico couldn't afford to engage in a standoff with this asshole.

He grabbed a nearby candlestick that had fallen off the cabinet and hurled it toward the kitchen door. The man emerged from behind the cabinet, firing in the direction Nico had thrown the candlestick. Nico took advantage of the diversion by firing at the man, then making a break for the kitchen door. The man stumbled back, clutching his chest, his eyes finding Nico's through the dark.

Dante?

The question was still ringing through his ears as he burst into the kitchen. He could hear the sound of gunfire outside, footsteps on the floors above, but he hurried out the terrace door to the SUV with darkened windows that stood waiting by the back door. He hated leaving his men, but nothing was more important than getting Angel out alive.

He was looking for Angel and Luca when Luca stepped out from behind the car. "She's inside," he said. "Told her to keep her head down."

Nico nodded, placing a hand on Luca's shoulder. "Thank you."

"No thanks necessary," he said. "What's the situation?"

"Men on the upper floors — not sure if they're ours or theirs — and two in the dining room. One of them's dead. I think the other one was Dante."

Luca couldn't hide his surprise. "Dante Santoro?"

Nico nodded. "I hit him, but I don't know if it took him down. Be careful."

"Will do." Luca glanced back at the house as gunfire burst from the top floors. "Now get out of here. Plane's waiting."

Nico opened the door, relief flooding his body at the sight of Angel in the passenger seat. He slid behind the wheel.

"I'll be in touch," he said to Luca before closing the door. He put the car in gear and glanced at Angel. "Put on your seat belt."

He heard the buckle click into place as he turned the car around and headed for the front of the house. They hit the front courtyard in a hail of bullets.

"Get down," Nico shouted at Angel.

She ducked, and he veered around the fountain and headed for the drive as bullets shattered the rear window.

Nico held his breath when they entered the path leading to the main gate. The trees on either side blocked out any light, and he had no way of knowing if more gunmen were laying in wait.

But it wasn't until the gate came into view that he saw what they were up against; six men standing in front of the closed gate with semi-automatic weapons. A quick rundown of their options left him with little choice. The iron fence surrounding the house was built to withstand severe force. If he tried to veer off road and crash through it, he and Angel might be killed. And if the fence didn't give and the impact didn't kill them, it would only be minutes until Carlo's men — if that's who they were — found them.

He pressed the button clipped to the visor and watched as the gate rolled open behind the men raising their weapons.

"Stay down and hang on," Nico ordered Angel.

He took aim at the gate and ducked his head as the men started firing. Then he floored it, trying to keep the wheel straight so it would take them through the gate. He couldn't have cared less about the men standing in front of it. They could move or die.

There was a split second when he wondered if they would make it. The car was barreling forward, bullets pinging off the hood, shattering the windshield. Then there was a sudden quiet, and they were skidding onto the private road outside of the house, fishtailing as Nico raised his head and corrected to keep them from sliding into the dense forest around the property.

He sat up and pressed the gas, relieved to feel the car respond even as wind whistled through the ruined windshield. Far behind them, he heard the sound of bullets, but the gunmen were too far back to do any damage.

He got off the main road leading from the house as soon as he could, winding his way toward the Thruway through the backroads. He half expected to see cars in the rearview mirror, but fifteen minutes later they were turning onto the highway, the road clear behind them.

He took a deep breath and looked at Angel. "You okay?"

She nodded, her eyes wide.

"Are you hurt?"

She shook her head, her eyes drifting to his thigh. "You've been shot."

He looked down at the blood soaking his slacks. "It's fine." He reached for her hand. "Let's just get out of here."

35

A private plane was waiting for them in Newburgh. They passed through customs and were on board before Angel had time to ask about her passport. Apparently, Nico's influence extended to the TSA. The pilot welcomed them aboard the luxury jet, and they were in the air less then ten minutes later.

Once they'd reached a cruising altitude, they went into the stateroom so Nico could change. Angel had to fight panic when he stripped off his bloody pants. The wound was only half an inch in diameter, but blood still streamed from it, and the skin around it looked raw and sore. She told herself it was the blood that made her woozy, not the thought of losing him. She ignored the voice in her head that called her a liar.

Nico inspected it dispassionately and declared that the bullet had gone straight through. He tried to dress it himself from an on-board first aid kit before Angel insisted on helping. She touched his skin lightly, cleaning the wound before slowly wrapping gauze around his leg. It was a different kind of intimacy, trying to keep from hurting him while he acted like it didn't hurt at all, both of them avoiding the subject of everything that had happened at the house.

When they were done, Nico poured them a drink. They downed the contents of their glasses, and he pulled back the covers on the bed so she could climb in. Then he stretched out carefully next to her and took her in his arms. Neither of them said a word.

She didn't think she'd be able to sleep, but the hum of the plane's engines coupled with Nico's solid presence slowly calmed the churning of her mind. Nine hours later, they deplaned and stepped out into the Rome sunshine. A car was already waiting, and Angel was surprised when Nico stepped forward, kissing the driver on both cheeks like an old friend.

"Buona giornata," he said to the stocky, older man.

"Buona giornata," the man repeated, his smile wide.

"Come ti va la vita?" Nico asked.

"La vita è bella a Roma," the man laughed.

Nico smiled. "Thank you for picking us up."

The man opened the back door, switching seamlessly to English. "Say nothing of it, my friend."

He put their bags in the trunk while Angel slid into the backseat. Nico followed, and the man shut the door and hurried around to the driver's side.

"This is Antonio," Nico said to her.

"It's a pleasure to meet such a magnificent woman," Antonio said, turning around to look at her.

"Stop flirting with my woman and drive," Nico said with a smile.

Angel looked out the window, feeling a perverse sense of pleasure at the idea of being Nico's woman. What was wrong with her? She was confused. Obviously. She hadn't even tried to run back at the house in New York. True, she'd been half asleep, not even sure the men invading Nico's property were there on her father's behalf.

But that wasn't it, was it? Not if she was honest with herself. Part of her — a big part — wanted to stay with Nico, rebelled at the idea of leaving him even as she knew it was inevitable. At some point she would have to learn the truth about her father, and there were only two ways it could turn out; either Nico was right and her father was a killer, or he was wrong and Nico was a liar. Was there any way forward for her and Nico in either scenario?

She thought about David. It had only been four days since she'd last spoken to him, but it felt like a lifetime. She missed him so much it hurt. She needed someone to talk to, someone who could give her perspective. She'd been too close to Nico for too long. She'd lost touch with herself, with the person she was before, and no one knew that person better than her brother.

She was pulled from her thoughts by the streets of Rome, vibrant on the other side of the window. Stylishly dressed people mixed with tourists as scooters weaved in and out of traffic. In the distance, she could make out the dome of Vatican City and the sun-burnished stucco of Rome's older buildings. She felt suddenly ashamed. Despite her heritage, she'd never even been to this country, didn't speak a word of Italian. She'd been sucked into the apathy of post-college life, drifting through the days and weeks. She wished she could do it again, go back to the naive Angel who had no way of knowing how drastically things would change. But that Angel was gone forever. Whatever happened, nothing would be the same.

Antonio chatted idly in Italian with Nico, pausing to shout at taxis and mopeds, on the way into the city. Angel's stomach was rumbling by the time they pulled up next to the entrance of the Waldorf, and she realized she hadn't eaten since lunch the day before.

Antonio retrieved their bags from the trunk and handed something to Nico, then kissed him on both cheeks.

"Stammi bene, amico mio," he said.

Nico patted his shoulder. "Anche tu."

He took Angel's hand and led her into the hotel, seemingly unworried that she might try to escape. The realization annoyed her. He thought because they'd slept together she was his, that she didn't still want to get away from him. And she'd let him think it.

They passed the front desk and headed straight for a bank of elevators.

"Don't we have to check in?" Angel asked. She was trying to maintain some kind of control over the situation, even if it was just to ask questions instead of just following along in Nico's wake.

He flashed the little envelope Antonio had given him; their room key.

"Taken care of," he said, stepping into the elevator.

They ascended to the top floor and exited into a private entry. Angel had to fight not to gawk at the luxurious room stretched out in front of her; an open living and dining room furnished with eighteenth century antiques, damask draperies, and fine art. Beyond the living room, she could see a bedroom with red walls and plush bed linens.

"What is this?" she asked, dropping her duffel bag on the floor.

He furrowed his brow. "What do you mean?"

"This… this room. What is it?"

"It's the Petronius suite," he said simply. "I thought about a smaller hotel, but I think this is safer. And Raneiro knows we're coming. That will offer us some kind of protection in his city."

She walked to the glass doors at the far side of the room and stepped out onto a balcony that seemed to teeter at the top of the world. A whirlpool bubbled on one side, and a row of lounge chairs lined up to take advantage of a breathtaking view of the city.

"We won't be here long, but I hope you'll be comfortable while we're here," Nico said.

She turned to find him leaning in the doorway. She almost thanked him, then remembered her earlier resolve to keep things in perspective. Still, it wasn't easy to keep her distance. He was a beautiful man. The urge to go to him, to link her arms around his neck and press her mouth to his, was almost overwhelming.

"Why don't you shower and change," he finally said. "I think you'll find everything you need in the duffel bag. If there's anything else, let me know and I'll see that you have it."

He turned away.

"Where are you going?"

"I'm not going anywhere until I know you're safe," he said. "I'll be making calls in the study if you need me."

36

The master bedroom was every bit as plush as the rest of the suite. There were not one but two massive beds in the middle of the large room, both of them surrounded by rich, scarlet wallpaper and flanked with polished mahogany end tables. She didn't even try to sell herself on the possibility of sleeping in one while Nico slept in another. What would be the point? She knew she would be helpless as soon as he touched her.

Opposite the beds, a chaise and chair were upholstered in red velvet and trimmed in gold leaf. A tray holding two glass bottles of Pellegrino, a small bowl of oranges, and a silver dome sat on a gilded table between the chairs.

She removed the dome to reveal four sandwiches made with thick, crusty bread, each of them oozing mozzarella and red peppers. She ate two of them standing up, guzzling the water between bites, and left the other two for Nico. When she was done, she spread the contents of her bag out on the bed.

There were three sets of underclothes, a pair of pants, three blouses, a T-shirt, and a skirt, all of them things she recognized from the stash of clothes Nico had placed in the Hudson Valley house. There were toiletries, too: shampoo and conditioner and high-end body wash, a hair brush, even face wash and make up that was way out of her price range in her normal life. Whoever had packed for her had done so carefully, and while the clothes would only get her through a couple of days before she'd have to repeat, it was more than she could have hoped for given their hurried escape in New York.

And there was something else in the bag; her passport.

She had no idea how Nico had gotten ahold of it. Presumably, he'd sent someone to her apartment. It should have given her the creeps, but instead she felt a rush of gratitude. The passport was her ticket to freedom. If she could get away from Nico, she could warn David, tell him to go into hiding while she figured out what was going on with their father.

She tried not to think about the other fear uncoiling in her belly; that if Nico were right and her father was willing to use her as a pawn in their war, he might be willing to use David, too. Which meant Nico wasn't the only thing to fear when it came to David's safety.

And maybe not even the thing to fear at all.

She didn't really believe Nico would hurt David — not after he'd promised not to — but the distance between them gave her additional comfort. It would take Nico awhile to get to someone in the states who could then get to David. If she acted fast enough, David could be gone by the time anyone reached him.

A dull ache began behind her eyes as she went round and round the possibilities.

What a fucking mess.

She took the passport and her toiletries and retreated to the bathroom where an enormous tub with whirlpool jets called her name. An hour-and-a-half later, she emerged from the bedroom clean and freshly dressed. The remaining sandwiches and water were gone. Nico must have come in while she was in the tub.

She found him sitting on the balcony, gazing out over Rome as the sun went down, lighting the city on fire in a wash of oranges and golds. She took the chair next to him and stretched out her legs, bare under the swingy black skirt she'd found in the duffel bag, along with an off the shoulder blouse. Nico reached for her hand.

"Feel better?" he asked, rubbing his thumb against her palm.

The sensation was simple but erotic, stoking the fire of her desire for him until she felt the familiar beat between her legs. "Much."

He smiled. "Good."

"Thank you," she said. "For packing my things, or having someone pack them, or... whatever."

"Of course."

"How did you know?" she asked. They'd only been at the Hudson Valley house for a day. Nico had seemed confident of their safety, yet he'd had bags packed and ready for both of them, plans for their escape waiting in the wings.

"I didn't," he said. "But I said I'd keep you safe, and that's what I mean to do. The bags — and everything else — were a precaution."

"How did they know where to find us?" she asked. "My father's men, I mean."

A shadow passed over his face.

"What is it?"

He hesitated, seeming to choose his words carefully. "The two men in the dining room on our way out?"

She nodded.

"One of them was Dante."

Her heart seemed to skip a beat. "But… I thought those men were with my father."

"That's what I assumed," he said, his gaze traveling over the city as it sank into darkness, lights coming on like stars in a vast night sky. "Now I'm not sure."

"It couldn't have been my father," she said. "Not if Dante was there."

Nico didn't say anything.

"Wait a minute… What happened to Dante after… after what he did to me?" she asked.

"I took care of it."

She sat up. "How did you take care of it, Nico?"

"No man hurts what is mine," he said, his voice hard. "I made sure Dante wouldn't hurt you again."

"But he doesn't work for you anymore." It wasn't a question. She hadn't seen Dante after the day he'd almost forced himself on her in the basement.

"No, he doesn't work for me anymore."

She leaned back in the lounge chair, letting her eyes travel over the city below. Dante obviously had an ax to grind. If he was at the Hudson Valley house the night it was invaded, he was either working for her father or he was working for someone else. And the former was a lot more likely than the latter. Was she ready to accept the fact that her father was the kind of man to work with someone like Dante Santoro?

"What does it mean?" she asked.

"I don't know," he said. "But I'm going to find out."

They sat in silence for a few more minutes before Nico spoke again.

"Let's go out." He opened her hand and kissed her palm. "I want to show you Rome."

It felt foolish and careless, pretending they were just like everyone else. But she was starting to realize that being foolish and careless was sometimes the only thing left to do when you didn't know what life was going to throw at you next.

She smiled at him. "Okay."

They took a taxi to the other side of Rome, and she almost lost her breath when they emerged outside the lit up Colosseum. It rose into the night sky, a broken, oddly eerie monument to the past.

They turned away from the main entrance where a group of tourists were preparing for a nighttime tour and headed instead for a darkened, seemingly deserted gate. She was about to suggest it was locked when a security guard emerged from the shadows. A quick conversation in Italian followed between the him and Nico. Nico handed the man a wad of cash, and the gate opened before them, as so many doors did when she was with him.

Nico reached for her hand as they stepped into a darkened tunnel, leading her into the Colosseum's interior, through tunnels and passageways etched with the hands of time and weather and history. He spoke softly as they walked, telling her about the history of the Romans and the mighty battles waged by gladiators fighting for their very lives. She'd taken a class in Roman history, but there was something different about hearing the stories fall from Nico's lips through the hushed darkness of the abandoned Colosseum.

They walked into the arena, sticking to the shadows in case they came upon the tour group. Enclosed and maze-like, it was nothing like she imagined, and she was standing in awe, looking up at the night sky far above their heads when she felt Nico's finger run across her collarbone.

She turned her attention away from the sky to him. It wasn't as hard as it should have been. He held her eyes for a minute, his mouth turning up slightly at the corners. His hand traveled around her neck to the back of her head, and then he was backing her against one of the old travertine walls, his body shaping itself to hers as he captured her lips with his mouth.

He kissed her gently at first, his tongue sweeping her mouth, exploring like it was the first time he'd tasted her. She wrapped her arms around his neck, leaning into the kiss, wanting all of him. He was already hard, and she felt a flush of heat between her legs as he rubbed against her through the thin fabric of the skirt.

He pulled away, breathing hard, his eyes dark and glassy. Cupping her jaw, he rubbed his thumb over her bottom lip. "What have you done to me?"

She shook her head. Whatever she'd done to him, he'd done in equal measure to her.

He took her hand. "Let's go. If we stay here I'm going to ravish you in this sacred historical sight."

"If we stay here, I'm going to let you do it."

They traced their way back to the gate. For a split second, she thought it might be locked, but when Nico gave it a shove, it opened.

"Let me guess," Angel said, "Your friend the security guard?"

"I'll never tell," he said, holding the gate for her.

They walked around the Colosseum to the Via Ostilia where Nico led her under a tiny stucco archway to a small trattoria called Il Bocconcino. The place was lively with locals, laughing and speaking animatedly in Italian. Nico greeted the maitre'd like an old friend, and the tall, balding man shouted to the back of the restaurant. A moment later a round man with smiling eyes emerged with open arms. He embraced Nico warmly and ushered them to a cozy table out back under a canopy of greenery lit with white Christmas lights.

A series of people proceeded to make pilgrimages to their table, all of them treating Nico like a long-lost son, brother, or uncle, all of them speaking Italian so fast that Angel gave up trying to figure out what they were saying, choosing instead to nod and smile while they exclaimed over her, gesturing to Nico with wide eyes.

Nico took it all in stride, rising to kiss and embrace each visitor until things finally settled down and they were brought two bottles of red wine. They were served several courses of mouth-watering food, including a salad with thin slices of duck, saltimbocca so tender it seemed to melt in her mouth, buttery gnocchi, tiramisu dusted with fresh ground cinnamon, fresh figs, and the deepest, darkest espresso she'd ever tasted.

By the time they were finished, she was stuffed and sleepy, teetering dangerously on the edge of a food and travel-induced coma. They said a goodbye, a process that took nearly half an hour, and wandered out into the street.

"That was amazing," Angel said, leaning her head on Nico's shoulder as he took her hand.

"I'm glad you thought so," he said.

They walked a bit more, and Angel let everything go as she soaked in the sights and sounds of Rome. Even the air was different here, scented with bay and oranges and a slight undercurrent of motor oil from all the cars and scooters that zipped past on the boulevard.

It was after one in the morning when they got back to the hotel, and they stumbled into the room, drunk on food and each other and Rome.

"Want to soak in the hot tub?" Nico asked, kissing her inside the doorway.

She shook her head. "I just want to go to bed."

He lifted her into his arms and headed for the bedroom. "Your wish is my command."

37

They were finishing breakfast on the balcony when the phone rang inside the room. Nico dropped a kiss on Angel's head on the way in to the suite. A few minutes later, he returned trailing Luca.

Angel was up and and hugging him before she knew what she was doing. "Luca! You're okay!"

He laughed. "So it seems."

Angel stepped back, trying to cover her embarrassment. She hadn't realized how much she'd come to like him. "I'm glad. But what are you doing here?"

"I asked him to come," Nico said. "We may need him."

She didn't know whether to be pleased by his use of the word "we" — it was the first time he'd referenced them as a team — or scared of whatever he expected to come next.

"Why?" Angel asked. "What's happening?"

"I'm going to see Raneiro. Luca is taking you shopping."

Annoyance flared inside her. Is that what he thought? That she wanted to go shopping while he tried to figure out where her father was hiding?

"I don't think so," she said. "I have as much at stake as anyone. I'm not going to forget about your accusations toward my father just because I have a chance to buy some new shoes."

"Of course not," he snapped. "But Raneiro will never allow you in our meeting. If your father isn't in Italy, we'll be leaving tonight, and you may need some things for whatever comes next."

She crossed her arms over her chest, and he walked over to her and rubbed her shoulders. "I know this is important to you. I'd bring you with me if I could."

"He's right," Luca said. "Raneiro might as well be the Pope for all the security surrounding him. They won't let Nico in if you're with him."

"I'm Carlo Rossi's daughter," she said.

Luca shrugged. "Raneiro doesn't know you. You have to be vetted to get access to him."

Nico kissed her cheek. "Go with Luca. Get some things to replace what you left in New York. I'll have news by tonight."

She sighed. "Fine. But I want to know what's going on— assuming I'm more to you than just a kidnap victim."

His eyes flashed, and he dropped his arms from her shoulders.

"Keep an eye on her," he said to Luca on his way into the suite.

Luca nodded.

Angel picked up her coffee cup and walked to the edge of the balcony. The Vatican City dome glimmered under a brilliant blue sky dotted with fluffy white clouds.

"He's trying to protect you," Luca said behind her.

She turned to face him. "That's bullshit. I wouldn't even be here if it weren't for him."

"That's true," Luca said. "You might be dead instead."

"Right."

Luca took a deep breath, like he was trying to gather his patience. "You don't know what you're talking about, Angel. I know you think you do, but you don't."

"Maybe that's because Nico isn't telling me everything. Have you ever thought of that?"

His biceps bulged as he folded his arms across his chest, and his blue eyes darkened with anger. "Nico's still trying to get a handle on what's happening. When he knows something, he'll tell you."

"And I'm just supposed to be a good little girl until he does?" She couldn't keep the bitterness from her voice.

"That's right." His eyes dared her to challenge him. She didn't, not because she didn't want to, but because she couldn't think of anything to say that wouldn't sound completely ineffectual. He turned for the balcony doors. "I'll wait in the living room. Let me know when you're ready."

Sometime in the past week she'd stopped thinking of herself as Nico's prisoner. But here she was, still guarded by Luca, although Nico would undoubtedly say it was for her protection. It might even be true, but it was getting old. She had no idea what was going on behind the scenes; what kind of power did the man named Raneiro yield? Did he know where her father was? And if she called her father — not as a trap to help Nico but as a cry for help from his daughter — would he come out of hiding?

She didn't know, and it didn't seem like anyone else had the answers either. She finished her coffee in one long swallow and headed inside to get dressed. Nico wasn't going to change her mind. If she wanted any kind of control, she would have to find a way to take it.

An hour later, she was crossing the city in the back seat of a limousine. Luca sat quietly next to her while Antonio navigated the car across the Tiber to the Via Condotti. Angel was quiet, still thinking about what Luca had said at the hotel.

"Why do you care about him so much?" she finally asked.

He turned to face her. "Why do you?"

Her face got warm. "I don't know."

"But you do?" he prodded.

"I do. I just don't know what to do about it." She smiled a little. She didn't want to fight with Luca. "Your turn."

He looked out the window. "If it weren't for Nico, I'd be dead on the streets. Or worse."

"What happened?"

He lifted his shudders with nonchalance she didn't quite buy. "Drug addicted mother, abusive father. The usual."

"And Nico... helped you?"

He turned to look at her. "You don't just walk into one of the Syndicate's families. You have to be.. affiliated. Usually through generations. But Nico knew I was alone, and he vouched for me, gave me a family and a home. A lot of the guys still don't trust me."

She could hear the regret in his voice. "But Nico does, and I'd lay down my life for him."

She looked down at her hands as he continued.

"Taking you wasn't supposed to play out this way. Nico's going to the mat for you, Angel. He's putting his life at risk — and the lives of the rest of the family — by protecting you."

"It would be easier to be grateful if I knew what was going on. If I could talk to my father."

"I understand that," Luca said. "And I'm not saying you should be grateful. I get that your life's been turned upside down. I'm just suggesting you have a little faith. If Nico were anyone but Nico, you'd be in bad shape right now, if you were alive at all."

"Why is he doing this then?" she asked. "Why risk the safety and reputation of his men?"

Luca's mouth turned up slightly at the corners. "Deep down, I think you know the answer to that."

She didn't trust herself to keep her expression blank, so she turned her face back to the window. She did know. God help her, she did. Nico felt about her the same way she felt about him. It was complicated and dangerous, but there it was.

The turned onto a busy street, and signs for Gucci, Prada, and Escada passed by on the other side of the window. Antonio pulled next to the curb and came around to open the door. He smiled as they stepped out of the car.

"Vi aspetto."

"Grazie," Luca said. He gently took Angel's arm and guided her through the throng of shoppers lining Via Condotti.

They started at Valentino and worked their way through Hermes, Dolce and Gabanna, Philosophy, and Farragamo. She was embarrassed by the exorbitant prices at first; her father may have been wealthy, but Angel had never paid too much attention to labels. Now Luca calmly picked up the things that she liked and handed them to the sales clerks along with Nico's credit cards. After awhile, she got used to it, and she reasoned that while she was perfectly happy with her clothes in the states, it was Nico's fault she didn't have access to them.

By the time they got to La Perla, the sky had darkened overhead, and the air was heavy with unshed rain. Luca followed her into the store, his lean muscle and protective posture looking almost comical amid the lace bras and satin underwear.

She turned to him inside the door. "Um… How about I do this one alone?"

He scowled. "I'm supposed to be protecting you."

"You can protect me from out there." She pointed to the street on the other side of the glass window.

He rubbed his jaw, like he was trying to solve a complicated problem.

"Seriously," she said. "It's not like I'm going to ask your opinion on any of this stuff. I'd kind of like some privacy, you know?"

He sighed. "I'll be right there. Try to make it quick."

She waited for him to leave before turning to the carefully curated selection; beautiful bras and bustiers, tiny slips of silk that revealed themselves to be underwear, all kinds of garters and stockings. It took her twenty minutes to choose seven panties with matching bras. At the last minute, she added a simple black nightgown with slim straps from the rack. Nico would like it, and she could use something else to sleep in.

A tall, slender saleswoman escorted her to the dressing rooms and asked if she'd like water, wine, or coffee. Definitely not the mall in Poughkeepsie. She had declined and was closing the curtain on the fitting room when a click sounded from the end of a long hall leading to the back of the store. She peeked out of the dressing room and saw that it was a door with a bright red sign reading USCITA over it.

Exit?

She leaned back into the dressing room, her heart beating faster. Was that a door to an alley or rear entrance?

She fished in her bag and pulled out her passport. It had been a last minute thing, adding it to the little purse. Now she wondered if it was some kind of divine intervention. She could make a break for it. Get to the American Embassy. Call David, then her father. Find out for herself what was going on.

Nico…

She couldn't think about him right now. If she did, she'd never leave.

She took a deep breath and slipped out of the dressing room, hurrying down the hall before she had a chance to change her mind.

Please let it be unlocked, please let it be unlocked...

It was, and a moment later she was stepping out onto a narrow cobblestone street that ran behind the shops on Via Condotti. She only hesitated a second before she started running.

38

Nico lifted his arms, allowing Raneiro's men to frisk him before proceeding into the house. He wondered if anyone was stupid enough to try and smuggle weapons into Raneiro Donati's private residence. If they were, Nico felt sorry them.

He'd been angry when he'd left the hotel, but now he regretted not saying goodbye to Angel. The rational side of his brain understood why she questioned him, even why she doubted him. They hadn't had the most auspicious beginning.

But the other part — the part that would die for her — wondered why she couldn't see what she meant to him. Why she couldn't trust him to do what was best. He'd kept her alive so far. Didn't she know that had become his sole purpose?

He'd left the city behind and made the hour drive to the coastal town of Ladispoli. Raneiro's villa was perched on the edge of the sea, surrounded by lush lawn and leafy trees on one side and the Mediterranean on the other, but Nico wasn't fooled by the picturesque location. Security cameras were spaced every few feet along the drive and throughout the house, the grounds patrolled by some of the most vicious men ever pulled off the streets of Sicily. He knew firsthand that Raneiro kept a store of munitions on the premises that would rival the stockpile of many small countries.

Finally Nico was given the all clear, and he moved past a beefy guard with a neck the size of a tree trunk and into the foyer, an elaborate three-story room with marble floors and gilded ceilings that made Nico's Hudson Valley house look quaint by comparison.

He stood with his back to the wall — force of habit — while one of Raneiro's henchmen stared at him from across the room. After about five minutes, clicking shoes echoed from somewhere in the house. The sound grew closer until a willowy blonde in a black skirt suit appeared from the hall.

"Mr. Donati will see you now."

Nico followed her to the second floor and a library as big as the suite at the Waldorf.

"Would you care for something to drink?" the blond asked.

"I can get it," Nico said, sinking into the familiarity of the room. "Thank you."

She nodded. "Mr. Donati will be right with you."

She disappeared into the hallway, and Nico crossed the room, remembering the many conversations he and Raneiro had in the room following the death of Nico's parents. Raneiro had been his savior, the only person he'd trusted in the wake of the loss that still felt like a knife to the gut.

He poured himself a Scotch from the bar and walked to the wall of windows overlooking the water. He knew from Raneiro that the villa was old, but it had been carefully and lavishly renovated. It was the sole occupant of this stretch of coastline, and Nico had spent many hours walking the beach below, climbing over the scrubby coastline while he plotted his revenge.

"Nico, my son." The voice came from behind him, and Nico turned to find Raneiro walking toward him with open arms.

"Raneiro." They embraced, and Raneiro kissed both of Nico's cheeks. "It's been too long."

"You've been busy," Raneiro said, studying his face.

"Yes."

Tall and lean, Raneiro Donati was a man who could easily be mistaken for a wealthy executive. But Raneiro had come up on the streets of Sicily in a hard-scrabble life that had included several brushes with death, and the Armani suits hid a dangerous man capable of holding his own with any of the men who worked for him. It was why he inspired such loyalty; he had a sixth sense for finding people like him, people who were alone in the world, people who had learned to do whatever must be done to insure their survival. Raneiro gave them a sense of belonging, educated and clothed them, made them loyal to the Syndicate and its families — and most of all to him. Every one of his men would die for him, and everyone in the Syndicate knew it.

One of many reasons Raneiro had been in charge for as long as Nico could remember.

"Let's sit," Raneiro said, patting him on the back.

They moved to a grouping of sofas and chairs in the middle of the room, and Nico took a long drink of his Scotch, bracing himself for the conversation to come.

Raneiro let the silence stretch between them before speaking. "It seems things are a bit… unstable in New York."

Nico nodded, staring down at the amber liquid in his glass. "You could say that."

"The kidnapping of family members is a violation of our code," he said simply.

Nico swallowed. "So is the murder of family members."

"We heard your case after the death of your parents," Raneiro said. "You have no proof."

"It was him," Nico said, trying to keep his voice even. There was nothing to be gained by being disrespectful to Raneiro. "Carlo Rossi."

"We have protocol for resolving disputes," Raneiro said. "You know this, Nico."

"I can't let him get away with it," Nico said softly.

"That's not your decision." Raneiro's voice was firm.

"No, it will be yours after I bring you evidence of his crimes." The words came out harsher than he intended, and Nico took a deep steadying breath. "I'm sorry, Neiro. But I can't let it stand."

Raneiro leaned back against the couch. "And now you have his daughter."

Angel's face flashed before him; the way she looked when he moved over her, the peaceful expression on her face when she slept, the way she gazed at him in the few moments she was able to forget what was between them.

"Yes."

"Have you harmed her?"

"No,'" Nico said fiercely. "I would never hurt her."

The corners of Raneiro's mouth lifted in a smile that was equal parts disappointed and chilling. "Then what is the point in taking her?"

"I…" Nico sighed. "I was going to use her to force Carlo to come forward with evidence of his crime."

"And now?"

"The bastard doesn't seem to care," Nico said. "In fact, he seems to think she's disposable."

Raneiro waved off the concern. "I don't have children, Nico, as you know, but if I had a daughter, I would sooner kill her than leave her to someone who might do worse."

The words made Nico's stomach turn. "The one person in my family who tried to hurt her was quickly corrected."

"But Carlo doesn't know that, does he?" Raneiro asked.

"I wouldn't be so sure," Nico said. "He seems to know a hell of a lot."

"You think you have a mole," Raneiro stated.

"I know I do. The first time — at Headquarters — I thought it had been a lucky guess. But the assault on the upstate house…" Nico shook his head. "No one knew we were there. Luca and Carmine had put the word out that I'd left the country."

"Could it be that some of your men are discontented with the changes you've made to your organization?"

Nico stood, pacing. "If they're discontented, they can leave. It's nothing to me. My results speak for themselves."

"You're on the run with Carlo Rossi's daughter," Raneiro observed. "Under attack from your own men, in violation of the Syndicate's code of conduct. Are these the results you're referring to?"

"My results are increased profit and decreased liability," Nico hissed. "Minimal exposure to legal action and income streams that were only a pipe dream two years ago."

Raneiro nodded. "All true. And yet you risk it all by taking — and keeping — Angelica Rossi. I sympathized when I thought you were going to use her, although I didn't agree with the strategy, but it's my understanding that she remains in good health. It does beg the question of purpose, not that I'm eager to bring you up on charges before the Syndicate."

Nico tried to find a way to explain the situation that would appeal to Raneiro's business sense, but in the end he could only tell the truth.

"I love her."

Raneiro didn't say anything at first, and Nico wondered if this was how it would end. One of Raneiro's men would take him out, dump into the sea.

"How do you see this ending?" he finally asked.

Nico thought about it, wanting to be honest. "I find Carlo, get the evidence that he killed my parents — along with whoever helped him — and let the Syndicate handle it from there."

"And the girl?"

The question gutted him. Whatever happened, at the end of it all Angel would have to live with it.

"I hope she can forgive me," Nico said. "That she can find a way to move forward."

"It's quite a lot to ask," Raneiro said. "Under the circumstances."

"Yes."

"What makes you so certain Carlo still has the security tape? It seems more likely he would have gotten rid of it after it came up at the original inquest."

Nico shook his head. "Someone's working for him. Someone from my family. No one would get rid of something so incriminating when it could be used to keep a traitor in line."

He seemed to think about it. "Perhaps."

He rose from the sofa and crossed to a 17th century writing desk, then bent over it and scrawled something on a piece of paper. He crossed the room and handed it to Nico.

Tell him what you know.
RD

Nico looked up at him. "What is this?"

"Take it to Farrell Black," Raneiro said. "But this is as far as I go to mediate your dispute, Nico. You must understand this." He clapped a hand on Nico's shoulder and squeezed. It was just on the border of painful, and Nico forced his expression blank. "It ends there, however it ends."

Nico nodded, leaning in to embrace him. "Thank you, Neiro. Thank you."

"Don't thank me until you find out how it ends," Raneiro said. "Sometimes the thing we want most is our undoing."

Nico was still thinking about Raneiro's words when he walked back into the hotel an hour later. What did Nico want most? That was easy.

Angel.

But getting there meant dealing with Carlo, and the outcome of dealing with Carlo was a wild card.

Could he let it go? Walk away and try to build a future with Angel, if she'd have him?

Every ounce of his being rejected the possibility. His mother had been kind and gentle, and while his father may not have been perfect, he'd honored the Syndicate's code. Neither of them deserved death at the hands of a treasonous coward.

He would have to talk to Farrell Black. Find Carlo. Fight for Angel, whatever came next. And at least now he had another move to make, thanks to Raneiro. His mood lifted at the thought. He would take Angel to dinner, make love to her. Tomorrow they would leave for London.

He was already itching to see her when he stepped off the elevator into the living room of the suite. But then he saw Luca, sitting on the sofa with his head in his hands.

"What is it?" Nico asked.

"It's Angel," Luca said. "She's gone"

39

She leaned against the hotel, water streaming down her face. Sometime after she'd left La Perla, the sky had opened up, drenching Rome's streets with rain. She had no idea where she was going. She had intended to get a taxi to the American Embassy. Instead she'd walked the streets, a pit of emptiness opening inside of her at the realization that she was really leaving Nico behind. He would come back from his meeting with Raneiro to find her gone.

She was terrified of his anger, but it was the thought of his grief that undid her.

Luca had been right; against all odds, she and Nico were one and the same. Her desire for him was matched only by his need for her. She knew instinctively, was as sure of it as she'd ever been sure of anything. If the thought of leaving Nico made it hard for her to breathe, she could only imagine it would be the same for him.

She had worked the problem in her head for hours; Nico's accusations, the invasion at his headquarters when her father's men had been willing to let her die, her father's unwillingness to give Nico what he wanted in exchange for her safe return. Nothing added up the way it should, and there was only one person who had the answers.

She wanted to believe her father would come if she called, but she wasn't sure of anything anymore. Except Nico. Strangely, he had become the one certainty in her life. If he said her father had killed her parents, it was either true, or the evidence was so compelling that Nico had every right to think it was true. Either way, she had to know. Nico hoped Raneiro would lead them to Carlo. If he had been right, it meant that Nico was the fastest way to the answers she needed. And probably the safest, for her and for David.

She stepped into the lobby of the hotel, ignoring the glances of passersby as she dripped water on her way to the elevator. She was getting ready to press the Up arrow when she realized she didn't have an elevator key to the suite.

She backtracked to the front desk and asked an elegant man with an aquiline nose to ring Nico's room and let him know she was there. He spoke quickly and quietly into the phone, then instructed an older man at the concierge desk to take her upstairs.

She emerged from the elevator into the hushed atmosphere of the suite. Nico sat on the sofa, his eyes full of anguish, while Luca glared daggers at her from across the room. The silence seemed to magnify as the elevator dinged shut behind her.

"I'm going to my room," Luca said.

A few seconds later, she heard the door close to the second bedroom.

Nico had dropped his head into his hands, shielding his eyes from her. There was something so defeated in the posture, something so unlike him, that she was overcome with regret.

She set her bag on the table by the elevator and crossed the room, stopping when she was directly in front of him. She pushed her hands through his hair, pressing his head into her stomach. They stayed that way for a long moment before Nico looked up at her, his gaze fierce.

"You came back," he said.

"I came back."

His hands ran up the back of her legs to her waist. He lifted her wet shirt, leaving a chaste kiss on the cold, damp skin of her stomach. The touch of his lips, hot and electric, sparked a fuse inside her, sending a stream of fire between her legs.

He stood, lifting her into his arms and carrying her to the bedroom. He held her eyes as he lowered her to her feet, then proceeded to strip off her shirt. She shivered in her bra, damp from the rain.

"You're cold," he said, stripping off his own shirt and wrapping his arms around her.

She sank into his imposing warmth, letting him envelop her, blocking out everything but the heat between them. She belonged with him. She knew that now.

He looked down at her, tracing her jaw with his thumb. When he spoke, his voice was husky. Was it desire or emotion? It didn't matter.

"All this time, I thought I had nothing left to lose."

"We both have something to lose now," she said softly.

He held her face in his hands, his thumbs touching the corners of her mouth as he slanted his lips over hers. She opened to him without hesitation, desire and familiarity and something too close to love to be called anything else winding itself through her body as he slipped his tongue in her mouth. She welcomed him, meeting the stroke of his tongue with her own, twining her fingers in his hair, pulling him so close she didn't know where he ended and she began.

"Angel…" He pulled back to look at her. "My Angel."

She ran her hands down the sculpted ridge of his chest to the bands of muscle that narrowed into the waist of his jeans. She undid the button and slipped her hand inside, holding her palm against the silken skin of his erection.

"I just want you to fuck me now, Nico."

His eyes seemed to flare; the panther in the moment before it grabbed hold of its prey. He unhooked her bra as he claimed her mouth all over again, backing her onto the bed. He peeled off her wet jeans, then shed his pants. She sucked in her breath at the beauty of his rigid cock. He could have been a Roman god, and her body responded with a rush of wetness to her sex.

She lifted a hand. He took it, and she pulled him onto the bed, letting him cover her body with his own. The feel of him, heavy and hard, between her legs was almost more than she could bear, and she lifted her hips, feeling like she would die if he didn't enter her.

"Not yet," he said. "I'm going to remind you who owns you."

He lowered his head to one breast, closing his mouth around the nipple and sucking while his other hand gently thumbed the other one.

"Nico…" She arched her back, wanting to disappear into the heat of his mouth.

He pulled back, licking and nipping until she was writhing for him. He moved down her body, trailing kisses across her stomach, dipping his tongue into the well of her belly button until she gasped with the pleasure of it.

She was soaked by the time he worked his way over the mound between her legs. He nibbled at the virgin skin on the inside of her thighs, running his tongue toward her center, stopping just before he got there.

"Please…" she moaned.

"Please what?" he asked, kissing the fold at the top of her thigh.

"I want to feel your mouth on me." She was lost to her desire, no trace of shame or inhibition left. She wanted him to occupy every inch of her.

He spread her legs and blew softly. "You're so beautiful, baby. Your pussy is so beautiful."

She felt his tongue along the folds of her sex, and he slid his fingers inside her while he closed his mouth around her clit. She clutched at the sheets as she lifted her hips off the bed, meeting his mouth, feeling around the edges of the explosion brewing in her body.

She lowered her hands to his head, and he moved his fingers while he teased the tiny bud with his tongue. She gasped, half out of her mind with desire as she climbed the mountain to her orgasm.

He flicked his tongue lightly over her, then locked his mouth on her and sucked, repeating the motion until her climax became a forgone conclusion. She wanted to draw it out, to keep his mouth on her forever, but her body had a mind of its own, and she felt herself teeter on the precipice of release as she tried to hold on.

"I'm going to come, Nico," she said.

"That's right," he said. "Come for me, baby. I want to taste you."

The words sent her over the edge, and she rode the waves of her orgasm as he buried his face in her, covering her with his mouth while his fingers coaxed every last spasm from her body.

She shuddered, sensitive to his touch, but then he kissed his way up her body and captured her mouth in his. She could taste the sex on his tongue, feel the pressure of him between her legs, and she was suddenly and inexplicably ready for him again.

She reached for him, positioning him at her opening, and was relieved to realize he'd already put on a condom. She wasn't sure she could have waited. He pushed into her the slightest bit, and she gasped, arching toward him, wanting to pull him closer, wanting to feel every inch of him.

"Mine," he said gruffly, looking into her eyes.

"Yours."

He plunged into her, and she cried out, wrapping her legs around his hips, meeting him thrust for thrust as she lifted her arms to hold onto the headboard, wanting him to have access to the deepest recesses of her body.

"Fuck, Angel," he said. "You're so wet. So tight."

"It's for you," she gasped. "All for you."

He pumped into her faster, driving himself toward his own release while she climbed again with him. He reached down, drawing one of her legs over his shoulder while he drove into her. The new angle opened her further, and she gasped as his body rubbed against her clit in time with his thrusts. She met him at the top, both of them balanced on the razor's edge in the split second before they spilled over it. He let out something like a growl, and she kept moving, milking him while he throbbed inside her.

When it was over, he covered her face with kisses and brushed her damp hair back from her face.

"I love you, Angel. I've never loved anyone until I saw you."

She took his face in her hands, stilling his movements. "I love you, too."

She didn't know what it meant. Didn't know if there was a future for them.

But she knew it was true.

40

They arrived in London around noon the next day. This time they were met by a hired car, and Angel couldn't help wondering who handled the details of Nico's life so seamlessly.

They made their way into the city under gloomy skies. Nico held her hand as if he were afraid she might disappear. Something had changed between them. She'd had a chance to leave and had come back to him. Now she had resigned herself to her feelings, and his presence suddenly seemed more protective than oppressive. The same couldn't be said of Luca, who hadn't said more than two words to her since they'd left Rome.

They exited the car in front of a flat near St. James park. Luca carried their suitcases, procured sometime while they'd been in Rome, up the stairs, then disappeared into one of the back bedrooms.

"I need to talk to him," Angel said, when Nico took her in his arms.

He kissed her gently on the mouth. "He'll come around."

"He's always been good to me, and I put him in a bad position by leaving like I did."

"His pride is wounded," Nico said. "You gave him the slip."

"I guess I did."

"Did you really tell him you wanted privacy?" he asked, the corners of his mouth turning up in a smile.

She grinned. "I did, but not because I was planning to ditch him. That was spontaneous."

"Well, good thing you had most of your shopping done by then," Nico said. "We're going out tonight. You'll need a dress."

"Can you be more specific?"

"We're going to Farrell Black's night club."

"Farrell Black?"

He nodded. "He runs the London division of the Syndicate. Raneiro says he has information about your father."

The thought caused a knot of anxiety to form in her stomach. But this is why they were here. It was time to see it through. She couldn't hide behind her naivety forever. Whatever she found out about her father's role in the death of Nico's parents, he was not the man she believed him to be. The newspaper articles had made that clear, and her father's unwillingness to meet Nico's demands in order to insure her safety only crystallized the picture they painted. She had been living in a fantasy world. It had been okay when she didn't know better, but she could no longer justify her obliviousness.

"I wouldn't normally take you," he continued. "But I need Luca, and I don't want to leave you here alone."

"I'll be ready," she said.

He held her tight, looking down at her and kissing her again, lingering over her lips. "You should rest. It might be a long night."

"If you stay, I won't rest," she said, her body already quickening at the thought of him inside her.

"Don't tempt me." He kissed her forehead and took a step away from her. "I'm going to make some calls, make sure everything's okay back in New York. Do you need anything?"

She shook her head. "I'm good."

He closed the door behind him, and she walked to the window and looked out over London. She could make out the roof of Buckingham Palace, and beyond it, the spires of Westminster Cathedral and the muddy water of the Thames. She suddenly wanted nothing more than to wander the city arm in arm with Nico, laughing and talking and collapsing into bed at the end of the day. Instead, the meeting with Farrell Black and the truth about her father loomed in front of them like a death march.

A blanket of exhaustion dropped over her, and she closed the curtains and pulled off her shoes, then stripped and crawled beneath the pristine white covers of the bed in the master bedroom. She sank into the pillow with a sigh and closed her eyes.

It was dark out when Nico's voice pulled her from the blackness. "Time to wake up, Angel."

She let her eyes adjust to the darkness in the room. "What time is it?"

"Just after nine," he said. "I've ordered some food. I thought you might like to eat before you get dressed."

Her stomach grumbled at the mention of food. She hadn't eaten since breakfast. "That sounds good," she said. "I'm starving."

He bent to kiss her. "Good. Eat then. The food's in the kitchen. I'm going to shower."

She was tempted to join him, but another growl of her stomach made it clear that her priorities were out of whack. She threw on her clothes and found Luca sitting at a modern dining table covered with food.

She took a seat on one of the upholstered chairs. "What's all this?"

"Indian," he said, not looking up from the tattered book in his hand.

"What are you reading?"

"Utopia."

"A little light reading, huh?"

He didn't say anything, and she put down the spoon she was using to serve herself tandoori chicken and looked at him.

"Luca."

He didn't look up.

"Luca," she said more forcefully. "Come on."

He raised his gaze to hers. His blue eyes were icy. "What?"

"I'm sorry, okay?" She hesitated. "You can't be mad."

"I can't?"

"No. You guys have been holding me hostage for over two weeks. Didn't you think I might want to go home at some point?"

"I was responsible for you."

"I know," she said. "And I'm sorry if I got you in trouble." She smiled. "At least I came back."

"Why did you?" he asked.

She rubbed the corner of a cloth napkin between her fingers. "I love him, among other things," she said softly.

"Good."

She looked up and was relieved to see the kindness had returned to his eyes. "Good?"

He nodded. "Are you here to stay?"

"I'm not sure," she said. "I think… well, I think we have to see what happens with my father. It's… complicated."

Gray, she thought. Not black and white. So very gray. All of it.

"Don't leave again," he said. "Not like that. He was crazy with worry."

Something in her heart twisted at the knowledge. "Deal."

They finished dinner in companionable silence, then Angel went to change. She chose a slinky black dress by Tom Ford. It had long sleeves, but with a hemline that brushed her upper thighs and slits cut into fabric at her shoulders and arms, it was anything but dowdy. She slipped on a thin black thong, skipping a bra in a nod to the back of the dress, which dipped low enough to brush the top of her ass. She finished it with a pair of gold Gucci heels, then wrapped her hair in a loose bun at the nape of her neck. She kept her face bare, with only dark, smokey eyeliner, several coats of mascara, and a careful swipe of red lipstick.

She was admiring her reflection in the mirror, reveling in the way the silk dress skimmed her bare body, hinting at what was underneath rather than making it obvious, when Nico's arms slid around her waist. He met her eyes in the mirror.

"You're the most exquisite woman I've ever seen."

She turned in his arms, taking in the tailored slacks that hugged his strong thighs. His eyes seemed lighter than usual, the amber standing out against the fitted, midnight blue button-down stretching across his shoulders and back.

"You don't look so bad yourself," she said softly.

He ran his hands down her back to her thighs, then slipped them inside the dress to cup her ass. It was like lighting a stick of dynamite attached to her core, and she felt herself grow wet as he pulled her against the rigid length of him.

"This was a bad idea," he murmured, looking into her eyes.

"What was?" she asked, breathless.

"Coming to check on you."

She let her hand travel down the iron plane of his stomach and pressed the flat of her palm against his erection. "I'm glad you did."

He groaned and stepped away, holding up his hands in a gesture of surrender. "We have to get out of here," he said. "Now."

She smiled. "If you say so."

He narrowed his eyes. "You're a wicked little thing."

She headed into the hall, casting a glance at him over her shoulder. "Maybe."

"You're killing me, Angel." His voice followed her into the hall, and she couldn't help laughing a little. For once, they were just like everyone else, and she realized this is what it would be like to be with Nico without all the bullshit between them.

Hot. Sexy. And yes, fun.

Would they get there? She hoped so. She really, really hoped so.

A car was waiting out front, and they made their way through town with the London eye lit up and looming in the rear window. Luca looked sharp in a fitted suit. His dark hair was combed back, highlighting the angular lines of his face. He was a good-looking man, every bit as handsome as Nico in a different way. She wondered idly if he had a woman in his life.

They finally stopped in a seedy area that stood in stark contrast to the sanitized cleanliness of the parts of the city meant for tourists. Nico slid out of the car and took her hand. Luca followed, and Angel didn't think it was her imagination that the atmosphere had gotten significantly more tense.

"Stay by my side," Nico said. "Unless I tell you otherwise."

She wanted to bristle at this commanding tone, but then they stepped up to a large metal door guarded by two men with dead eyes and arms as big as her waist. She stepped a little closer to Nico. She thought they might be questioned going into the club, but one of the men nodded at Nico and opened the door without a word.

Interesting.

They stepped into a stairwell lined with purple lights. Music pumped from somewhere beneath them, vibrating the ground. Nico started down the stairs, and Angel had never been more glad to feel Luca's presence behind her.

They emerged into a large warehouse space filled with writhing bodies dancing to the music that invaded the space from invisible speakers. At the front of the room, a massive movie screen was playing Scarface on mute. A giant pile of cocaine sat in front of Al Pacino, the movements of his mouth working in strange synchronicity to the music in the club.

Nico stopped in front of a small man wearing a headset and sunglasses. Without a word, the man hooked a thumb to a staircase at the back of the cavernous room.

Nico took Angel's hand and started through the mass of bodies, the crowd seeming to part in front of him like he was the Messiah himself. They passed several more men on their way up the stairs but proceeded without incident down a long hall that seemed to wind its way into the bowels of the building. The music faded slightly, the bass pounding like an electric heartbeat in the background.

They came to the end of a hall and a door guarded by four men holstered with semi-automatic weapons. One of them had a scar that ran the length of his face under eyes that made Angel shudder.

Dead. Soulless. All of them.

She'd thought Nico and his men were imposing — and they were — but Nico's operation looked nothing like this. Here she knew there would be no mercy, no New Age attempt at reconciliation or pacifism. Here violence wouldn't be a last resort but a opening salvo to any kind of engagement.

She swallowed hard as one of the men opened the door. Then Nico was pulling her into a room beyond the hall. The door shut behind them with a heavy thunk that made Angel think of the door to a tomb.

Clearly, not your average warehouse door.

She didn't know what she was expecting, but the room was nothing like any of the places she'd seen belonging to Nico. Instead they could have been in any abandoned faculty building. It was large and bare, the furniture old and mismatched. The air was heavy with smoke, and Angel caught a whiff of something earthy and bitter.

A man stood behind a rusted steel desk, and she had to fight the urge to recoil.

He was massive, at least a couple inches taller than Nico's already impressive height, with a scar just above his left eye. His hair was cut close to his head, his face shaded with the kind of five o' clock shadow she'd never seen on any of Nico's men. Violence emanated off him in waves, a tsunami of psychic misery that pulled at her like a riptide.

Nico was the iron fist inside a velvet glove, danger masked with refinement.

This man was something else entirely.

There were no guards inside the room, but Angel wasn't comforted by the thought. This was not a man who was afraid. Of anything.

"Farrell," Nico said, stepping up to the desk.

"Vitale."

There was no warmth between them, none of the brotherhood that was so evident when Nico talked to his men. Farrell's eyes traveled unashamedly over her body, and she felt Nico tighten next to her.

"I didn't expect to see you in this part of the world," Farrell said in a British accent that looked way too refined for the kind of man he was. He sat down behind the desk. "Heard trouble's brewing across the pond."

Nico didn't sit, and she tried to follow the train of posturing; who was more important, who was making a point or taking a stand through their actions. It was like trying to decipher an argument in a mysterious language.

Nico handed him a piece of paper. Farrell held Nico's eyes for a few seconds before reading it. When he looked up, his expression hadn't changed a bit. His gaze returned appreciatively to Angel.

"So this is Rossi's daughter."

Angel flushed, although she couldn't have said if it was because of his frank appraisal or because he was yet another person connecting her father to this world.

"It is." Nico's voice was hard as granite.

Farrell nodded, and for the first time, a trace of humor showed in his eyes. "You know what you're doing here, Vitale? Seems like you might be off reservation on this one."

Nico held his gaze. "Raneiro doesn't seem to think so."

Farrell glanced back down at the piece of paper. "Or maybe he's just speeding along your untimely demise."

Nico didn't say anything, and Angel forced herself to remain still, tried to make her face impassive in the ensuing silence.

Finally, Farrell leaned forward and scrawled something on the piece of paper Nico had handed him. "Word is he's at a safe house. You didn't hear it from me." He slid the paper across the desk but didn't let go when Nico tried to take it. "But I'm not with you on this. Understand?"

"I don't need you on it." Nico's voice was flinty. "I just need you to keep your men out of the way until it's over."

Farrell let go of the slip of paper, and Angel glanced around Nico to see what was written there; 21 George Row.

Nico pocketed it, guiding Angel in front of him as he and Luca headed for the door.

"Does she know what's going to happen to dear, old dad when you find him?" Farrell asked behind them.

Angel looked back at Farrell, now holding a lit cigar, then up at Nico.

"Let's go," Nico said, ushering her out the door.

41

They rode back to the flat in silence, although Nico had a feeling that wouldn't have been the case if Luca hadn't been with them.

Fucking Farrell Black.

Angel waited until they were behind closed doors in the bedroom of the flat to ask the question he'd known was coming.

"Are you going to kill my father?" she asked, folding her arms over her chest.

He walked to the dresser and removed his cuff links. "That's not my intention, no."

"What does that mean, Nico?"

He turned to face her, forcing himself to remain calm. "It means that my intention is to obtain evidence of his part in my parent's murder and then hand it over to the Syndicate."

She scowled. "You don't sound convinced."

"I'm convinced that is my intention," he said carefully. "Because it is."

"Then why did Farrell seem to be saying otherwise?"

The torment in her eyes sliced through his soul, but he hadn't lied to her yet. He wouldn't start now. "Because Farrell knows how these things sometimes go down."

"And how is that?" she asked.

Nico took a deep breath. "These are not good men, Angel. Your father -"

"My father isn't a good man," she finished for him. "Isn't that what you want me to know?"

"No. Not what I want you to know."

"But what you believe is true."

He chose his words carefully, not wanting to hurt her. "There are all kinds of men in this business. Some are more... selective than others in choosing their income streams."

"Income streams?" Her laugh was brittle. "You're not an investment banker, Nico. You're a criminal."

He flinched, then hardened his heart. "I've never lied about what I am, Angel."

She stalked to her suitcase and took off her shoes. "No, you just wrap it all up in a designer bow and hope no one will notice."

He turned away from her. "You're not being fair."

"None of this is fair," she said.

"No."

She turned to face him, her face streaked with tears. "I know my father isn't a perfect man. The evidence is pretty much irrefutable. But he's my father."

"I know," Nico said. "Believe it or not, I understand the bonds of family more than you might think."

She seemed to consider his words. "Then I guess we'll just see what happens."

He started unbuttoning his shirt. "You have my word that I'll tell you everything. Luca will be there, too, so you can ask him for his version after it all plays out if it makes you feel better."

She went still. "What are you talking about? I'll be there with you, Nico."

"No."

"No?" She shook her head in disbelief. "You don't get to tell me no."

"The hell I don't," he said, stripping off his shirt.

"He's my *father*, Nico."

"I think we've established that. And we've also established that this is an extremely dangerous situation. I can't risk having something happen to you."

"That's not your decision to make."

"You're entitled to your opinion."

"It's not an opinion," she said. "You may own me in the bedroom, but it's not a literal interpretation of the word."

"I'm not taking you with us," he said simply. "And Luca won't take you. So you're not going."

He walked into the hall and shut the door behind him. The flat was quiet, and he poured himself a drink and opened the doors to the balcony off the living room.

The lights of the city glimmered in the darkness, London's monuments lit up like trophies to the past. He loved Europe, loved the history of it, but sometimes he was fucking tired of looking behind him. Angel made him want to look to the future, and Carlo Rossi was standing in his way.

He hated telling Angel no, wanted to give her everything she asked for, everything she wanted and more. But this was one thing he couldn't — wouldn't — give her. The potential price was too high. Not just death, but the probability of seeing her father at his worst. Of watching Carlo Rossi do what Carlo Rossi did.

And that had never been pretty, even before the situation with Angel.

It was a fool's errand, trying to protect her from the truth, but ever since he'd met her, all he'd wanted was to keep the light burning in her eyes. He'd even posted someone near her brother's school, hoping to insure the safety of the person who seemed to matter most to her. But he couldn't save her from everything. She would find out. When this was all over, she would find out the kind of man her father was. There was nothing Nico could do about that, but he could control the how of it, could try and insure that the blows were delivered in a way she could bear.

And he would keep his word. He would make every effort to keep Carlo alive, to pass the burden of responsibility in deciding his fate to the Syndicate where it wouldn't be connected to him and to Angel and to the surprising thing that had begun to build between them.

He finished his drink and went inside to find his rosary, pushing aside the feeling that he was no longer in control. That he was on a journey with an ending he couldn't shape and probably wouldn't like.

42

Angel was up with the sun the next morning, her eyes dry and gritty. Nico had come to bed at some point after she'd turned off the light. He'd reached for her, and she'd gone to him without speaking. This was how it was with them. How it had to be. A separation of their undeniable feelings and everything that should have made those feelings impossible.

In bed they belonged to each other. Time would tell about the rest.

She sat on the balcony while Nico and Luca plotted out how to get into the safe house. Their murmured conversation was irrelevant to her, and she spent the day lost in her own thoughts.

"You'll be okay while I'm gone?" Nico asked when night finally fell across the city.

"I'll be fine," she said. And she would. She had to believe she would.

He cupped her face and ran his thumb along her cheek. "I love you, Angel. Don't forget that in all of this."

She stretched to kiss him softly on the lips. "Don't you forget it either."

He nodded, seemingly satisfied, and left with Luca. She waited a half hour before leaving the apartment and hailing a taxi.

"Twenty-one George Row," she said to the driver.

He looked back at her. "George Row? In Bermondsey?"

"I… I guess."

"You sure that's where you want to go, luv?"

She sat back in the seat. "I'm sure."

He sighed and started the meter, then pulled out into traffic.

She looked out the window, her mind turning to her father. She hadn't seen him in at least six months. It made her feel shitty, despite everything she'd learned about him. Had he always been this man? Or had he become this way after her mother died? Was there any way back from all of this? Would he be happy to see her? She hoped so, especially since she planned to walk up to the door and knock. Luca and Nico had gone to great lengths to plan their entry to the safe house in a way that allowed for the possibility of armed guards. Angel was hoping her status as Carlo Rossi's daughter would make her entrance considerably easier.

She thought back to that day at Vitale headquarters, the day her father's men had come for her. Nico had been right; they'd been willing to sacrifice her. Could she really count on her father's love to keep her alive?

It didn't matter. This was the end of the road. She had to know who her father really was, and she wasn't going to get it secondhand from Nico or Luca. She had no doubt they would tell her a version of the truth, but it would be watered down, filtered through the lens of their desire to protect her.

People will tell you who they are if you listen.

It was time for her father to tell her who he was.

They'd been driving about twenty minutes when the car pulled over to the side of the road next to a row of rundown brick houses.

"I can wait if you won't be long," the driver said, turning around to look at her.

"It's okay," she said. "I'll have a ride back." She passed him some cash she'd found on Nico's bedside table. "Thank you."

He hesitated, then nodded and put the car in gear. She watched him drive away before turning to the row houses in front of her.

43

Nico ducked through the window in front of Luca, careful not to knock anything over as he slid to the floor. The house was small and shabby. No surprise. Carlo was a lot less likely to attract attention in a neighborhood like Bermondsey, although Nico had no doubt it was well below Carlo Rossi's usual standards. The realization gave him a hit of pleasure; Carlo had been afraid of him.

Very afraid.

Some kind of comedy was on the TV beyond the kitchen, and Nico used the laugh track to cover his steps as he inched forward toward the noise, wanting to get a handle on how many men were in the house. They'd seen one posted near the front door on their way to the back of the house, and he assumed Carlo had at least one man with him at all times. That meant he and Luca would be outgunned by at least one man.

But they had the element of surprise, and that gave them some advantage.

He flattened himself against the wall between the kitchen and the living room. A commercial was playing on the television, and he held his breath, hoping Carlo and his men didn't decide to use the opportunity to take a leak. A couple minutes later, the show they were watching returned, and Nico peered out into the living room.

Three men; Carlo and two others.

Carlo sat on the sofa with a sandwich in his lap while an overweight man took up space at the other end. Next to it, an old recliner was occupied by a beefy guy with a bald head. A cross tattoo snaked up the back of his neck.

Nico pulled back into the kitchen and held up three fingers to Luca, standing on the other side of the doorway. Now Luca would know how many men they were dealing with.

Luca nodded, and Nico raised five fingers and started counting down on them.

5... 4... 3... 2... 1

They came through the door at the same time. Carlo's guards were on their feet, guns pointed at Nico and Luca before Carlo even knew what was happening. Lazy.

"I wouldn't," Nico said, pointing his gun at Carlo's head while Luca aimed at the shorter of the two men. "You might be able to take us, but at least one of you is going along for the ride. Besides, we just want to talk."

Carlos stood, brushing crumbs off his perfectly tailored trousers. "Nico Vitale. If you'd wanted to make a social call, you should have let me know. I would have cleaned up a little."

He had changed in the year since Nico had seen him. His face had grown thinner, his hair grayer, and there were lines etched around his eyes that Nico didn't remember. He was still tall, imposing in the way that tall men are, even when they were lean like Carlo. But he didn't look well.

This is Angel's father. His Angel.

He pushed the thought aside. Carlo was a murderer, and that was the only way Nico would afford to think of him.

"Give me the tape," Nico said. "Give me the tape and I'll let you live."

"This again?" Carlo held up his hands in a gesture of confusion. "I told you in the Syndicate's hearing, I have no idea what you're talking about. They believed me. Why can't you?"

"Because you're a murderer and a liar. They may not know it, but I do."

"Yes, but it's not what you think you know that counts, is it? It's what you can prove," Carlo said calmly. "And right now, you can't prove a thing, while I can most certainly prove that you kidnapped my daughter."

His mention of Angel made Nico see red. "You don't deserve her."

Carlo's brow furrowed, like he was trying to complete a complicated math equation in his head. "That's interesting."

"Shut up." Nico cocked his weapon, and everyone went still.

"Give us the tape," Luca said. "At least you'll live."

"I'm afraid I really don't know what you're talking about," Carlo said. "But if you won't listen to reason, I have no doubt Raneiro and the Syndicate will understand my position. You kidnap my daughter, come in here, hold me at gunpoint... " He shrugged. "A man's got to do what a man's got to do." He glanced at his men. "Do it."

44

She walked up to the door, glancing around for any sign of danger. But it was just a house, at least from this vantage point. She took a deep breath and knocked.

A moment later the door was opened by a thin man with mean eyes. He looked her up and down. "Yeah?"

"I'd like to see Carlo Rossi," she said. "I'm his daughter."

The man's expression changed, the light of interest coming into his eyes. "Carlo's daughter?"

She nodded.

"Stay here." He shut the door.

She looked around, half expecting someone to come at her from behind or shoot from the street. It was too normal for all the preparation Nico and Luca had done, although she doubted they'd knocked on the door.

The door opened, and before she knew what was happening, she was being yanked across the threshold into a cramped entryway. It wasn't until the door was slammed and locked behind her that she realized the man standing in front of her was Dante.

She had a flash of his rough hands on her breast, his leering face looming over her in the basement at Nico's headquarters. She shrunk back instinctively, every cell in her body rebelling against his proximity.

He grabbed her arm and brought his face close to hers. "Looks like the kitty cat has finally come home."

"This isn't my home," she choked out. "And you better take your hands off me. Now."

He stared her down before holding up his hands with a smile. "Hey, now we know who's side you're on. No hard feelings."

"I am not on your side, Dante. And I never will be. Now take me to my father."

Dante laughed, then looked at the thin man who had first opened the door. "Do you believe this broad? Mouthy, isn't she?"

The other man nodded. "Uppity, too."

Dante sighed. "True, but she is the boss's daughter. We better let him decide what to do with her."

The words send a trickle of ice water into her belly. As if her father would decide to do anything to her. As if he wouldn't just let her go when she wanted to because she was his daughter.

"Come on," Dante said. "He's in the living room."

She followed him down the darkened hall into the house.

* * *

Nico was weighing his options, trying to figure out if he could hit one of Carlo's men before they took him or Luca down, when Angel stumbled into the room. She looked back, and Nico saw that she'd been pushed by Dante.

When he followed her into the room, Nico saw that Dante had a gun in his hand. And it was pointed at Angel's head.

Fuck.

* * *

She should have been scared by the gun pointed at her head, especially since it was wielded by Dante. But there was no room for fear. She was mesmerized by the scene in front of her: Luca and Nico with their guns pointed at two men whose guns were pointed back at them, her father standing like some kind of benevolent king in the center of it all.

"Angelica," Carlo said, crossing the room to her. "You're finally here."

He tried to embrace her, but she stood stiffly in his arms. She already knew this man wasn't her father. Not the father she thought she knew.

He put an arm tightly around her shoulder and faced Nico. She had the sense of the gun at her back, the feeling that Dante was still pointing it at her head without comment from her father.

"I think it's time for you to leave now, Nico," he said. "Angelica and I have a lot of catching up to do. It seems a lot has happened in the past couple of weeks."

"Give me the tape," Nico said.

"I'm afraid you're being short-sighted." Her father glanced at Dante. "You have a loyalty problem, but you also have a brand ID problem."

"Brand ID?"

Her father nodded. "We don't do modern, Nico. It's not what our business is about. And while I admire your financial acumen, the truth is that your methodologies will kill our organization as we know it."

"Now you're the one being short-sighted," Nico said. "My organization is thriving. And if I have a loyalty problem, it's only with men who no longer suit the needs of my business. Outdated and obsolete. Good riddance."

Angel stood very still, her father's arm too tight around her shoulders.

"You're rationalizing," he said. "It was a fault of your father's, too,"

"What are you talking about?" Nico asked.

"Didn't you know? Your father had been petitioning the Syndicate for years to alter its code of conduct. It seems bleeding hearts run in the family."

Nico turned his gun on Carlo.

"Don't," Luca said.

"We tried reasoning with him." Her father didn't seem at all concerned by the gun pointed at his head, and he warmed to his subject as he continued. "We reminded him about tradition and ritual, the need to make people feel like they belong to something special, something… apart from the modern world. But he wouldn't listen. He'd gone soft, and he wanted to make the rest of us soft, too. But our business is no place for soft men, Nico. I think deep down you know that."

"I'm not going to stand here and discuss business practices with you," Nico said. "Give me the tape."

"That would be foolish," her father said. "And I am not a foolish man. Besides, I wasn't alone that night, and Dante here has entrusted me with the confidentiality of the security tape. What kind of leader would I be if I violated that trust?"

She closed her eyes as the words worked their way into her mind. Nico had been right. Her father had murdered Nico's parents in cold blood. And Dante had helped him do it.

"Motherfucker," Dante cursed behind her.

Nico pointed his gun somewhere beyond her head, and she realized he was aiming at Dante. She saw the fury in his eyes and knew that if she hadn't been there, he would have burned the whole place to the ground even if he had to burn with it.

She should have been wrecked by the proof that her father was a killer, but instead a kind of peacefulness settled over her. Now she knew. Now she knew and she had to get out of here, tell David, find a way to move forward with Nico.

She let her eyes skim the room, trying frantically to find a way to get out alive with Nico and Luca. It didn't look good. Presumably, Dante still had his gun aimed at the back of her head while her father had a death grip on her shoulders. Nico was pointing his gun at Dante while Luca held down the two other men, and her father's men had their weapons aimed at Luca and Nico.

Everyone had a gun pointed at their head.

"I think the best thing for everyone involved is to call a truce," her father said. "What's done is done. We can hash out the future of the Syndicate through proper channels, let bygones be bygones. I have my daughter back. If you choose to go peacefully, I'm willing to set aside this little incident."

"No fucking way."

She knew from the tone of Nico's voice that walking away wasn't an option. Not without the proof he needed to avenge his parents, and not while she was being held at gunpoint.

"It's okay." She looked in Nico's eyes. "Just go. He's not going to hurt me."

She tried to send him a message with her eyes. *Leave me with him. I'll try to find the thing you want.* He didn't seem to notice.

"No."

She heard a click near her head and looked sideways to find another gun pointed at her head, this time by her father.

* * *

The gun had appeared out of nowhere. Nico had been so focused on Angel that he hadn't seen Carlo pull the weapon out of his waistband. Now Angel had two guns pointed at her head, and he had no idea how he would get her out alive. He and Luca were outgunned, but not by much. The bigger problem was Angel, and he almost couldn't see straight through his fear for her.

He met her gaze and didn't know if he should be comforted or terrified by the strange calm there. She didn't think her father would kill her, but she was wrong. Carlo Rossi would do what he had to do to make it out alive, and if his survival was called into question, he would take the offensive rather than wait for things to play out according to Nico's timeline.

The realization clarified his options. He had the same options; wait for Carlo to make a move or make it himself. He could take Carlo. After that, Dante would only be concerned about his own skin. He wouldn't bother killing Angel to make a point. Men like Dante didn't do things on principle because they didn't have principles. They only did things to achieve their desired goal, and right now Dante's desired goal was survival.

If Nico took Carlo and Dante fled, Luca would take the other two, starting with the one pointing his gun at Luca. By the time the other one spun on him, Luca would have brought him down.

It made sense. It was viable. But it was risky. Nico didn't have a problem gambling his own life, but he couldn't gamble Angel's, even if the odds were in their favor.

He was still trying to come up with another option when something crashed from the front of the house. Everyone turned toward the hall.

* * *

She was trying to gauge Nico's next move so she could help, even if it was just to get out of the way, when she heard the sound of splintering wood from the front of the house. She barely had time to register that something was happening before four enormous men dressed in black SWAT-type gear exploded into the room.

Her ears rang as gunfire exploded over her shoulder, and she watched as the two men who had been pointing guns at Nico and Luca dropped to the floor.

Farrell Black turned his weapon her way, pointing it at her father, but he was already dragging Angel back toward the hall, the gun still pointed at her head, while Dante fired at Farrell and Nico and the others.

Then everything seemed to slow down and speed up at the same time. The gunfire dropped into the background, guns flashing in silence as everyone fired. She heard a thump behind her and twisted to see Dante on the floor, scrambling backward toward the front door as he continued to fire, blood seeping through his shirt.

They were close to the door now, her father's hand a death grip on her upper arm, the gun still pointed at her temple. She looked down the barrel of Nico's gun and knew he was pointing it at her father. She shook her head, wanting to tell him not to fire, she would go with her father, she would be okay.

But a moment later all the sound seemed to come back into the room. The muzzle of Nico's gun flashed while she screamed, and her father's hold on her arm loosened. Then he was falling to the ground, his forehead marked by Nico's bullet.

45

She and David stood by the grave long after the others had left. The funeral had been well attended in spite of his violent passing. Many of the people who had expressed their condolences knew her father from his legitimate business or his church. It was only the somber men at the back of the cathedral that she'd marked as belonging to the Syndicate. Nico hadn't come, and while she was relieved — it wouldn't have been appropriate — she also felt like someone had carved out her heart with a dull blade.

"You okay?" David asked.

She looked up into his eyes, blue like their father's, though that was where the resemblance ended. David's eyes were gentle, completely lacking the shrewd violence she'd seen in her father's before his death.

She nodded. "You?"

He sighed and put his arm around her. "It's just… did we ever really know him?"

She'd asked herself the same thing at least a hundred times in the five days since her father's death. He had been a killer. But he had also been a husband and father. A businessman and a parishioner. Would they ever have known him? Did you ever really get to know anyone?

"I don't know," she finally said.

They stood in silence a moment longer, looking at the headstone.

CARLO ANTHONY ROSSI
Husband and Father

It seemed terse, but it was the best they could do under the circumstances. It would probably take them a long time to reconcile all that he'd been.

"Look who's here," her brother said.

She looked up to find Nico standing near a tree some distance away. She couldn't see his face clearly, but her heart still clutched in her chest at the sight of him. She would recognize him anywhere; the regal set of his spine, the lazy grace with which he stood.

"Want me to take care of it?" David asked.

She tried to smile up at him. He was her younger brother, but somewhere in the course of everything that had happened, he'd grown up.

"I got it," she said. "I'll meet you at the car."

He hesitated, then headed for the limo parked by the curb.

Angel walked across the grass, heading for Nico. The closer she got, the harder it was to breathe. It had been easier to tell herself she didn't need him, that her feelings had only been twisted and magnified because of the circumstances, when she didn't have to look at him. But now he was right in front of her, his lion eyes veiled, his elegant body draped in a suit of black wool.

"Hello," he said, handing her a white rose. "I'm sorry for your loss." His words were stiff, but a moment later he cleared his throat, and when he met her eyes his vice was hoarse with emotion. "I'm so sorry, Angel."

She nodded. "I know."

"He had a gun pointed to your head, and I..."

"He wouldn't have hurt me."

"You don't know that." The steel had returned to his voice.

"I do."

He looked down at her. "Can't we find a way to start again? Put this all behind us?"

Tears stung her eyes, and she shook her head, forcing down the emotion welling in her throat. "I can't, Nico."

He hesitated, then nodded. She knew it was only his pride that kept him from arguing the point. His pride and his love for her. The pain in his eyes almost undid her, but she'd already made her decision, and she knew it was the right one in spite of the vacuum already opening up inside of her at the thought of being without him.

Nico.

"If you need anything — ever — I'll be here," he said fiercely.

She nodded, wishing she could find the words to explain. To tell him she needed him, but she couldn't look at him without thinking about her father, and she couldn't think about her father without remembering him as he'd been when she was little, back when her mother had been alive and they'd been happy and it had seemed like he was a good man.

She would have to reconcile all of those parts of him somehow, just like she'd have to reconcile the Nico who had loved her so tenderly with the man who had killed her father. Just like she'd have to reconcile the part of her who had loved both her father and the man who killed him.

"Ange."

She turned to find David looking at her with concern. She held up one finger and returned her eyes to Nico, drinking him in, wanting to remember.

"I have to go," she said.

"I know."

She stretched to kiss him on the cheek. "Goodbye, Nico."

She hurried toward David before she could change her mind.

"Goodbye, Angel."

The words were said to her back, and when she turned around, he was holding his cheek where she'd kissed him. She forced herself to keep walking, her father's voice echoing in her ears.

People will tell you who they are if you listen.

Nico Vitale was a criminal and a gentleman. A lover and a fighter.

He had shown his enemies his wrath, and he had shown her more tenderness than she'd ever experienced in her life.

He had almost destroyed her, but he had saved her, too.

She was listening, but all she heard was silence.

Let others know how you enjoyed this book by leaving a review.

READ ON FOR A SNEAK PEEK OF FEARLESS, BOOK TWO
IN THE MOB BOSS SERIES, OR
ORDER IT NOW FOR MORE NICO, MORE ANGEL, AND
MORE SMOKING HOT ROMANCE.

You can also preorder SAVAGE for more of the down and dirty
Farrell Black.

If I was Superman, Jenna was my Kryptonite.

Farrell Black is dirty, dangerous, and holds nothing sacred. Growing up on the mean streets of London, he clawed his way to the top of a criminal empire with nothing but sheer force of will and the determination to need no one.

Ever.

Then he met Jenna Carver, and all bets were off — until the day she walked out of his life without a backward glance.

Leaving him was the hardest thing she'd ever done.

As a kid, Jenna knew how people looked at her. Like she was stupid. Worthless. Poor. So she spent her life working to become someone else. Then she met Farrell Black, and their all-consuming passion blew a hole in everything she thought she knew about herself.

Until she was forced to make a terrible choice.

Now Jenna is back in London for her father's funeral, desperate to avoid the one man who can banish her hard-earned reason in favor of red-hot ecstasy. But when her father's death is tied to an abuse of power at the highest levels, she has no choice but to ask Farrell for help.

As they work together to find answers to a puzzle that could have dangerous implications, desire threatens to undo them both — **and forces Jenna to choose between keeping the secret of a lifetime and having the one man who can command her body and soul.**

Continue reading for a free sneak peek of FEARLESS.

Fearless Sneak Peek

Angel Bondesan watched her brother, David, in the living room of her apartment. She felt a rush of affection for him, his light brown hair falling into his face, narrow shoulders working while he stuffed clothes into his duffel bag.

They'd spent the last few months going through their father's things, talking about all the clues they had ignored that might have led to the truth about him. Angel had sobbed on David's shoulder when she missed Nico so much she felt like a gutted animal, and he'd been just as patient about listening to her rail out loud when she could muster her rage against Nico.

David had his own unfinished business with their father. Would he have eventually accepted David's sexual orientation? Did he love his son at the end?

People will tell you who they are if you listen.

It was something their father used to say, but now he was dead, and none of their questions about him would ever be answered.

David had insisted on spending spring break with her, and they'd passed the time taking long walks by the river that wound through town, talking and laughing, getting stoned, watching movies, and eating ice cream.

"Are you sure you have to go?" she asked.

"Classes start up again tomorrow." He turned to look at her, his forehead creased with worry. "But if you need me here, you know I'll stay, Ange."

The nickname caused a lump of sadness to rise in her throat, and she had to fight the urge to beg him to stay. He was her little brother. It wasn't his job to take care of her.

She smiled. "No way. I'll just miss you, that's all."

"Come stay with me anytime," he said. "Brad's a douche, but he won't mind, mostly because he'll spend the whole weekend hitting on you."

She wrinkled her nose. "Ew."

It was more than the fact that David's college roommate was an idiot. After the weeks she spent with Nico before Thanksgiving, every guy she met seemed like an ineffectual little boy. It didn't matter if they were thirty or if they were college guys like Brad, she felt nothing but a kind of benevolent pity for them. She'd only dated one man since she'd come home, a thirty-year-old music producer working on an album in one of the Hudson Valley's many small studios. But there hadn't been even a flicker of the heat she'd felt with Nico. She tried to tell herself that was a good thing. What she'd had with Nico was unhealthy, dangerous. It had killed her father, and it had almost destroyed her.

It was an unconvincing argument, even to herself. It was hard to settle for an unlit match when you'd had a wildfire.

"Well, the offer stands," David said, zipping up his duffel.

"Thanks."

He checked his phone. "You ready? The bus will be here soon."

She nodded, crossing the room and grabbing her keys. "Let's go."

They left the apartment and made their way down the narrow flight of stairs. The air was still wet from winter, slowly warming under the weak April sun. The streets were already teeming with students returning from break, and Angel felt an unkind hatred for them as she and David nudged their way around the crowds converging on the narrow sidewalks. She'd chosen to stay here before Nico's men had kidnapped her, but now it felt like purgatory. She was no longer the naive girl who believed her father was simply a wealthy real estate developer. Now she knew the truth; Carlo Rossi had been head of the Boston division of the Syndicate, a worldwide network of organized crime.

And he'd killed Nico's parents in cold blood.

It was hard to come back to the place where she'd once been so innocent. Hard to face her own denial and the loss of the person she'd once been. But the truth is, she didn't have anywhere else to go. She and David had inherited all of their father's property, including the apartments in Boston and New York City, but those places were too close to her father's work — and her father's work was too close to Nico Vitale.

Nico...

She pushed him out of her mind and turned her attention to the crowd gathering outside the bus station. "I hope you can get a seat," she said.

"I'll be fine," David said.

"You have your ticket?" she asked.

He pulled it from his bag. "Got it, Mom."

She smiled. "Very funny."

He looked at her for a long moment. "You sure you're okay, Ange?"

She nodded. "Yep."

He tipped his head. "Liar."

She leaned in to hug him so he wouldn't see the tears in her eyes. She was fine as long as nobody called her on her bullshit, as long as she didn't have to think about whether she was fine. But whenever someone got too close, she recoiled. Talking about her feelings meant talking about Nico, and that was like probing an open wound. Better to leave it alone. Maybe it wouldn't get better that way, but it wouldn't get worse either.

David squeezed her hard. She breathed in the scent of him; security and comfort and the aftershave he'd worn since he was sixteen.

He pulled back to look at her. "Promise you'll call if you need me."

"I promise. You?"

He nodded. "I promise."

"And don't let that asshole, Jacob, fuck with your head," she said. "You deserve better."

David had only come out a few months before their father's death, and he was still figuring out how to navigate the dating landscape at college. It had been a relief to listen to his guy problems instead of rehashing her own.

Not that she had any problems in that department. She and Nico were done. Because there was no way you could love the man who killed your father, even if your father had been a bad guy. Even if he'd been a criminal who had held a gun to your head.

She and Nico were done because that's the only thing they could be.

She and David turned as a bus pulled into the parking lot spewing black smoke.

"That looks good for the environment," David said.

Angel laughed in spite of herself. "When you're a famous writer, you can buy yourself a Prius."

"Deal." The bus pulled to a stop at the curb, and a few people got off before the crowd started climbing the stairs to board. He looked down at her. "I guess this it."

She forced herself to smile. "I guess so."

He wrapped her up in another hug. "I love you. Everything's going to be okay, I promise."

She didn't know if it was true. Didn't know if it could be true. But it was nice to have someone say it.

"I know," she said, giving him a final squeeze before she stepped back. "Now go on. Get a window seat."

He nodded. "See you in a few weeks."

"Margaritas and tacos," she said.

"Don't forget cabana boys," he added.

She grinned. "Can't wait."

They'd wanted to take a trip together over the summer, and while David had suggested Europe, Angel couldn't imagine going back to Italy or England without Nico. They could have gone somewhere else — Europe was big enough — but Mexico seemed like a safer bet. There she wouldn't have to remember Nico kissing her in the shadow of the Colosseum, wouldn't have to remember their final night together in London.

"I'll text you when I get in," David said, stepping on the bus.

She nodded, waving to hide the lump in her throat. She was being dumb. She'd lived alone for years before Nico had her kidnapped. But she and David had spent the last few months cleaning up their father's affairs, and she hadn't had much time to be alone with her thoughts. The magnitude of the trust left to them, the investments and charitable contributions and property, was overwhelming.

Then there were the businesses — both legal and illegal — to untangle. Angel had left most of that to Frank Morra, her father's Consigliere, but she knew that Raneiro Donati was putting pressure on him to get a permanent power structure in place.

And you did not mess with Raneiro Donati.

The problem was that there had been no Underboss in place at the time of her father's death. He'd been arrogant right up until the end, sure he'd be around to run his empire for a long time to come. Angela and David still didn't know what to do about it. How did you dissolve an illegal enterprise as big as the one run by Carlo Rossi without implicating every involved —from the soldiers who did his killing to the secretaries who had no idea they were covering for one of the country's most notorious mob bosses? She and David had managed to issue an edict against several heinous income streams — human trafficking, high-interest loans to those who couldn't afford to repay them, the bullying of store owners to pay for protection — but Angel had no doubt there was plenty left to clean up. They would have to figure it out — and soon — but for now she presumed the remaining illegal business interests were still running under the auspices of the legitimate real estate company owned by her father before his death.

Owned by her and David now.

How would they untangle the illegal business interests from the legitimate ones?

She watched the bus pull away and waved until she lost sight of David's face. Then she started walking back into town for her shift at the record store. It was as good a place as any to distract herself from the mess that was her life.

2

Nico shuffled on the balls of his feet, moving quickly around the sparring ring at the center of the renovated gym. He was alone, the room dark around the spotlight inside the ropes, and he moved into a series of sweeps and knee jabs designed to disarm an enemy.

It had gotten harder to find sparring partners in the months since he'd started practicing Eskrima, a form of martial art that was so deadly it had been outlawed when the Spanish invaded the Philippines. He should have stopped sparring with his men long before he sent one of his soldiers to the hospital with a concussion. He had seen the looks on their faces when they worked together, knew his obsession was becoming dangerous. Then he'd gotten caught up in the moment, transported back to the dingy living room in London when Carlo Rossi had put the gun to Angel's head. A red wash of rage had blanketed his mind, and the next thing he knew, he was staring down at Paul, unconscious on the floor of the ring after a wicked elbow jab Nico had landed to the back of his head.

Nico had been horrified. Holding his own with the men was one thing; making them victims of his obsession was another.

Now he practiced only with his coach or when he was alone, reliving the scene with Angel's father over and over again, imagining an outcome in which he'd managed to disarm Carlo, even seriously injure him, rather than putting a bullet through his brain. Maybe then Angel would have forgiven him. Maybe they would even be together now.

"Boss?"

The voice caught him off guard, and he spun on his feet, ready to fight as he faced the door. He dropped his arms when he saw who was standing there.

"Luca." He hadn't been aware that he was breathing hard, but he was aware of it now as he spoke. "Is everything okay?"

Luca nodded. "Just here for the briefing."

"Is it that time already?" Nico asked. How long had he been in the gym?

"Ten past eight," Luca said.

Nico ducked under the ropes and grabbed his towel off one of the hooks. He wiped his face, then draped it over his bare shoulders as he crossed the floor of the gym.

"Is Vincent here?"

Luca nodded.

"Let me clean up," Nico said. "I'll meet you both in my office in ten minutes."

Luca held the door as Nico moved past, and Nico wondered if he was imagining the concern in his Underboss's eyes. It didn't matter. He wouldn't give credence to Luca's worry by addressing it. He was fine. Well, maybe not fine. He missed Angel. Missed her so fucking much that he felt like a sinkhole had opened up inside of him. Everything that mattered had been sucked into it, and he was still standing on the edge, peering downward, thinking maybe he should just jump in and get it over with.

He shook his head. That was weakness talking. His business — and his men— needed him, now more than ever.

He hustled up the stairs to his office suite and turned the shower on cold. Stripping off his shorts and tank top, he stepped under the spray, forcing himself to stand there until he was shivering. It was the only thing he seemed to feel, and he waited until his skin turned numb to climb out and towel off.

He walked into the adjoining bedroom and slipped on a clean pair of trousers and a short sleeve T-shirt. He avoided his apartment now, preferring the smaller, more intimate suite of rooms at his headquarters in Brooklyn. Here he could almost fool himself into thinking he was something other than alone, could almost feel part of the business he'd rebuilt in the wake of his parent's execution style murder at the hands of Angel's father.

Angel…

He had a flash of her, standing on the beach with her golden hair blowing around her face, her eyes as green and fathomless as the sea stretching out in in front of them. The memory hit him like a punch to the gut, and he was torn between wanting to hold onto it and wanting to banish it forever.

He chose the latter — or tried to anyway. It's not like she had given him a choice, and while he'd be lying if he said he didn't hope she would change her mind, banking on it would be foolish.

And he'd done enough foolish things because of his feelings for Angel Rossi.

He finished getting dressed and pulled a revolver from the top drawer of his desk. He still preferred to avoid the use of weapons, but he couldn't afford to stand on principle in such uncertain times. He was getting ready to close the drawer when his gaze settled on the rosary inside the drawer.

There had been a time when the meditative nature of the beads had soothed him, when his visits to empty churches all over the city had allowed him to feel closer to his parents. Now those things only made him bitter. What was the point in comfort if it only allowed you to pretend everything would be okay when it was all going to shit anyway?

He closed the drawer with a slam and made his way downstairs to the second floor conference room. Headquarters was quiet this time of night, with only the rhythmic hum of the machines in the cyber lab and the soft murmurs of the few people who stayed overnight to keep an eye on things. There were others in and around the building — more so in light of recent events — but they were all out of sight.

"Luca, Vincent," Nico said, sweeping into the conference room.

"Hi, boss," Vincent said.

He was a large man, and Nico had been embarrassed when he realized Vincent's blank face hid a keen intellect. Nico prided himself on seeing below the surface of things, and it bothered him that he had unfairly judged one of his soldiers. He'd rectified the situation immediately, moving Vincent into Luca's position when he made Luca his Underboss. That had been a forgone conclusion. Luca had stuck with him through the fiasco with Angel, had watched Nico's back when everything went to hell in the London flat.

But Vincent had been a surprise. He'd taken a bullet wound to the head — just a graze, but still — during the altercation with Carlo's men when they tried to rescue Angel. Since then he'd proven himself an asset in the management of sensitive issues that forced Nico to walk the moral line that was part of his next generation mob family.

Nico took a seat at the head of the table, Luca on his right and Vincent on his left.

"Tell me," he said.

Luca cut a glance at Vincent before returning his eyes to Nico. "Three more hijacked shipments, four men missing, possible breach of one of the databases."

"Four of our own?" Nico asked.

"And six more from other East Coast families," Luca said. He hesitated. "One of them from the Rossi family."

Nico tried to hide his alarm. He'd assumed the attacks on the Vitale family were isolated, aimed at him in the wake of Carlo's death. But that would mean they were perpetrated by someone in the Rossi family. That theory went out the window if they were losing people, too. He wondered if Angel knew. Word was Frank Morra was running things, and somehow Nico didn't see Frank keeping

Angel and her brother apprised of the situation. Then again, Angel probably wanted nothing to do with it all anyway.

"Any sign of Dante?" he asked, revisiting an early theory.

"Not since the sighting in Brazil," Luca said.

Nico drummed his fingers on the conference table. His mother would have said Dante was like a bad penny, turning up everywhere. But the London police had placed guards by the door of Dante's hospital room, and Nico had been sure he would be sent away for a long time. He'd been enraged when Dante escaped, and he'd spent the next month milking every source he had for information. He'd even assigned someone to keep an eye on Angel, just in case the bastard tried to fuck with her. Nothing had happened, and a few weeks later, they'd gotten word that Dante was in Brazil. They hadn't heard a word about him since, and Nico forced himself to open his mind to other possibilities.

"What do you make of it?" he asked Vincent.

"It can only be one of two things," Vincent said. "Either the men are being taken as some kind of message, or…"

"Or?" Nico prompted.

"They're leaving voluntarily."

It was possible. Not everyone had been a fan of his twenty-first century vision of the business. Maybe the turf war with Carlo had pushed them over the edge. Carmine, his Consigliere and most trusted advisor, had warned him there might be dissent in the ranks. Raneiro, too.

Raneiro Donati. What would he make of this? As Nico's mentor and head of the Syndicate, the international organization that ruled over every organized crime family on the planet, Raneiro would have to know what was going on. But Nico had avoided asking him for help, knowing his patience had run thin in the wake of what happened in London. Nico hesitated to involve him again in business that should have been well under Nico's control.

And it would be. Nico would do whatever was necessary to see it done.

"Have you talked to the families of the missing men?" Nico asked Vincent.

"Claim to have no knowledge of their whereabouts."

"All of them?" Nico asked.

"All of them," Vincent said.

"Do you believe them?"

"I do."

Nico filed that away for later consideration and turned to Luca. "Tell me about the data breach."

"Sara Falco says there are signs that someone was trying to break through one of the firewalls."

"Trying?"

Luca shrugged. "She said it didn't look like anyone had gotten in, but I thought I should mention it."

"Because you think it's all connected," Nico said.

Luca sighed. "I think it's possible."

"How good is Sara?" Nico asked.

"Very good," Luca said. "She was in the Bureau's cyber training unit when we got her."

Nico shuffled the pieces inside his head. "I'll meet with Frank tomorrow. See if I can get a read on what's going on inside the Rossi family. In the meantime, I want a detailed report from Sara on the possible implications of the data breach and all the ways we can get in front of it."

"What about the hijacked shipments?" Vincent asked. "The men are worried."

"I pay them to transcend emotions like worry." He heard the steel in his voice and took a deep breath. He demanded total loyalty, total strength in his men, but alienating them wouldn't accomplish anything. "Tell them it's under control. No violence unless their lives depend on it."

"We're losing money - " Luca started.

"I don't care about the money," Nico cut him off. "Let's try to keep things from escalating until we can figure this out."

Luca nodded.

"Is there anything else?" Nico asked.

He suddenly wanted nothing more than to retire to his bedroom upstairs. To close his eyes and let the dreams of Angel come. It was the only time of day he could think about her without feeling weak. No man was in control of his dreams.

Luca shook his head and was rising to stand when a shrill ring sounded from his pocket. He removed his phone, looked at the display, and scowled.

"What is it, Morelli?"

Luca's face turned two shades paler, and a pit of dread opened up in Nico's stomach. His first thought was Angel. Could something have happened to her?

"What? Where?" Luca cut his gaze to Nico while he listened to whoever was on the other end of the phone. "Thanks for letting us know," he finally said. And then, "No, he's right here. I'll tell him."

He disconnected the call and turned to Nico. "It's Carmine. He's dead."

3

"Why don't you just call him?" Lauren asked the question from across the record store where she was alphabetizing a new shipment.

"What would be the point? Nothing's changed," Angel said.

She sprayed the glass door at the front of the store with window cleaner, then used long strokes to wipe it off. She'd quit her job at the Muddy Cup as soon as she'd gotten back from her father's funeral. She would never be able to work there again, never be able to lock up at night without thinking about the moment she'd been kidnapped by Nico's men. It didn't matter that Luca, one of her abductors, had become a friend during her captivity, or that she'd fallen in love with Nico. Dante was still out there, and even though Luca told her he'd been spotted in Brazil, the knowledge that he was free bothered her like an itch she couldn't scratch. She didn't want to relieve the moment it had all began, and she was grateful when Lauren put in a word for her at the record store.

"Perspectives change," Lauren said, dropping the last record into place. "Sometimes things look different after some time has passed."

"He killed my father," Angel said softly.

"But he did it to protect you, right?"

Angel could feel her friend's eyes on her back. Lauren was right, but it wasn't that simple. Angel had told Nico not to fire, had told him to leave, that she would be okay. Now it was impossible to know if he'd pulled the trigger to protect her or if some part of him — maybe a big part — had done it to avenge the murder of his parents.

It's not like she would blame him. Even outside the context of the law, unsanctioned killings of Syndicate family members were forbidden. Her father had killed Nico's parents to gain a foothold in the New York City territory. He'd done it for greed, plain and simple. She could understand why felt the need for vengeance.

"It's more complicated than that," Angel said, crossing to the register. She avoided Lauren's eyes as she put the window cleaner under the counter.

"Maybe," Lauren said. "I just hate to see you like this."

Angel tried to laugh. "Like what?"

Lauren shrugged, her curly brown hair bouncing around her shoulders. "Sad. Sadder than usual."

"What's that supposed to mean?" Angel asked.

"You've always been sad, Angie," Lauren said. "But this feels different."

"My dad was murdered," Angel said.

Lauren knew that much; that Angel had been kidnapped and held for ransom. That she'd fallen in love with the man who had held her captive. But Angel had been spare with the rest of the details, telling Lauren that things had gone bad at the end and Nico had saved her life but accidentally shot her father. She hadn't told Lauren the rest; that her father had been a notorious mob boss. That compared to him, Nico looked almost like an upstanding citizen. Her father may have given her and David a different last name to protect himself, but in the end it had saved them from being associated with the Rossi crime empire. It was the only saving grace in a long line of shitty things that had happened since Nico's men grabbed her last October. The fact that the showdown with her father's men had happened in London helped; US news outlets weren't interested in much if it didn't happen within their country's borders.

"Have you thought about counseling?" Lauren asked, joining her behind the counter.

"I'm not ready to talk about it like that," Angel said. The words came out with more vehemence than she intended, and Lauren held up her hands in a gesture of surrender.

"Just a suggestion."

Angel sighed. "I know, and I appreciate that you care. I just need some more time to figure things out."

Lauren grinned. "Maybe some Thai food will help." She dug around in her bag. "I'll go pick up lunch."

"Let me give you money," Angel said, reaching for her bag.

"I got this one," Lauren said. "You can catch me next time."

Angel smiled. "Thanks."

"No worries." She headed for the door. "Back in fifteen minutes."

The bell on the door jingled as she stepped outside, and Angel was left alone in the quiet of the empty store. The majority of their customers were college students looking to kill time, but every now and then a collector would come in to buy one of the more valuable LPs. George, the owner of the store, must have made his money that way, because the store was nearly always empty.

She put Brand New on the turntable that was hooked up to the speakers, then started sweeping the old linoleum floor. She'd learned the hard way that silence was the enemy. That was when thoughts of Nico came creeping back, when she would see his panther eyes darken with desire as he tucked a piece of hair behind her ear, feel his breath on her lips in the moment before he lowered his mouth to hers. Then everything would come back to her — the safety she'd felt in his arms even when it didn't make sense, the completion she felt when he drove into her, making her his in a way no man ever had, in a way she feared no man would again.

She sang along to the record, slowly letting go of her thoughts. She'd protested the first time Lauren showed up at her apartment, determined to take Angel to her weekly meditation class. But it had been surprisingly helpful, and before long Angel actually looked forward to the sessions. It was the only time silence was tolerable, and willing her mind blank had become a kind of contest to see how long she could go without thinking of Nico.

The bell on the door rang, and Angel was surprised to see that Lauren had already returned.

"That was fast," Angel said. But she knew right away something was wrong. Lauren's eyes were wide, her chest rising and falling like she'd been running. "What's up?"

Lauren set her bag on the counter, then met Angel's eyes. "That guy... the one who kidnapped you..."

"Nico?"

Lauren nodded. "Nico Vitale, right?"

Fear unspooled in Angel's stomach, and she fought against the tide of panic. Had something happened to him? "What's going on?"

"I was waiting for the food," Lauren said. "They had the TV on the news. They showed his picture..."

Angel forced her voice steady. "What are you saying?"

"Someone close to him was killed. They're talking about the mob, Angel. Using words like execution." Her face was a mask of shock and worry. "Is that true? Is he part of the mafia?"

"What else did they say?" Angel asked, already rushing to grab her bag.

"Angel... this is not - "

"Just tell me what they said, Lauren," Angel snapped. "Please."

Lauren took a deep breath. "They said he's in hiding."

Angel headed for the door. "I have to go."

ORDER FEARLESS NOW

Or get more Farrell Black with SAVAGE, the first book in the London Mob series.

If I was Superman, Jenna was my Kryptonite.

Farrell Black is dirty, dangerous, and holds nothing sacred. Growing up on the mean streets of London, he clawed his way to the top of a criminal empire with nothing but sheer force of will and the determination to need no one.

Ever.

Then he met Jenna Carver, and all bets were off — until the day she walked out of his life without a backward glance.

Leaving him was the hardest thing she'd ever done.

As a kid, Jenna knew how people looked at her. Like she was stupid. Worthless. Poor. So she spent her life working to become someone else. Then she met Farrell Black, and their all-consuming passion blew a hole in everything she thought she knew about herself.

Until she was forced to make a terrible choice.

Now Jenna is back in London for her father's funeral, desperate to avoid the one man who can banish her hard-earned reason in favor of red-hot ecstasy. But when her father's death is tied to an abuse of power at the highest levels, she has no choice but to ask Farrell for help.

As they work together to find answers to a puzzle that could have dangerous implications, desire threatens to undo them both — **and forces Jenna to choose between keeping the secret of a lifetime and having the one man who can command her body and soul.**

Please find me online. I'd love to get to know you!
Website
Facebook
Twitter
Instagram

Acknowledgments

Making the decision to branch out from traditional publishing wasn't an easy one. Despite the increasing difficulty of swimming in the big pond, there is a kind of safety net of agents and editors and copyeditors and booksellers and librarians. They are the very best traditional publishing has to offer, and I've felt lucky to work with so many of them over the years.

That said, I've been overwhelmed and surprised and humbled by the Indie publishing community, by the many people who have rooted for me and offered me advice and helped me bring this book to market. However you publish, it takes a village, and I've been so fortunate to find one in the Indie community that is every bit as meaningful as that in the traditional publishing community.

Thank you to my agent, Steven Malk of Writers House, who continues to support me in all endeavors, no matter how rogue they may seem.

Thank you to M.J. Rose, one of my favorite writers and the Patron Saint of Authors everywhere. M.J. has probably helped thousands of us along the way, and she never seems to tire of giving me a boost, spreading the word, providing timely marketing advice, and generally making me feel like I can do anything. It is not an understatement to say I might not have written this book without her support. Pay it forward for me by checking out her work, will you?

Thanks to Nazarea Andrews, K.P. Simmons, Jessica Collins, and everyone at Inkslingers PR who have helped get the word out about this book. You made it so easy for me, even when I came in under the wire and probably made you crazy with my ridiculous timeline.

Thanks also to all the bloggers and reviewers who are so passionate about reading and who continue to spread the word. I'm not sure the Indie book community would exist as it does without you.

I owe a special debt of gratitude to the thousands of people on Facebook and Twitter who have made my writing life less lonely and who are willing to support every book I write. You not only buy my books, you spread the word, swag bomb your hometowns on release day, review my work online, and generally make my world a nicer place. I'm very lucky to know you.

Lastly, thanks to my mother, Claudia Baker, for seeing me through the practical and logistical challenges of supporting my family with my work, and to my father, Michael St. James, who generously gave me the use of the family name for my adult book endeavors.

And of course, to Kenneth, Rebekah, Andrew, and Caroline, who remain the reason for everything I do.

Made in the USA
Lexington, KY
12 February 2017